THE MONKEY HOUSE

A NOVEL BY
BOYD TAYLOR

The Monkey House
Copyright © 2015 by Boyd Taylor

Katherine Brown Press
Austin, TX
KBTPress@ymail.com

Editor: Mindy Reed, The Authors' Assistant
Cover Designer: Douglas Brown, Album Artist
Interior Designer: Danielle H. Acee, The Authors' Assistant

First Printing 2015

ISBN: 978-0-9894707-1-1

PCN 2 0 1 5 9 3 8 6 8 5

Printed in the United States of America

I think that I shall never see
A billboard as lovely as a tree
Perhaps, unless the billboards fall,
  I'll never see a tree at all.

  ~Ogden Nash
from "Song of the Open Road", 1933

Other books in the Donnie Ray Cuinn Series:

The Hero of San Jacinto
The Antelope Play

CHAPTER ONE

AUSTIN
TWO YEARS EARLIER

Moonlight filtered through the large oak trees, casting wavy shadows on the small group of men, all dressed in black, who stood silently outside the Monkey House. At their leader's signal, they crept to the large wooden gate at the back of the three-story enclosure. The chimpanzees stirred, a questioning call from one, but otherwise there were only the usual sounds of the colony at rest.

The leader pointed at the chain that held the gate closed. A man appeared beside him, a large bolt cutter in his hand. Quickly, as the animals began to chatter nervously, the man placed the bolt cutter on the chain and snapped the chain in two. The noise from inside the compound grew louder. The men pulled the gate open and ran into the building, opening the gate to a large common cage at one end of the building. As they opened the enclosure, a light came on in the custodian's building on the opposite side of the Monkey House.

The intruders hurried through the foliage, out of the compound and back the way they came. As they ran, they heard the first of the chimps swinging overhead, swinging out of captivity, swinging toward freedom.

Austin Globe Standard, Saturday, February 2:

CHIMPS ESCAPE ANIMAL COMPOUND IN WEST AUSTIN

A number of chimps escaped from the Primate Preserve on the Hieronymus Parcel in West Austin last night and still remain at large in the Old Enfield and Tarrytown neighborhoods of West Austin. A spokesman for the Primate Preserve said that "only a couple dozen" of the chimps escaped, out of the one hundred or so that are housed at the Preserve. He said that law enforcement officials had captured several of the escapees, and that he was sure the others would be found "before long."

Austin Globe Standard, Sunday, February 3:

TARRYTON RESIDENTS IN UPROAR AS CHIMPS RUN LOOSE

State and local officials sought to reassure Austin residents that the chimps running through their neighborhoods, perching in their trees and scavenging for food, were not dangerous and would all be returned to captivity soon. Meanwhile, beleaguered officials of the Primate Preserve defended the company's program of biomedical research on the animals, claiming that it had been responsible for "enormous health benefits." Officials at the National Institutes of Health, which provides fifty million dollars a year of funding for the preserve, said that the Primate Preserve had been inspected regularly and that the chimps were handled according to the protocols in place. "Of course," the NIH spokesman said, "we deplore the escapes, but there is no reason to believe that there is any public health concern." They did advise residents to avoid contact with the animals. "That is only common sense. They are not domestic animals or pets. They are chimpanzees." He said that the enclosure from which the animals escaped held chimpanzees not part of any ongoing research program. He said the chimps in question were not infected with any contagious disease and presented no health risk. Sheriffs' deputies patrolling the West Austin neighborhoods denied they were under orders to shoot to kill.

Residents expressed surprise that the experimental lab had been allowed to operate in their neighborhood. A city official said that the land was leased to the Primate Preserve many years ago. "The monkeys were there first, before most of those houses were even built." According to public reports the Primate Preserve is a consortium of drug companies created in the 1970s. The Preserve is on the Hieronymus Parcel, a large tract of land on the banks of Lady Bird Lake in West Austin, near the Tom Miller Dam. The preserve employs more than one hundred staff and faculty, including veterinarians, animal care staff, basic scientists, research technicians and administrative staff. Its programs involve research that requires nonhuman primate models of human diseases such as cancer, hepatitis, HIV, diabetes and obesity.

Mayor Leaf Granderberg, who lives in the area, and whose grandson took a picture of two of the chimps in his backyard, said while the research is important, there has to be a better location for it, and promised city action "to get that place shut down." Save The Chimps (STC) a group of retired university academics and local activists issued a statement deploring conditions at the Preserve, calling for its closure and resettlement of the animals to a safe environment that respected rights of non-human primates.

Austin Globe Standard, Saturday, February 9:
LAST CHIMP RECAPTURED
TARRYTOWN BREATHES EASIER
National Guard troops captured the last two escaped chimps yesterday from a greenhouse on an Old Enfield estate, where they had taken refuge amid blooming fruit trees. "They looked really healthy and didn't want to leave," the guardsman said. STC and other community groups vowed to fight until all the animals are freed from captivity. Local residents, even those supporting the research, called on the city to close down the facility. "It's a safety issue," hair stylist Bon Chance said from his salon two blocks from the Hieronymus Parcel.

"My customers are afraid." He claimed a chimp snatched the Birkin handbag of a well-known West Austin matron. "She was livid. That chimp just laughed and ran off with it. Can you imagine?" City officials were studying the matter and there was talk of creating a commission to investigate.

Austin Globe Standard, Saturday, March 2:

NIH REDUCES FUNDING FOR CHIMP RESEARCH

The National Institutes of Health announced that it was sharply reducing funding of testing on chimpanzees. "Americans have benefitted greatly from the chimpanzees' service to biomedical research, but new scientific methods and technologies have rendered their use in research today largely unnecessary. Their likeness to humans has made them uniquely valuable for certain types of research, but also demands greater justification for their use. Greatly reducing their use in biomedical research is scientifically sound and the right thing to do." The NIH denied there was any connection between its decision and the escape of chimps from the Primate Preserve in Austin. Officials of the preserve said they were considering their next move.

Austin Globe Standard, Saturday, March 21:

PRIMATE PRESERVE TO CLOSE

NEIGHBORS CALL FOR PARK LAND IN ITS PLACE

The Primate Preserve notified city officials that it was closing the Primate Preserve, which has conducted biomedical research on nonhuman primates on the Hieronymus Parcel on Lady Bird Lake for decades. The National Institutes of Health has decided to cease funding most primate research and the Austin consortium will close its Austin facility immediately. Resident animals will be relocated to a non-testing preserve in Louisiana.

The H.H. Company, the Austin non-profit company that owns the Hieronymus Parcel said it was commissioning a study of possible uses for the parcel "consistent with the intent of Hiram Hieronymus." The Parcel was left to the company for charitable purposes by Hiram Hieronymus, a wealthy Austin benefactor, who also donated land and an endowment for the Cartwright House, a retirement home located across from the Parcel.

ccccc

It had been six months since the closing of the Primate Preserve. Professor Ralph Rothschild picked up the old set of binoculars from the table beside his chair and moved outside to the railing at the edge of his apartment balcony. It was mid-afternoon, and the professor had on his usual dress: A corduroy jacket with elbow patch sleeves, a neatly pressed white Oxford cloth shirt and a red tie. The stocky eighty-year-old's thick hair was completely white and his salt and pepper mustache was mostly salt now. His vision was not as good as in his boyhood days in France and his hearing came and went but his mind was quick and his memory still accurate (unlike many of his colleagues who also resided at the Cartwright House).

From his sixth floor vantage point he could watch the activity on the Heironymus Parcel across the road. Children parked their bikes beside the Monkey House, shuttered and fenced off ever since Primate Preserve closed. They played on the ropes and swings once used by the chimps, which had been salvaged by city park personnel and moved to the center of the parcel of land. The high chain link fences had been removed, but rusting poles were a reminder of the days when the chimps had played there.

This morning something was different. Through his binoculars Professor Rothschild saw two men with yellow fluorescent vests. One held a surveyor's rod and the other, a hundred yards away, took sightings with what the professor supposed was a theodolite. He knew the word, from the Greek for *sight*, or was it? He remembered an argument years ago at the Faculty Club between a slightly tipsy engineer and an indignant Latin professor about the derivation of the word, but he could not bring the details to mind. *It's a transit, really; isn't that what we Americans call it?* he wondered.

"Dorrie Louise," he called. "Come see this. There are surveyors over on Hieronymus. What do you suppose that's all about?"

"Papa, look who's here."

He turned, but held on to the railing to keep his balance. In the doorway stood a tall, slightly stout but still athletic man with ruddy cheeks and a familiar shock of black hair. He stood beside Dorrie Louise with his arm around her shoulders. "Hello, Professor," he said. The warmth in the voice was still there.

"Wesley, my word, is it really you?"

The former All-American football player smiled. "I saw this in a bookstore and thought of you." He handed the retired poet a thin book. The professor's hands trembled slightly when he took it.

"Sorry. I'm afraid it may be Parkinson's but they say it is not, that it is just age. Doctors!" He looked carefully at the book. "It's *The Marble Faun!*" He opened the book slowly. "My word," he said. "I do believe it is a first edition. A First of Faulkner's first." Ralph Rothschild was a poet, but he was also known in severely selective English Literature circles as an expert on the poems of William Faulkner. He was surprised that Wesley had remembered that. He had a way about him, this football player.

Wesley laughed. "It better be. That's what the man in the bookshop said. I saw it, thought of you and had to get it for you."

The professor shook his head. "No, Wesley, it's too much. I couldn't possibly accept it."

Wesley winked at Dorrie Louise. "Tell him I can afford it, Mrs. Smith. Besides, they won't give me my money back."

The slight woman smiled. "Call me Dorrie Louise, Wesley. I'm divorced from Mr. Smith now." She fluttered around the small apartment and brought out glasses and a pitcher of tea. "Papa always adored William Faulkner. I never could seem to get past the first chapter. What was it called, Papa? *I Lie Dying,* or something like that?"

Professor Rothschild looked up from the book. "*As I Lay Dying,* Dorrie Louise. But his poems. Ah, his poems. Imagine. A first edition of *The Marble Faun.*"

They sat around the worn dining table they had brought with them from The Haven after Dorrie Louise sold the old hotel and moved herself and the professor to the apartment at the retirement home.

"This is nice," Wesley said, looking around. There was a picture of Lena, the professor's deceased wife, in a place of honor on the living room wall. "Lena," Wesley said, "She was something."

"Papa and I miss her so much."

He turned to Dorrie Louise. "I drove by the old hotel the other day. I bet it was a hard decision to sell it. A lot of memories."

"It was, but Donny Ray thought it was a good deal, and Papa and I agreed it was time for Papa to be where he could be looked after if something should happen to me. Do you know how many years I lived there?" She sighed. "Before I married Mr. Smith?"

"And how many more years Donnie Ray lived there, when you moved out to the country."

"That was so hard, Wesley. But Lena convinced me that it was best for Donnie Ray to go to school in town." She looked at Papa fondly. "She and Papa were so good to Donnie Ray. They raised him like he was their son. I promised Lena that I would look after Papa, and that's what I'm doing. Though truth be told, he doesn't take much looking after."

Papa looked up. "The women in my life tell me what to do and I learned long ago it is best to obey."

Wesley sat down in the old recliner and thumbed through a Cartwright House brochure. "Very nice." He looked around at the roomy apartment. "So you and the Professor are living in sin?"

Dorrie Louise giggled. "Oh, Wesley. It's all very proper. We have separate bedrooms and bathrooms. It's lifetime care, you know. There are two hundred apartments. And we have fruit, lots and lots of fruit." She pointed at a large bowl on the table. "Would you like a banana? Or an orange?" She pointed a large bowl of fruit in the center of the table.

Wesley smiled. "No thanks." He put down the brochure. "It's a great location, right in the center of town and just a few miles from the University."

"Yes, and the wonderful thing is that so many of Papa's old friends are here. Everywhere you turn, there's a professor of something. Brilliant people."

Papa looked up again. "At one time they were brilliant. It would be wonderful if only scholars and teachers lived here. Unfortunately, all the administrators have also made their way here: deans, provosts, the whole lot. It's almost as if I never retired." He smiled. "Except I do not have to meet classes any longer." He frowned and said, "Wesley, come out on the balcony. What do you think those men are doing?" He pointed at the men in yellow vests, who had moved further away, down the street.

"It looks like they're surveying the Hieronymus Parcel, Professor."

"Yes, I think they are."

"Getting it ready, I imagine. I've heard the H.H. Company is going to sell it."

"You have heard that?" Papa sighed. "Dorrie Louise, we need to have a STC meeting. Get me the list. I need to tell them there is activity on the Hieronymus Parcel."

Wesley watched the men through the binoculars. "STC?" he asked, handing the binoculars back to the Professor.

"It is the name of our protest group."

Wesley looked at him blankly.

"STC was formed to fight the operation of the Primate Preserve."

"You were involved in that?"

"Yes. STC stands for Save The Chimpanzees."

"I recall that a bunch of them escaped. Did they ever catch them all?"

Papa picked up a writing tablet and started making notes. "Oh, yes. I recall there was some disagreement about whether there were twenty-five or twenty-six chimps that escaped. STC did not orchestrate the escape, although we have been accused of that, but certainly the escape was a triggering event. After twenty five chimpanzees ran loose in West Austin for forty-eight hours almost everyone agreed the primate laboratory did not belong here."

"That must have been something to witness. I was in Houston then."

"STC opposes using chimpanzees for research purposes, infecting the poor creatures with diseases and testing vaccines on them." He shuddered. "Barbarous."

"They were there a long time. I remember Donnie Ray and I used to take dates over there so the girls could hear the monkeys carrying on all night." He lowered his voice and whispered to the Professor. "Some of them really loved it."

"Hmm," Papa said. "You are a very interesting man, Wesley, with unusual experiences. You are correct. The preserve was there a long time. It was receiving fifty million dollars of federal funding, and of course drug company money. Everyone approved of it, except of course, the chimpanzees."

"Did the H.H. Company get a piece of that?"

"Of the grant money? Oh, I imagine so. At least, they always argued that that was what allowed them to support all manner of charities."

"Doesn't Dockery Ashley run the H.H. Company?"

"Yes, Judge Ashley is the president."

"So your group of protestors shut down Judge Ashley's favorite project?"

"Don't underestimate the power of retired academicians, Wesley, in matters of protest. A Latin professor, an expert on Fifteenth Century Flemish history, a law dean, all sorts of talented people."

"And a poet."

"Well, yes. I did play a role. It was not easy, I assure you, but we were dedicated." His eyes brightened as he remembered the events. "The claim was that the use of animals was essential to finding a cure for AIDS and cancer but neither was ever established. At one time, there were over a hundred chimps there." He pointed at the land across the road. "They did develop a Hepatitis C vaccine. But at what cost? Those poor animals were deliberately infected with the most horrible diseases. Many were kept in cages all the time. The poor things were like children, trusting their keepers and all the while…"

"Oh come on, Professor. They're monkeys. If they can help humans, shouldn't we use them?"

"In the first place, Wesley," the professor said, " we are not speaking of monkeys. We are speaking of chimpanzees."

Wesley smiled tolerantly. "There's a difference?"

"Indeed. They are both primates, but chimpanzees are a type of ape, closely related to humans, which is what led to their being used for medical research? Many kinds of monkeys exist, but their brains are smaller, and they are a different primate group."

Wesley winked at Dorrie Louise, who smiled at him. "Why is the building over there called the Monkey House? Why not the Chimp House?"

Papa said, "The Primate Preserve had monkeys there for many years, mostly rhesus macaque monkeys they were breeding for laboratory use. That program was stopped some time ago. The National Institutes of Health finally admitted that most chimpanzee research was unnecessary. When the government cut off the funding, the fight was over."

"What happened to the chimps?"

"They were sent to a real primate preserve in Louisiana."

"So you won."

Papa returned to his notes. "We won the battle for the chimps. Now we must win the battle for the Hieronymus Parcel. It is too precious to use for office towers and multi-million dollar high-rise apartment complexes. It would make a wonderful park. The Monkey House could become an arts center. The employee housing could be saved, updated, used as affordable housing for people who cannot afford to live downtown."

"Good luck with that, Professor." He looked at Dorrie Louise. "He's something, isn't he?"

"A man with a mission. Save the Hieronymus Parcel," she said to Wesley with a smile.

They went into the kitchen and left Papa to his phone calls. Wesley shook his head. "Austin's never gonna stop growing, There's some amazing new projects ready to come online."

She ignored his comment. "How are you, Wesley? Happily married?"

"Oh, sure," he said. "Cindy's a great girl. Just a great girl."

"Children?"

Wesley sighed. "Not yet. But we're still trying."

"Are you, Wesley?" Dora asked. "I see the articles in those magazines at the checkout line at the grocery store. You and your wife are in there a lot."

Wesley shrugged. "They exaggerate."

"Do they? What I read was that you two are in the middle of a break-up. Is that true, Wesley?"

"I still have my hopes. But her friends turn her against me, telling her I'm sleeping around. My friends tell me she's crazy jealous and generally bitchy."

"Those are not very nice friends, are they?"

"Another thing: the Patson family is well-lawyered, and I won't come out of a divorce in very good shape." He gazed out the kitchen window. A stray cloud crossed in front of the sun, offering a moment of shade. "You know who Tommy Thomas is?"

"No," she answered.

"He's always been the go-to lawyer for the University's football players. Always. Well, I called him to ask what I should do, you know, in the event there is a divorce, and he said he couldn't advise me."

"Why in the world?"

"Nobody wants to cross her family."

"They're very wealthy, I guess."

"You could say that. Anne Morgan Patson, you know, Cindy's mother, is like the richest woman in Texas. Oil money. Tommy Thomas doesn't want Anne Morgan for an enemy. No lawyer in Houston does. At least, none of the good ones. Ann Morgan loves a good fight and she's hardly ever lost one."

They stood silently. Dorrie Louise broke the silence. "You should talk to Donnie Ray about this. He's a very good lawyer."

"Oh, I can't do that, Dorrie Louise. He won't talk to me."

"What happened between you and Donnie Ray, Wesley? You were best friends. All that partying and double dates. I worried at the time that you two were partying too much, but that was the happiest I ever saw him. He won't tell me a thing about what happened between you."

"I made a big mistake. I admitted it. I asked him to forgive me, more than once, but he never would."

"That doesn't sound like him, to bear a grudge." Dorrie Louise said.

"He bears one, I can swear to that. Did you know he wrecked my car?"

"Donnie Ray wrecked that beautiful blue car?"

"Yep. My Beemer. Drove it right off Coyote Hill out on 2222."

Dorrie Louise sighed and brushed back her hair. "This humidity," she said. "He never said a word about wrecking your car."

"It doesn't matter." He bounced on his toes, still light-footed enough to remind any fan that he had been an All-American football player for the

University. "We need to change the mood. I want you to see my new car. It's a Ferrari."

"Is it blue? I loved that blue car."

Wesley grinned. "It is. Come on. I'll take you for a ride." He led her back into the book-lined living room. "We'll drive out and look at my new development. And then we'll all go to dinner." He spoke to Papa. "There's a new Hungarian place on South Congress. How does that sound to you for dinner, Professor?"

Papa looked up from his notes. "Hungarian, you say? I've never had Hungarian food and I'm not of a mind to start now. No, if you're free for dinner, I insist you join us here."

Before Wesley could object, Dorrie Louise said, "He wants to show you off, Wesley. You're a real life celebrity at the Cartwright House. It will thrill Papa to bring you to dinner."

Wesley escorted Dorrie Louise to the parking lot where his expensive blue Ferrari glittered in the sun. He helped Dorrie Louise in and then lowered himself effortlessly into the sports car.

"Goodness," Dorrie Louise said over the roar of the engine. Wesley sped out of the parking lot, leaving a sonic boom behind. "That'll knock them right off their rockers," she said with a laugh.

Wesley steered sharply onto MoPac and quickly got the low-slung car up to eighty. He wove in and out of the morning traffic, swerved sharply onto the Capitol of Texas extension and then onto Ben White. In a matter of minutes, they were on the Interstate, heading south.

"'Where are we going?" she asked, shouting to be heard.

"*Universe Race World.* Have you heard about the Grand Prix race-track being built past the airport? I want to show it to you." He slowed the Ferrari onto a bumpy farm-to-market road. The sports car shook with every pothole. Dorrie Louise braced herself against the jolts. Wesley slowed down and pulled to a stop on a knoll that overlooked the site of the race-track. He unfolded a large map. "Over there" he said, pointing to the north, "where the big dirt movers are, they're building a 3.4 mile state-of-the-art, circuit track. The elevation will change about a hundred and thirty feet.

It's being designed for all classes of racing, but the big deal will be with the Grand Prix. This is the first track in the U.S. built especially for Grand Prix racing."

"It certainly will be large," she said.

Wesley laughed. "Large? Yes. There'll be a tower and an amphitheater. But think about this: its capacity will be one hundred and twenty thousand people."

"No!"

"Yes! Can you imagine getting that many people out here from Austin to see a race?"

"I cannot. How are they possibly going to do it?"

"They have lots of plans, of course, but let me show you what the governor and I are planning." He turned the car around and sped down the road a few miles, then slowed and turned onto a gravel road. "Here we are."

Dorrie Louise stared at the scrubby land. A few goats were sheltered under an oak tree. There was a windmill in the distance. "What is this place, Wesley?"

He helped her out of the Ferrari. "Imagine it, Dorrie Louise, a four-lane expressway running from the Interstate right through here, and then, all the way to the Circuit of the Americas. Over there," he said, pointing to their left, "a world-class resort hotel. Over here, a Jack Nicklaus golf course. A helipad. Trees and beautiful plants everywhere you look. No expense spared."

"Really? It's hard for me to visualize."

"Not for me. Bob Braeswood and I have an option on this land."

"The governor?"

"His term is up. He and I are doing this. We're calling it *Austin Next*. You get it? The next big thing in Austin. The next generation of Austin. Right here. This land. All ours. It'll make history." He turned to her, eyes flashing. "This is a huge deal." His jaw tightened. "A huge, huge deal."

"It must be very important to you." She leaned against the sports car, squinting at the land. "You can visualize it all, can't you?"

"Every detail. This is mine, my deal. There won't be a dime of Patson money in it."

She touched his arm. "That's important…that your wife's family isn't…involved?"

He nodded his head. "Yes. It is. I don't have anything of my own, Dorrie Louise. I'm on an allowance. A kept man. Cindy and her mother watch me like hawks. Any time I do something that doesn't please either one of those women, there's hell to pay."

"Is there hell to pay often, Wesley?"

"You know me, Dorrie Louise. I can't resist a pretty face."

She smiled. "You're a married man, Wesley. It's about time for you to settle down."

He helped her back into the car and squatted by the door. "So I've been told. It didn't have to be this way. I should be in Congress now, making plans to succeed Bob Braeswood as governor. If Donnie Ray had only . . ."

"Why did Donnie Ray wreck your car, Wesley? What really happened between you?"

"I made a mistake, and he couldn't forgive me. In fact, he bad-mouthed me to important people, and I lost my chance to run for Congress." He stood up and shielded his eyes against the afternoon sun. "*Austin Next* will fix all that. It'll make me a rich man, and I can do what I want. What *ever* I want."

He got back in the car and turned on the ignition. Over the roar, Dorrie Louise said, "Tell me what happened, Wesley. I need to know."

"Ask Donnie Ray." He turned in the seat, and backed the Ferrari around on the gravel road. "I never meant to hurt him. Never."

"Let's call him, Wesley. Let's call Donnie Ray. I do so want you two to be friends again. You meant so much to each other."

"I don't know. I doubt he would even speak to me."

"He'll speak to you. Stop this car and give me your phone."

❧❧❧❧❧

In his office in the Panhandle town of Velda, Don R. Cuinn, attorney at law, recognized his mother's familiar voice. "Where are you, Mama? Is everything all right?"

"Yes, it certainly is, Donnie Ray. Guess who is sitting here beside me?"

"I give up."

"We're in a beautiful blue car, just as nice as the one you wrecked."

"It's a Ferrari," Wesley said loud enough to be heard.

"Don't tell me you're driving around with Wesley Bird in a blue Ferrari. You're not, are you? Please tell me you're not."

"Donnie Ray, Wesley forgives you for wrecking his car. He wants you two to be friends again."

"Jesus Christ, Mama. Let me talk to him."

She handed Wesley the phone. "I told you he'd talk to you."

Wesley winked at her and said, "Hello, *Crud*. What in the world are you doing way up there when you could be in Austin with me and your Mama, drinking *mojitos*?"

"No, Wesley. The question is, what are you doing, riding around Austin with my mother?"

Dorrie Louise opened the car door and climbed out. She smoothed her dress and stuck her head in the window. "I'm going to walk down there," she said, pointing to a culvert across a stream, "and look around. When I get back, I want you two boys to be friends again. Okay?"

Don waited a minute and then asked, "Is she gone?"

"Yeah," Wesley replied.

"Good. Now listen to me Wesley. I want you to leave my mother alone. Do you understand me?"

"Donnie Ray, I can't believe you're still mad. Whatever I did, you wrecked my car, screwed me over with Sawbucks Banjo, kept me from being elected to Congress, and let me get married to Cindy. Aren't we about even?"

Memories rushed over Don, memories of the day when he discovered that Wesley had played him; guiding him to a forgery in the State Archives that made the attorney general's ancestor out to be a drunkard liar; arranging for him to write an article about the incident ridiculing the attorney general's claim to be a descendant of a true Texas hero; getting that article published in Drayton Philby's magazine *Texas Today;* gleeful when the article played a big part in Bob Braeswood defeating the attorney general for governor; all that planned by Wesley, his best friend, the brother he never had, his mentor and confidant, who promised to always have his back.

"No. I did not screw you over with Banjo. I told Drayton that the article I wrote for his magazine was based on a forgery that you were responsible for, and Drayton was so angry, he told Banjo you were a bad actor. Which you are, by the way."

"Donnie Ray, everything I did, I did for us. We had something special. Remember how we promised to look out for each other?"

"I remember. You're the one who forgot."

"Not true, son. Not true. But think about all the good times: the partying, the fun, the girls. Remember election night? How great was that?"

"We had some good times," Don admitted. "And yes, until the end you looked out for me. I appreciate that."

"I'm still looking out for you, D. Ray. This land deal I'm working on is going to be immense. You're a lawyer now, right?"

"I have a license."

"Are you any good? I'll bet you're a great lawyer."

"I'm not too bad," Don said.

"This deal is Bob Braeswood and me. We could use a general counsel. Come to work for our company and we'll give you profit participation in the deal."

"No."

"No? You don't even want to know how much you could make? You'd rather stay up there in a rinky-dink town than live in Austin and get rich? Not to mention getting to see me every day?"

Don laughed, despite himself. "Wesley Bird, I would rather have my balls chewed off by a rabid groundhog, than go into business with you. You are a low-down, thieving, cheating, skirt-chasing son-of-a-bitch."

"Oh," Wesley said. "I see. Well, that doesn't mean we can't be friends, does it?"

Don laughed again. He had missed Wesley. "I guess we can be."

ᕫᕫᕫᕫᕫ

The Cartwright House was into the ninth decade since its establishment by Hiram Hieronymus as a retirement home for retired Methodist clergy and their widows. It had gone through several metamorphoses, each with new buildings and changes in its mission. Now it included two new residential towers alongside the original one. It was the retirement home of choice for University faculty and administrators. State politicians who preferred to retire in Austin rather than return to Muleshoe or Rusk flocked to it. Old Austin families had entrusted several generations of elderly mothers and aunts to the care of its staff. It had an incomparable location, across from Lady Bird Lake, close to doctors' offices and shopping malls and convenient for family members who lived nearby in upscale West Austin. It had three hundred apartments for senior living and over five hundred residents.

The dining room was decorated in the style popular in country clubs in the 1970's: expanses of carpet with an almost oriental design, but dark enough to hide food stains; chandeliers with ornate brass fittings. The wait staff was recruited from Third World countries and trained by the manager of dining services to provide the attentive service the residents expected. The staff, wearing black and white uniforms, carried trays and stored walkers. Small hard-of-hearing women sat erectly at dining tables with white tablecloths, smiling with feigned interest at their dinner partners.

Dorrie Louise had been right. By the time she and Professor Rothschild escorted Wesley through the dining room doorway, the University's All-American tight end was recognized and a buzz spread across the room. Dorrie Louise checked them in and waited for the waiter to find them a table. "The food here is very good," she said to Wesley.

But he couldn't hear her. Retirees, prominent men from the University, surrounded him. They were all laughing like schoolboys, clapping him on the back, shaking his hand. Wesley's team had won the school's last national championship at the Sugar Bowl. Listening, it seemed all of them had been in the stadium when Wesley caught the game-winning touchdown pass. Paul Stinson, the retired dean of the Engineering School, ninety-six years old and still alert, even though profoundly deaf, was recounting the game's last two minutes to Maurice Richard, the retired provost of the University and to St. Livermore Berkeley, the retired dean of the Law School.

Richards looked at Wesley and smiled. "We were at the game, Wesley. In fact, the three of us were sitting together. Paul just doesn't remember that."

Berkeley patted Papa on the shoulder. "Hello, Ralph. Can we convince Wesley to re-enroll? Coach Jones needs some help."

Papa shook his head. "Come on, Wesley. The dining room closes at eight. No food for late-comers, even you."

"Just a minute, Professor," Wesley said. "Let me speak to Judge Ashley. And I think that's Coach Wisconsin's widow, isn't it?" He turned and waved to the heavy-set, balding man who was watching from a long table at one end of the room. Ashley returned the wave and motioned for them to join them.

"My, my," Dorrie Louise said, "we've never been asked to sit with Minerva Wisconsin."

By the time they arrived at his table, former county judge Dockery Ashley had conferred with Minerva Wisconsin his hostess, and the self-appointed first lady of Cartwright House. She shooed away enough less important residents to make room for Wesley, Papa, and Dorrie Louise. She placed Wesley between herself and Judge Ashley. Dorrie Louise and Papa were relegated to the end of the table, next to Wilda Ashley, Judge Ashley's peckish wife. She nodded at the two of them and continued her conversation with Charles Cowlson, the retired dean of the History Department. Papa nodded to Judge Ashley, who did not speak.

Minerva Wisconsin's booming voice carried to the end of the table, "Of course we will beat Baylor. We always beat Baylor." Wesley and Judge smiled at each other. Thrice widowed, Minerva Wisconsin's most recent husband had been the late Jack (One-Eye) Wisconsin, the famed defensive back and safety, who despite having sight in only one eye, was an All-American at the University; later he was an All-Pro, and eventually head coach at Pittsburgh. Being the widow of the famed Coach Wisconsin lent Minerva precedence on matters athletic or so she believed. In between comments about the year's football team and its woefully inadequate coach, Jonesy "J" Jones, Minerva tended to her other duties, not the least of which was observing the scene before her, noting wait staff errors or breaches of the dress code in a small notepad. She shared her sightings of lapses in service or resident attire at regular meetings with Billy Boykin, the portly manager of Cartwright House. Minerva pushed her chair back discretely, rose, blew a kiss in the general direction of Judge Ashley, and walked to the end of the table. "Do change places with me, Wilda," she said to Mrs. Ashley. "I want to talk to Ralph." She took the other woman's chair and turned to Papa. "Tell me what books you've been reading, Ralph? Have you seen any plays? I love the theater."

Rather than sit where Minerva had directed her, Mrs. Ashley drained her glass of Vodka, nodded primly and tottered across the dining room. "Poor Dockery," Minerva whispered to Papa. "She was very wealthy and considered quite a catch when they married."

Papa grunted. "I have not had much contact with the judge...or his wife."

"A good wife is the key to a man's success, so they say."

Papa raised his glass. "To success."

They clinked glasses. Minerva Wisconsin smiled "When will your next volume of poetry be published, Ralph? I love poetry."

"Do you? Most people do not."

"I'm not like most people. But when?"

"Oh, never, I suppose. There is very little market for my sort of work."

"Oh, but there should be." She lowered her voice. "Send me the manuscript. Jack Fellows at the university's press is a very good friend."

"You're very kind, Mrs. Wisconsin. But really..."

"Call me Minerva. Kindness has nothing to do with it. I am a supporter of the arts: the symphony, the opera, the ballet, I support them all. Why not poetry? I'll call you tomorrow. Perhaps we can discuss it over tea."

Papa blushed and turned to his mushroom soup.

At the center of the table, Judge Ashley and Wesley ate their soup. Ashley ate hungrily, without speaking. He boasted a muscular rotund body; big but not fat, set off by his shaved round head. He finished his soup with a final swipe of his spoon and said to Wesley, "Your mother-in-law, Wesley. What is she up to these days? Busy with the Houston arts scene?"

"Anne Morgan's more interested in making money than giving it away."

"Like her father. I worked with him on a few projects." Judge retained the aura of power. For decades, he was one of the most powerful men in the capitol city. During his terms as county judge, he spearheaded the change away from the city's distrust of growth, turning it into a Mecca for developers and land speculators. Welcoming, let alone seeking out new industries, was anathema to the city's Old Guard. However, they soon took their place among the wealth seekers, converting their land holdings and rundown properties into shining examples of the new Austin. At one time the judge had been the face of the new city, no matter who was mayor, or president of the university, or speaker of the house, or even governor. He knew every legislator, every regent, every lobbyist, and every important donor across the state. He vetted appointments for every governor, regardless of party, but Bob Braeswood's election had made public what insiders had known for some time: Ashley's days as a master powerbroker were over. The newcomers had their own ways of exercising power, and Ashley's brand was old-fashioned, crude, even. When he was finally deposed as county judge, his golden parachute was presidency of the non-profit H.H. Company, the owner of the Hieronymus Parcel, and the source of funds for many local charities. "It is," he said, "my way of giving back to the community." In fact, it was his main source of income, now that his wife Wilda's inheritance was spent. Running the H.H. Company provided a large annual salary, an expansive downtown office, club memberships, and the other trappings of power that Ashley had become accustomed to.

Wesley broke off a piece of his Parker House dinner roll and spread butter on it. "Anne Morgan," he said of his mother-in-law, "may have inherited the largest oil fortune in Texas, but she'll leave the earth with a lot more than she inherited. I can't get her to even look at my projects."

"I hear that you and Braeswood have something in the works, out by the new motorway."

20

Wesley pushed his plate away and looked down at a plate brimming with meatloaf and mashed potatoes covered with dark gravy. "*Austin Next*, we're calling it."

Ashley leaned in close. "You ought to look into the Hieronymus Parcel," he whispered.

"So the rumors are true? You're opening it up to bidders? That'll bring out a shitload of protesters, pardon my English."

"We have no choice but to sell, Wesley. The H.H. Company lost its major source of income when we lost the damned monkeys. We have to sell or close up shop. Yes, there will be protests. Many of them from people in this room." He frowned. "They want us to give the land away. Give it away! Use it for hiking trails and picnics. Ridiculous! But fortunately, I still have some influence. We'll keep them quiet. Even your friend, the professor, over there."

"Professor Rothschild is a poet," Wesley said. "I've known him for a long time. Maybe I could speak to him."

"Any help would be appreciated, Wesley. I don't like to be a schoolyard bully, beat up on the defenseless." He nodded with a thin smile and turned to his meatloaf. "This has been a good talk. Maybe your mother-in-law would be interested in bidding on the Hieronymus Parcel."

Wesley answered softly, "Yes. She might be interested. The question is, do I want to let her in?"

Ashley chuckled to himself. He knew how little influence Wesley had in the Patson Empire.

CHAPTER TWO

THE PRESENT

It was a clear sunny day, crisp and calm. Dave Lewis turned to the others and said, "I've lived in the Midwest too long. The sky here is scary."

Don smiled. "I know what you mean." He looked at the endless horizon and the startling blue sky and remembered how strange all the openness felt when he first moved to the Texas Panhandle. Now, he hardly noticed it, unless someone reminded him, like the newspaper executive from Akron, Ohio, whom he had just met. *Did he come all the way down here just for the funeral?* Don wondered.

The paper's Velda editor, Charlton Denning, was taking everything in, whispering notes into his phone, waving at his staff photographer. "This is different from any funeral I ever attended," Denning said, excitedly. "Or even read about. It'll be our headline story in the *Sun* in the morning. It'll probably be picked up by the wire services," he said to Lewis.

They were standing in a large gravel parking lot carved out of the Texas Panhandle caliche. In front of them, folding chairs for the invited guests, all one thousand of them, had been arranged in a semi-circle in front of a wooden platform. On the platform was a pulpit and chairs for the celebrants officiating at the funeral: a Catholic Cardinal, a Jewish Rabbi, probably the first ever to visit Velda, and of course, the pastor of the First Baptist Church of Velda. The church where Sawbucks Banjo, world famous oilman, television personality, fund manager, and kingmaker, had been a member, a large donor, and even an occasional worshiper. The First Baptist choir, (augmented by fifty professional singers flown in from Dallas) were gathered on risers to the left of the platform. To the right of the platform was the Fightin' Titan Marching Band, which had arrived by bus the night before from Sawbuck Banjo's alma mater, Central Southwestern Kansas College. The Banjo Sports Arena, (home of the Fightin' Titans championship basketball team) the Banjo School of Free Enterprise and the Banjo Library, all assured that Banjo's fame would endure as long as Central Southwestern Kansas College did. It also guaranteed that if Banjo's funeral directions called for the marching band to be at his memorial services, they would be there, even if they had to march two hundred miles.

The college's ROTC Honor Guard flanked the platform, carrying the flags of the United States of America, the State of Kansas, and of Banjo Enterprises.

The wooden platform itself had been erected in front of the passageway in to what appeared to be a large earthen mound. On top of the mound were solar panels and skylights.

Lewis turned to Charlton Denning. "Charlie, did Sawbucks build himself a tomb, or what?"

The Fightin' Titans began to play a Bach cantata. The brass and oboe echoed across the canyons and, most of those in attendance would say later, were surprisingly effective.

Charlton Denning waved to the photographer to move to the other side of the crowd. "Dammit. He needs to get a shot of the TV cameras. Look at that. The networks are all here. Even ESPN." Finally satisfied with the photographer's location, he turned back to Lewis. "This is the largest underground dwelling in the United States! It is completely solar powered! It has its own water well! The rooms are fifty feet underground! The temperature down there is a constant sixty-five degrees!" He rolled his eyes at Lewis. "We've run at least five features about it over the years. One when it was built by a Crackstone manager, Jessie somebody." Seeing Lewis' blank stare, he added, "Crackstone Industries, biggest employer in Velda, until they got taken over by the Swiss."

"Ah," Lewis said.

The band was winding down and the Baptist preacher was testing the microphone. Charlton lowered his voice. "When that guy Jessie was transferred, Crackstone bought the place. They used it as an office and some sort of environmental laboratory. Looked good in their annual report, I guess. When the Swiss took over, they didn't want it. Sawbucks Banjo ended up with it; he probably got it for next to nothing."

The Baptist preacher introduced the Cardinal, staring disapprovingly at his regalia. The Cardinal entertained the crowd with a lengthy remembrance of the deceased, including several humorous references to Sawbucks Banjo's tight way with a dollar.

"Did Banjo live here?"

"God, no. He claimed to be a resident of Velda, but he was hardly ever here. When he was, around, he stayed at his house north of here. Nobody could figure out why he wanted an underground house. I guess now we know." Charlton whispered in his cell phone to his photographer, "Get George and Laura; see if you can catch them laughing with Clinton."

Don scanned the crowd, noticing the row of West Coast celebrities up front. The vice president was there as, conveniently, the president was unable to leave Washington. He was negotiating an end to a hockey league player strike, and, as he told his vice -president, "I just won't be able to see them bury that son-of-a-bitch." Sawbucks Banjo was a vocal supporter of the other party. But the president had made Air Force One available to the vice president. Security concerns had delayed air traffic for several hours around the Amarillo airport. Satirical comments about the delays lit up social media, to the displeasure of the vice president, who was maneuvering to succeed the president.

"Why didn't they just rent Madison Square Garden? Or the National Cathedral?" Lewis asked.

Charlton laughed. "You had to know Sawbucks. It's a last show of his power, dragging all these A-listers to Velda. I mean really, Velda? To pay their respects? Even the ones who hated him are here."

After the music and eulogies and the mandatory forty-minute sermon by the Baptist preacher, (who knew a main chance when he saw one) the mass choir joined the college band in a rousing rendition of the Fightin' Titans alma mater, "Southwestern Kansas We Love Thee." Rabbi Bluestein from Los Angeles ended the service with an ecumenical prayer to, "Whatever God, if any, whom all here assembled worship, or do not, in their hearts."

Don said goodbye to the newspapermen. He compared the spectacle that the oilman had scripted to the simple memorial service at the state cemetery when his adoptive mother, Lena Rothschild, had died. He brushed away a tear, then looked around self-consciously. He didn't want anyone to think he was crying for Sawbucks Banjo, God rest his soul!

He motioned to Wiley Franklin, the young lawyer who was the only associate in the Rosen & Cuinn law firm. Together, they watched as the mourners waited in line to pay their respects. Don had come, not because he was a friend of Banjo or his family, which he was not; or because most everybody in the Panhandle would be there, which wouldn't hurt his visibility. He came because he wanted to see the mausoleum the famous man had built for himself out of the earthen house that rose out of the plains a few miles outside the town of Velda.

Don had been in the underground house, when it belonged to Crackstone Industries. He was curious to see what Banjo had done to it. And finally, of course, like the other mourners, he wanted to see for certain that Sawbucks Banjo was really dead.

Wiley wiped the dripping sweat from his forehead. "Chief," he said, "Didn't this place belong to Tommy Crackstone? How did Sawbucks come by it?"

Wiley had taken to calling Don *"Chief"* after Don took over the Rosen law practice. Don didn't like it. He also didn't like Wiley's badgering about moving back to downtown Velda from the firm's satellite office in Antelope City. That office was Don's, the only part of the practice's income that he didn't have to share with Jake Rosen under the agreement they made when Jake finally decided to retire.

"Bought it, I guess. Figured he'd need a gravesite somewhere. Although I believe he thought that he was immortal."

Wiley grinned. "Wasn't, was he?"

"It doesn't look like it. But we haven't been inside yet. Maybe he has a surprise for us."

The crowd parted to let the politicians, the movie stars, the Wall Streeters and other important grievers pass. They were shepherded into the earthen house first but they didn't stay long, and they smiled and laughed and chatted with their fellow luminaries when they came out. The other guests pressed forward. Don and Wiley stood in the shade of a large mesquite tree. A bird's nest perched wobbily on a high branch.

Wiley said, "Heard about any more layoffs? They let Jobie go. He came to the office the other day, really upset. Wanted to know if there was anything we could do about it."

Some time earlier, GFC, the American subsidiary of the Swiss company *Gesellschaft für Chemische*, took over Crackstone Industries in a proxy fight. The Crackstone heirs may have lost their company, but the takeover only made them richer. For Veldanians, it created a tsunami of uncertainty. Crackstone had been in Velda since the 1930s, and no one knew what the GFC's plans were for the local operation. According to the Chamber of Commerce, Velda could not afford to lose its largest industrial plant. Its members lobbied the city and county to give the Swiss tax abatements, hoping they would not leave. Other residents said they would be happy to see the air cleaned of the noxious fumes from the plant. Don would have sided with the latter group if he had not been owner of the office building that housed the GFC offices.

GFC had already cut their lease space in the building by a third, and no one in the company would tell him their plans. Don cursed Jake Rosen silently one more time. Jake had finally retired and sold the law practice to Don. But Jake kept a third of the profits for the next ten years, compensation for leaving his name on the firm and being available whenever one of his rancher clients wanted the original law product instead of the new younger variety. As part of the deal, Jake insisted that Don buy the Hansro Building and against his instinct, Don had agreed. Now, instead of being moderately well off as a result of a large fee he collected from

Elmer Thorpe for the sale of his water rights, Don was the Cuinn in the Law Offices of Rosen & Cuinn and the owner of an office building, which was losing its tenants in the middle of a town, which was losing it's biggest industry. *Not really the building's owner,* he reminded himself. The bank owned a lot more than he did. All Don had was the mortgage, which he suspected was underwater the day the loan was made. Jake Rosen was the deal-master.

"The guy they let go, Jobie, isn't he the black guy?" he asked Wiley.

"The only one out there, and they fired him. Six months' pay, and he'd been with Crackstone for fifteen years."

Don reached down and retrieved a paper napkin that had blown across the parking lot. "He probably should have taken the buyout."

"That's what that new Swiss manager told him. The one who took Chrome's place?"

Don nodded. He wadded the paper onto a ball and tossed it into a trash barrel. Chrome, the well-liked Crackstone plant manager, had been sent packing. Bill Dixon, the HR guy, had told Don over a beer at the Greeks that he was being paid well to stay around and help the new owners sort out whom they needed to keep and whom they could do without. "Consolidation and rationalization," Dixon had told him. "Those of us who have jobs will probably be in Lake Charles. The plant here is a keeper, but all the admin types, they're just fat as far as the Swiss are concerned." Dixon took a long swig of his beer. "Truth be known, that probably includes me."

Don was surprised that the Swiss had fired the only black professional in the plant office. He turned back to Wiley and said quietly, "Let's meet Jobie out at Antelope City. He may have a discrimination claim."

He knew what Wiley would say next. "It would be a lot easier if I was downtown."

"Easier for you maybe, but not necessarily for our clients. I'll bet Jobie came to the Antelope City office because there nobody would notice he was talking to a lawyer. Bring him back to your office. Set up a time with Faye."

Wiley grimaced. "Right. Chief. You're the boss." Almost as an afterthought, he asked, "Why isn't Jake here?"

"He's in Dallas."

"With the new widow?"

They were almost to the front entrance of the earth house. "I would guess so. Plus, he has some Hansard Foundation business with the tax guys down there." Major Hansard, the richest man in Velda had died at age ninety the year before. Except for a bequest to Bridget O'Neill, the major left everything to his foundation and named Jake Rosen as its trustee.

The line inched forward. The local state representative grabbed Don by the shoulder and whispered, "The governor's here!"

Don looked up and saw ex-governor Bob Braeswood exiting the tunnel. Behind him, smiling at Don, was Sid Banger. The emaciated political consultant whispered something to Braeswood, who looked up and smiled when he saw Don. Banger guided Braeswood toward Don and Wiley. There was no way to escape.

"Governor, you remember D. R. Cuinn, don't you? Wrote the *Hero of San Jacinto* article?"

Braeswood smiled. "Of course. Of course. Gave the attorney general what he deserved, didn't you? Sent him running back to West Texas."

"Payne died last year, didn't he?" Don said.

"Oh, yes, I think he did." Braeswood grimaced. "Great public servant, tragic loss." He looked at Banger and then back at Don. "It's too bad we didn't have you to help us during the last election." Braeswood had been defeated in a close election.

Don bit his tongue. *Need some more dirty tricks?*

The county's state representative had been listening, obviously excited at being so close to power, even ex-power. He was probably impressed that Don was on speaking terms with Braeswood. He broke the silence to ask, "Sawbucks Banjo was an early supporter of yours, wasn't he?"

"From the beginning. Great public servant. Tragic loss."

What Braeswood didn't say was that the oilman had supported both Braeswood and his opponent.

Banger stuck out his bony hand. "Let bygones be bygones?"

Don ignored the outstretched hand.

28

"Ralph Rothschild is related to you, isn't he? Are you giving him advice about the grand jury?"

"What grand jury?"

Braeswood said loudly, "Hillary," and joined the Clinton entourage.

Sid lowered his voice and pulled Don away from the others. "It's very sensitive." He glanced over at Braeswood. "The governor is distressed about it. Apparently your boy Wesley is in serious trouble. With the law."

"That doesn't surprise me, but what does that have to do with Papa?"

"I imagine he'll have to testify before the grand jury that's investigating Wesley's land deal. But then, I'm sure he told you all about it."

"Told me about what?"

"The investment Professor Rothschild and your mama made in *Austin Next*."

"You're such a shit, Sid." He started to leave and then turned back to the bug-eyed consultant. "Sid…"

"Yeah, old buddy?"

"Tell Wesley to stay away from Papa and my mother."

"Stay away? Wesley said they're like a second family to him. Why else would they have invested with him? And convinced other people to invest?"

Jesus. Can I be hearing this? "They're not his family. Just tell him to stay away."

Sid smirked and looked for the governor, who was talking animatedly with Hillary Clinton. "You'll have to tell him yourself. I don't see much of Wesley these days."

"Aren't he and Braeswood partners in that land deal?"

"No. Never partners. The governor is as innocent as the other investors."

Don nodded. "And your job is to make sure everyone believes that, right?"

"If it's the truth, it's easy. Not like the hatchet job you and Wesley pulled on poor Payne."

Don jerked away and got back in line. He motioned to his young associate, who had been standing apart, watching the celebrities. "Come on, Wiley. Let's see King Tut's Tomb."

Don couldn't concentrate on the displays inside the underground house: walls with war flags from the PT boat that Sawbucks captained in Vietnam; cases full of trophies won by sports teams endowed by Banjo at Central Southwestern Kansas; walls of enlarged photos of Banjo with world leaders; a replica of the trunk of Banjo's old Ford, out of which he sold his first deals; the well core from Banjo's big offshore discovery, the one that made his company. *What had Wesley done and why did Dorrie Louise not mention it? Don talked to her every Sunday.*

The glass casket was on a bier in the conference room where Don once sat. The college honor guard protected it against all enemies, and as Don recalled, Sawbucks Banjo had a few. Few mourners lingered in front of the exhibits. The honoree's puffy face was heavily made-up and was lit by an amber spotlight from high in the atrium.

Wiley whispered, "I hear they brought his make-up girl from the business channel."

Don didn't answer. *I needed to get out of here and call Dorrie Louise,* he thought.

"It wouldn't have hurt you to introduce me," Wiley said.

"To the governor?"

"Fuck the governor. To Sid Banger. I may want to run for office someday."

The thought of Wiley in public office almost made Don smile. "Oh, Banger." He pushed Wiley by the elbow toward the exit. "Believe me, you're better off. Let's get out of here."

"I sort of sensed you don't like Banger too much."

Outside, as his eyes adjusted to the bright Panhandle sun, Don saw Braeswood and Sid Banger standing by a limo, talking to the editor of the Velda newspaper and Dave Lewis. It was just like Sid to insist that Braeswood talk to the *Velda Sun. Hell, the Sun wasn't even influential in Velda,* Don thought.

CHAPTER THREE

Don poked around the kitchen, looking for a clean glass. He found one that was covered with dust, not dirt, and wiped it clean with a dishtowel. He opened the twenty-year-old refrigerator and wrenched an ice tray loose. For a rich man, the major had not believed in kitchen appliances. Of course the major had a man to deal with half-filled ice trays and dirty dishes. Until a month ago, Don had Bridget. Now all he had was the deed to the Hansro Building, more law office than he needed, the free use of the major's old apartment, and a past-due note at the Bank of Velda.

Bridget had warned him against buying the building. "Jake's using you. He's unloading his white elephant. You can't afford it."

"It's part of the deal," he said and refused to discuss it further.

Bridget had been right, as she usually was. Jake wanted to quit practicing law so he probably would have sold the practice to Don without Don buying the building. But Don desperately wanted the law practice. He wanted the sign on the door that said Rosen & Cuinn Law Offices; he was a chicken ready to be plucked. Too bad for Don. Jake Rosen was a champion chicken plucker.

Don wandered into the bedroom, set his Scotch on the rocks on the mahogany bedside table, and stretched out on the bed. He looked at the picture of Cecilia on the opposite wall. It was an enlargement of a picture he took of her outside their apartment in Mexico. While he and Bridget were together, he kept the picture in in his office desk. The night before Bridget left, she had said, "Before we make love, every time you pray to St. Cecilia, asking her if it's all right for you to do it."

He disentangled himself from her naked body and pulled on his shorts. "She's dead, Bridget."

"I know she's dead, Don. But she's not gone, is she? I can't compete with her."

After Bridget left him, he took the photo to Vera's Photos and had the enlargement made and framed. Then he hung it on the wall where he would see it every night before he went to sleep and every morning when he woke up.

"You're right, Bridget," he had told her. "I'm not fit to be lived with. Go find somebody else."

She had tried to make it work. She quit complaining about Jake. She and Faye, the law firm's office manager and secretary, tried to turn the major's apartment into a love nest. "We could raise a family here," Bridget had said. "It's big enough." *No family. No marriage. No future.* Don felt it in his bones, and before long, Bridget felt it too. He missed her.

Now, the Swiss had given up a third of their office space, and were obviously going to cut back even more. *Did Jake know? Of course he did. Jake always knew. Who else was interested in prime office space in downtown Velda?* Don couldn't think of anyone.

He stared at the phone. He needed to call his mother. What was Wesley up to? He thought he had Dorrie Louise and Papa taken care of, happy in their retirement home. Unfortunately, the residency agreement didn't cover Acts of Wesley.

Dorrie Louise answered on the first ring. "Hello, darlin'," she said.

"Do you always answer that way, Mama?" he asked.

"Oh, I'm high-tech, Donnie Ray," she said. "I saw you on the caller ID. Would you like for me to teach you how to use it? You can avoid people trying to sell you burial insurance."

Don smiled. "Well, I could use some help avoiding people, Mama. For example, I saw Governor Braeswood today."

"Really? In Velda?"

"That's right. At the Sawbucks Banjo memorial service."

"Oh, wasn't that nice." He could hear her speaking loudly to Papa.

"Papa, isn't that something? Governor Braeswood went all the way out to Velda to pay his respects to Mr. Banjo."

The professor mumbled something inaudible to Don. "Papa wants to know if Wesley was with him?"

"No. I don't think Wesley and Braeswood are on speaking terms right now."

Dorrie Louise repeated what Don had said. More mumbling on the other end. "Papa says if you see Wesley, to tell him to take care of business. Our dividend check is late."

Don's heart sank. *Please God, no.* "What did you do, Mama? Did you invest with Wesley?"

"Oh, of course we did. You should see how hard Wesley works. That poor thing. Did you know that rich wife of his divorced him? She left him with a lot of bills and he's working day and night to pay them off. And every month we get a nice fat dividend: ten percent on money that was just sitting in the bank, not earning anything. We can use that dividend. Our monthly fee here goes up every year, and Papa's pension and our social security barely cover it as it is."

"What scheme did he talk you into, Mama? Believe me, you cannot trust Wesley Bird."

"Oh, it's perfectly safe, honey. Don't worry about that. There's this big development that Wesley and the governor are doing, out by the new race track."

"*Austin Next*. I know, Mama. Listen to me. You cannot trust Wesley."

"But the governor is in it, Donnie Ray. Of course it's safe. The governor!"

"How much did you give him?"

She hesitated. "Papa, do you remember how much money we invested in Wesley's land development?" More mumbling. "Let's see. We had that money left from the sale of the hotel. Earning nothing, Donnie Ray. Now we get this big check, every month."

"How much, Mama?"

"Well, most of it, you know. Wesley said we ought to keep some for emergencies, that sometimes the dividend check might be late."

"Like this month!" Don could hear Papa this time.

"Now, Papa, it's only three weeks late."

Don sighed. "Why didn't you ask me first, Mama?"

"Oh, honey, I was there when you two made up, remember? Out at Wesley's property, we talked on the phone and you and Wesley reconciled, settled everything, Wesley told me. I'm so happy you two are friends again."

"Did you sign some papers, Mama?"

"Why yes, of course, it's all perfectly legal. And the governor is a partner, did I tell you that?"

"Send me the papers, Mama...by Express Mail. Get them up here right away."

"Well of course, Donnie Ray, if you want me to. I think I know where they are."

"Jesus, Mama."

"Don't swear, Donnie Ray. I hate it when you swear. Really, it's a wonderful arrangement for us. Besides, Wesley said he'd give us our money back, any time we wanted out."

"Call him right now and tell him you want your money back. And send me the papers. Today!"

"My goodness, Donnie Ray. Separating from Bridget has certainly put you in a bad mood."

CHAPTER FOUR

D on sat in the old wood chair, its arms still in need of tightening, at the same conference table, in the same conference room, converted from a supply room in Elmer Thorpe's old store, where Don had set up shop as a lawyer when Jake Rosen fired him…or he quit, depending on who was telling the story. When he moved back to Velda and took over Jake's practice, he installed Wiley in the Antelope City office.

Wiley had not changed things very much. Most notably, Maye, the office manager and Faye's twin sister, had retired again and returned to Amarillo, replaced by an attractive Polish girl. Something about the embarrassed way she greeted Don led him to suspect that the bedroom in the back of the office was getting some use on slow afternoons. *What the hell,* Don considered. *They're both single. And she is good-looking; Wiley's lucky. From what I've heard about Polish girls, there are probably wedding bells in Wiley's future.*

"Tell Don what you told me," Wiley said to Jamail Jobey, who was sitting across from them.

The well-dressed black man opened a folder and read through his notes. "It was on Friday, the 20th of last month. The guys from Zurich were in town and wanted to meet." He looked down at his notes and then spoke directly to Don. "It was about eleven."

"You keep good notes," Don said.

"An old habit."

"It could come in handy."

"You think so?"

"In case of litigation," Wiley said.

Don patted Wiley on the arm. "We're a long way from litigation. Go on," he said to Jobey.

"Yes. Anyway, I thought they were going to take me to lunch, maybe tell me what their plans were, whether I'd be transferred. You know, things like that. It never occurred to me…"

Don waited for him to go on, then asked, "I guess no lunch?"

"Right. Instead they sat me down and told me about the restructuring, having to find the best fit for the combined operation." He looked at his notes again, then sighed. "I still didn't get it. I know it sounds stupid, but I was still thinking it might be a promotion." He took out a freshly starched handkerchief and wiped his brow. "I have to tell my wife."

"You haven't told her yet?" Don asked.

"It's hard. I've never failed at anything. High school, college, business school."

"You haven't failed," Don said. "The new owners are screwing you over. Not just you. Lots of folks are losing their jobs."

"It sure seems like failure. Where are we going to move? We'll have to leave here, go somewhere I can find a job. We'll take a loss on the house, if anyone will even buy it. Six months' pay. All our savings, everything we've worked for. It'll all be gone."

"Six months pay?" Wiley was taking notes. "Where did that come from?"

"A month's pay for each year I worked for Crackstone, maximum of six months. Under five years, people will only get one month."

"That's cold." Don paused. "Do you have a contract?"

"A contract? No. As far as I know, no one has a contract."

Don turned to Wiley. "Get us some coffee, will you, Wiley?"

The younger man hurried out the door and Don pushed it shut with his boot. "Do you mind if I call you Jamail?"

"No, of course not."

"So tell me, Jamail. Do you believe they are letting you go because you are black?"

Jobey paused. They could hear Wiley and the blond Polish girl preparing the coffee. "I've thought about it. They never mentioned it, of course, but underneath, all the talk about downsizing, I felt like it wouldn't be happening if I wasn't black."

Don had prepared hurriedly for the meeting. He had never tried a race discrimination case, mainly because there were so few racial minorities in Velda. As far as he knew, Jobey was the only black professional in the county, and one of the few in the Panhandle. He had talked to a Houston lawyer who specialized in discrimination claims. He knew that Jobey's chances of winning a discrimination claim depended on the answer to the question he was about to ask: "Can you think of any instance, before this, of course, where the Swiss or Crackstone treated you unfairly because of your race?"

Jobey shook his head. "Crackstone, never, not once in over fifteen years. These guys, it's a feeling I got. The Swiss are very stern acting. It could just be that."

"Listen," Don said, looking at the door, "I think we can get you some more money. Not a big award, with punitive damages, but more than they've offered. This will be Wiley's case, and he'll do you a good job. He'll leave no stone unturned. But I'm just telling you that these cases are hard to win, without some pretty blatant evidence of race discrimination. Wiley will work with you, see if you can remember more that will help your case. Does that sound all right with you?"

"Is it worth it? How much will you charge?"

"We will do it on contingency. We will take a third of whatever we get you, over and above the six months' pay. As far as it being worth it, we'll make them squirm a little, if that's of any interest."

For the first time, Jobey smiled. "Let's do it."

CHAPTER FIVE

D on's unease grew as he read through the paperwork for the *Austin Next Limited Partnership*. He turned to the last page again, on the off hope that he had seen it wrong; that Papa and Dorrie Louise hadn't signed it, or had signed it improperly; but of course, their signatures were both there, with witnesses and a notary's stamp. He recognized the English professor's handwriting and his mother's precise lettering. No doubt they signed it. Without even calling him. The lawyer!

Their money was gone, and their faint hope of getting it back seemed to depend on the governor and Wesley making a success of *Austin Next*. It had been a long time since he had wished anything good for Wesley Bird, but he had to root for him now. "Just one more impossible play," he whispered under his breath. He hoped that the All-American's luck hadn't run out.

He opened his laptop and began a list of things to ask Dorrie Louise about. What she had sent him was a fairly typical limited partnership agreement. Papa and Dorrie Louise were limited partners. The good part of that was that they weren't responsible for any debts of the partnership. The bad part was that they had no say in how the partnership was managed. That was the responsibility of the general partner, which in this case was another limited partnership. He made a note to Faye to find out more about that partnership, Big Score LLP, from the Secretary of State. He supposed it was owned by Braeswood and Wesley, and was a way of diverting profits away from their investors. Of course, nowhere was there any mention of Wesley's promise to return Papa and Dorrie Louise's money if they wanted out of the deal. Even more ominously, nowhere was Braeswood's name even mentioned.

"Faye," he called. "Do you have a minute?" He forwarded his notes to her desktop. The office manager strode into his office with a new cup of steaming coffee. She sat it down on his desk, stacking a few papers in a neater pile to make room for the cup. "Yes, Mr. Cuinn?"

She steadfastly refused to call him Don. Faye was probably the only person in Velda who called him Mr. Cuinn. He handed her the papers his mother had sent. "Start a file on this, will you? And I've sent you my notes and some information I need you to get from the Secretary of State's office."

She thumbed through the papers quickly. "Your folks? They never leave old folks alone, do they?"

"I need to go down there and see what I can salvage."

"Monday? I'll get you a flight. A hotel? That place you like on South Congress?"

"Monday's fine. But let's find a new place to stay." The funky motel had been his and Bridget's place.

"Speaking of Miss O'Neill…"

"I wasn't."

Faye straightened the last remaining cluttered spot on Don's desk. "As I was about to say, since Miss O'Neill left us, the apartment has become, shall we say, untidy."

"And you know this how?"

She passed her hand over her thinning gray hair. Faye never seemed to worry about her appearance, unlike her twin sister Maye, who had shepherded Don through his early months of law practice in Antelope City. "I am the building manager and rental agent, aren't I?"

"You certainly are, Faye." He had given her the job of keeping the tenants happy and the offices leased, in return for a commission. She was waging an uphill battle, about to get worse with the Swiss cutting back on all sides, but Faye didn't shrink from a challenge. "And that gives you the right to prowl around my apartment?"

She ignored his remark. "I have access to all the property. Sometimes, I've shown the penthouse to prospective tenants, to let them see the view… from the deck."

The five-story building was the tallest building in Velda and it had unobstructed views of the entire county. He remembered the cocktail party the major held in the penthouse when he and Bridget connected for the first time. He remembered their nights together, after he bought the building and convinced her to move in with him; lying together on the chaise lounge on the deck, the moonlight almost as bright as day, playing off the shadows of her body; making love until the moon darkened and the early morning dawn broke.

Faye was still talking. "Thank goodness I inspected it before I showed it to the gas company people."

"And I suppose you noticed that all of Bridget's clothes were gone, that she's gone for good."

The frown grew deeper. "No, sir. What I noticed was dirty dishes and an unmade bed and dirty laundry in the washroom. That floor hasn't been mopped since she left. Mr. Cuinn, I will clean up your mess and straighten your desk for you here, in this office. But there is no way I will do your laundry or wash your dishes."

"Nobody asked you to, Faye."

"Now don't act hurt with me, sir. I suspect you're glad the O'Neill girl is gone. I could have told you it wasn't going to last."

"Exactly how could you tell, Faye? I thought it would last. I wanted it to last. Very much. What did you see that I didn't?"

"I'd rather not say."

"Do say. Tell me what made me unable to have a relationship with an attractive, funny, intelligent woman who cared for me?"

She paused and straightened the neat pile once again. "All right, then. Mr. Cuinn, I believe that you are a one-woman man, and that woman is dead. I'm sorry, but I do believe that is the truth."

Don turned away and stared out the window. When he turned back, she was still standing there. He said, "What are we going to do about the dirty dishes? I don't want to cost us a new tenant."

"I have a nice woman who will come in for a couple of hours every afternoon. She needs the work. Her husband has been laid off."

"The Swiss?"

"Who else?"

"By the way, we're suing them. Race discrimination."

"Don't tell me they fired Jamail Jobey? He has the most beautiful baritone voice." She sank down in the client's chair in front of his desk. "He's in our church choir. Oh my, they won't like it when their landlord sues them."

Don smiled. "I've turned the case over to Wiley. He gets to deal with them. I don't expect it'll amount to much." He handed her a case folder.

She fanned herself with it. "Oh my. All those empty offices."

"We'd have lost them anyway. They're leaving town. But you'll fill the building. I hear there's a new shale play, the north end of the county. Lots of oil men are probably descending on Velda as we speak."

"Let us sincerely hope," Faye said. She jumped up. "I need to call the gas company. Then I need to review our lease with the Swiss." She turned back to Don. "You have an appointment at ten. Charlton Denning."

"What's Charlton want? A quote about Sawbucks? He probably saw me talking with Governor Braeswood at the funeral."

"He wouldn't say. Just that it was a personal matter." She gathered up the files. "I hate people who won't say what their business is."

The chubby editor shuffled uneasily. He looked like he was about to cry. Don found a box of tissue he kept in his desk drawer for distraught wives who had discovered their husbands were cheating on them. For a small town, Velda had a lot of cheating going on. *Nothing else to do,* Jake had said. *Don't ever turn down a divorce. One side or the other. No matter. Just try to get them to reconcile. They'll love you for it and then one or the other will be back in a year or two, really angry. An even bigger fee.*

"Thank you," Charlton said, blowing his nose. He held the tissues at arms length. Don picked up his wooden wastebasket and handed it to Charlton, who folded the tissues neatly and laid them in the basket. "I really liked Dave Lewis. It goes to show you, doesn't it?"

Don opened his laptop and typed Charlton Denning's name and the date. He looked at Charlton.

"You think someone is nice, and then he does this to you."

"Start at the beginning, Charlton. What did this Lewis do to you?" *Car wreck? Certainly not an angry husband,* Don guessed.

"Dave Lewis is the managing editor of all the KL newspapers? KL, the company that owns the *Sun*. Named for its owner and founder, the great American Kingston Lehrer."

"Ah," Don said, remembering. "Didn't I meet Lewis at the funeral?"

"Yes. A war hero. Did you know he lost both legs in the Gulf War? Both legs below the knee, and he's out running marathons. I should have known there was something wrong. Nobody's that perfect." Charlton reached for another tissue. He took off his thick-lensed glasses and wiped his eyes. "I'm sorry I'm so upset. It's just that everything was going so well. I really believed that Graff and I had found the perfect home. Everyone has been so accepting. Except for Bert Martin, of course."

"Tell me what happened, Charlton, from the beginning." He looked at his watch. They had been at this for ten minutes and all he had was Charlton's name and the date. He added *Dave Lewis. KL Newspapers.*

"At the beginning? Well, at the beginning, Dave called and said he was coming down. That was unusual. He's only been here once since he took...ah got the job. Of course, there are two-dozen newspapers in the chain, and the *Sun* is one of the smallest, so you wouldn't expect him to be here all the time. I supposed he was coming for the funeral—"

"Sawbuck's funeral?"

"Well yes. But it turned out he didn't even know the biggest funeral in a decade was going to be here in Velda. The Clintons here. Goodness, you'd think he would have known."

"So if he didn't come for the funeral, what did he come for?"

"After the services, we went back to the paper and he closed my office door and looked very serious. Of course I knew it was important when he closed that door. I never close my door. Never."

Don made some more notes and waited.

"Could I have a Coke please? Diet? If you have it?"

Don got up and went to the door. "Faye," he called. "Can you find a Diet Coke for Mr. Denning?"

"Of course," she answered. "Should I change your eleven o'clock meeting with Wiley?"

Don nodded. "This may take a while."

They waited while Faye found the Diet Coke and poured it into a thin crystal glass. Charlton took a long sip. "What a nice glass," he said. "One of the major's?"

Don nodded. *Nothing says I couldn't have a nice glass myself*, he wanted to say, but instead he closed the door and asked, "Then what happened?"

"That's when he told me."

"Told you what, exactly? Tell me exactly what he said, Charlton. Please." *Please God, please!*

"He told me the company was making some changes and that Bum Peterson was coming in from San Diego to take over as editor of the *Sun*."

Don typed notes. *At last.*

"What else did he say?"

Charlton shook his head from side to side. "Bum Peterson. Bum Peterson! I knew him when I was night editor in San Diego. He's a total incompetent."

"Let's try this another way. For now, just tell me exactly what he said."

Charlton rattled the ice in his empty glass. "He said Bum Peterson was coming in as editor and that I was out."

"Did he say why?"

"I asked him. 'Why? Why are you doing this? Everything is going well here. We put the on-line edition in faster than any other paper in the chain. Ad revenue isn't down. I've done everything you asked to hold down expenses. Why are you doing this?' He wouldn't say, some nonsense about new directions and reducing costs, but of course I knew. It was Bert Martin."

Bert Martin ran a small chain of Panhandle discount stores, always in a scrap with the big box stores and ready to fight anybody who crossed him. Jake had represented him in a squabble when some of Bert's employees threatened to organize a union. He remembered that Bert had shown the employees no mercy when he won. "What's Bert's problem?"

"He hates gays. He must have threatened to pull his advertising, because the *Sun* has a gay editor. Or used to have. Now it has a fool. That ought to suit Bert just fine."

"Bert Martin buys a lot of ads?"

"Oh my God, yes. He runs those full-page ads fighting Wal-Mart and Costco, trying to stay in business. He's ferocious about it. You must have seen those ads."

Don didn't want to admit that he seldom read the local rag. He choked on the right wing politics and the slavish coverage of high school sports. "Why do you believe that Bert hates gays?"

"For one thing, he told me he did. He said he couldn't understand why Kingston Lehrer would have a queer running his newspaper. Whenever he sent in ad copy, he would address it to 'Head Gay.' I made a joke about it of course. I never dreamed he would go this far."

"But Lewis never said this change was because of Bert?"

"He's smarter than that. I should have seen it coming, ever since the Rotary Club asked me to join. Bert resigned. The president told me it was good riddance; they would rather have me."

"What do you want from me, Charlton?"

Charlton sat up straight and answered quickly. "I want my job back."

Don shifted to all caps and typed 'rehire' with a large question mark. "Do you have any reason to think that Lewis would do that?"

The editor shifted a little in the chair. "I doubt if he will. He's a Lehrer and they don't change their minds."

"He's a Lehrer, you say?"

"He married into the family. He's married to K.L.'s daughter."

"A little nepotism?"

"Oh, it's very much a family affair. Three daughters, three sons-in-law; all at headquarters. I never met the other two. They stay in Akron, sending memos to the local editors, telling us everything we've done wrong. But Dave Lewis, when he came along, I had hopes. He worked for the *Plain Dealer*. A reporter. At last, I thought, a newspaperman. Well, he's a tool, just like his in-laws."

Don thought a minute. "Suppose I talk to Lewis. We may have enough of a sexual orientation complaint that he'll reconsider. Or at least offer you a job somewhere else."

Charlton made a face. "We like it here, Graff and I."

"Graff is your partner? I think Bridget and I met him at the Community Concert."

"That's right! Jacobi, the pianist. Wasn't he wonderful?"

All Don remembered was falling asleep and Bridget nudging him. They laughed about it that night and she promised, 'No more Community Concerts.'

"I hear that Bridget has left town, moved to New Orleans?"

"News travels fast in Velda."

"I *am* a newspaper man."

Don stood up. "Let's see if we can keep it that way." He shook Charlton's hand. "But I wouldn't get my hopes up about your old job. Some more money maybe, or maybe a job somewhere else."

Charlton sighed. "I guess I'd better go home and tell Graff. His garden club meets this afternoon. I don't want him to hear it from one of the ladies."

"Like I said—"

"I know. News travels fast in Velda."

❬❬❬❬❬

Faye looked through his meeting notes. "You're going to cost us another client."

"Bert Martin argued about the bill on that union case for six months, as I recall. He's not a very good client."

"Well, he won't be one at all, if you take on Charlton Denning."

Don waved for Wiley to come in. "We're becoming specialists in discrimination cases, Faye. Race, sexual orientation. Do you know of a woman who's been discriminated against?"

She stood at the door. "I know one, and that would be me."

CHAPTER SIX

Faye reached Dave Lewis on the phone right away. After a few minutes discussing the Sawbucks Banjo extravaganza, Don said, "I have a client named Charlton Denning, Mr. Lewis. I wonder if we can meet and discuss Charlton's situation?"

"You know, I'd be happy to do that, but I'm on my way to Austin. Can we discuss it on the phone?"

It certainly is a strange day, Don thought. "That's interesting. I'm going to Austin myself. Maybe we could meet down there."

"I'll be busy fixing a magazine, or should I say, trying to fix it. But listen, if you can be ready in an hour, you're welcome to fly down with me on the company plane. We can talk on the trip down."

Never turn down a ride on a client's plane, Jake had said. He hadn't mentioned an adversary's plane. "I'll meet you at the airport," Don said.

❮❮❮❮❮

The Lear 70 was waiting on the taxiway at Audie Murphy Airport, the gangway down and the auxiliary engine on. Dave Lewis came out of the small tin shed that served as the airport office. He had a cup of coffee in one hand and a phone in the other. He was muscular, like a middleweight boxer. His light hair was cut very short, and his face sported fashionable stubble. He wore tailored jeans and a well-worn leather jacket. He pocketed his phone, extended his hand, and smiled. "Hello again, Don."

"I hope I haven't held you up."

"No. I think Brewster's getting his flight plan filed. Let's get aboard." He motioned toward the gangway.

A rangy man trotted from the shed. He reached for Don's duffel bag. "Let me have that, Mr. Cuinn."

"This is Brewster, our pilot. He and Al will be taking us down to Austin." He pointed to the man who looked like a younger brother of Brewster visible in the cockpit. Don shook the pilot's hand and handed him his bag.

Brewster jumped up the gangway and motioned for them to follow. "About an hour and a half, Mr. Lewis, depending on traffic. We'll be at forty thousand feet going down to Austin. A few thunderstorms on the way, but we'll be able to avoid them, I think."

The cabin of the sleek jet was fitted out with facing leather seats, a table between them, on each side of the narrow aisle. Two more seats were behind them. Lewis settled into the front-facing leather seat on the left and motioned for Don to sit across the aisle from him. "A few bumps makes it fun, don't you think, Don?"

Don buckled his seat belt. "If you're happy, I'm happy."

Brewster revved the engines and the plane shuddered like a race-horse waiting for the gate to open. They sped down the runway, a short one, Don remembered too late. They lifted off the ground just as they ran out of runway. Don could see Webster's oil field equipment yard below the wing tips as they left the ground. Webster's yard and the other light indus-try warehouses around the airport fell away below them and disappeared beneath a bank of clouds. "It needs it all, doesn't it?" he said to Lewis. He had to speak loudly to be heard over the roar of the engines.

"Not really," Lewis shouted back. "It only needs about forty-five hun-dred feet. The runway here is a good fifteen hundred more than that."

The plane seemed to Don to make an almost vertical ascent, too fast to be bumpy. *This must be like riding a rocket to the Space Station.*

Within minutes we were at cruising altitude. The pilot leveled off, cut back the thrust, and turned off the seatbelt sign. Lewis motioned to the service bar. "Have a drink? Or coffee?"

48

"Thanks, I'm fine," Don said. He looked around at the leather and wood interior. "KL newspapers must be doing well."

Dave smiled. "Not really. The plane is my brother-in-law's toy. I needed the plane to get in and out of Velda, so Tom had to fly commercial. It serves the little prick right. He's in New York, talking to bankers, I'm in Velda." He smiled. "Excuse me. I kind of like the town. I grew up in a small town myself."

"Still," Don said. "A company that can afford a Learjet can afford to be generous with a faithful employee with almost twenty years' service."

"Time for business, is it?" Lewis pulled up his pant legs. The prostheses beneath his knees gleamed. "Let me take these off. I travel better without them." He unstrapped the artificial legs and tossed them on the floor. He rubbed his stumps and sighed. "Better." He looked over at Don. "Do my stumps bother you? I can cover them."

"Oh, no, it doesn't bother me at all." Don said. *I'm accustomed to flying at five hundred miles an hour in a metal tube with a man with bionic feet. Jesus, what a negotiating technique.*

"It's closer to fifteen years than twenty." Lewis lifted his left stump and massaged it.

"Even so. Firing him?"

Lewis pushed his seat forward and rested what remained of his legs on the seat opposite him. He motioned at the titanium feet, fitted into a pair of dress shoes. "God, it's a relief to get those damned things off." When Don didn't reply, he said, "How well do you know the newspaper business, Don?"

"Not very well," Don said.

"Our advertisers are very important to us. Subscribers pay hardly anything for a paper, compared to what it costs to put one out. We try to keep the guys who pay the bills happy."

"Just because one advertiser hates gays . . ."

"Is that what you think? That I let Charlton go because he's gay?"

"That's what Charlton thinks. He believes that one advertiser who hates gays complained and you caved."

Lewis smiled. "It wasn't that way at all. Our editor represents the company in the community. We have to have an editor who is accepted by the community. In this case, someone who is accepted by Velda."

"And Charlton Denning isn't?"

"We had a delegation come all the way to Akron, demanding to see Kingston Lehrer himself, complaining about Denning. We can't ignore that."

Don looked out the window. All he could see was a thick layer of sudsy clouds beneath them. There might as well not have been any land down there. "How many people were in this delegation, Dave? You don't mind if I call you *Dave*, do you?" *Especially seeing that I'm Don to you.*

"Sure. Call me whatever you like. Now what was the question?"

"How big was the delegation?"

The pilot pulled back the curtain to the cockpit and called back. "Better buckle up, gentlemen. A little chop up ahead. ETA is forty minutes."

"Thanks, Brewster," Lewis said. He turned in his seat and stared at Don. Finally he said, "I have no idea. I was out of town. When I got back, the Old Man was livid."

"Livid? I think that's the first time I ever heard anyone use that word."

"If you knew Kingston Lehrer, you'd hear it all the time. He said that I let the situation at one of our papers…in one of our towns…get into a mess. 'Go down there and straighten it out,' he told me. So that's what I did."

"Just following orders, like the guards at Auschwitz, is that your story?"

Lewis's face turned red. He reached for his artificial legs and strapped them on, tugging on the straps with a grunt. "You're a civil sort of guy, aren't you?"

Don said, "If I could prove to you that most of the business owners in Velda like Charlton and don't give a damn whether he's gay or not, would that make a difference?"

Lewis pulled his pant legs down and leaned back in the seat. "Probably not."

"He's a good editor."

"Bum Peterson will be a better one."

"Really? Carlton says his name is accurate."

50

Lewis smiled. "I'll bet. Let me ask you this. Does Charlton have a regular golf game? Is he in the weekly poker game at the country club? Does he hunt or fish? Does he go to every football game and basketball game? Can he tell you the details of every Super Bowl game?"

"I don't know."

"Bum Peterson does all those things. He's a man's man, and he'll fit in just fine in Velda."

The engines roared as they began their descent. They were in the cloud layer and there was a flash of lightning in the distance. Don leaned across the aisle and spoke loudly enough to be heard above the engines. "You don't know a damn thing about Velda. Folks respect Charlton. They accept him despite your paper's goofy politics. Hell, they even invited him into Rotary."

Lewis smiled. "That's an exclusive group?"

"Pretty exclusive. They've never asked me."

"Oh?"

"Only one member per firm. My partner, Jake Rosen, belongs."

The engines went quiet as they broke through the clouds. Don could see they were over Lake Travis, headed toward the city. The hills were green and dotted with hundreds of houses and apartment buildings. Highway 183 was crowded with cars, moving slowly in both directions, even on the toll road extension. Don looked at his watch. *Not even rush hour and cars everywhere. Some things don't change.* "We'll sue."

"You'll lose."

"Find him a job somewhere else."

"I thought of that. Didn't work."

"Your father-in-law?"

The plane veered north, then southeast, settling onto the approach to the airport. The University tower and the domed state capitol were visible on the right side of the plane. Don tried to spot the old Haven Hotel where he grew up.

Lewis brought his seat upright and tightened his seat belt. "I'll tell you what I do know something about. We keep a shitload of lawyers on retainer. Six of them are defending lawsuits against the paper right now. We've never lost a case, not once since I've been there. We do not settle. We'll spend a hundred thousand dollars to keep from paying out a thousand. So all you get out of this deal, my friend, is an airplane ride."

Don shook his head, trying to think of a response. "We can get a friendly jury in Velda."

"Yeah, sure," Lewis replied. "Be my guest."

The landing was smooth, Don supposed. It was like landing on an aircraft carrier, all speed, a smooth touchdown and a brick wall when the engines were reversed and they braked to a stop. He was glad he had buckled up tightly. The private plane hanger stood apart, austere and unadorned, the opposite of the main terminal with its live music, murals, Earl Campbell memorabilia and Salt Lick barbecue.

Standing outside, they shook hands. "I'd offer you a ride, but that's my local editor over there. We're late for a meeting and need to discuss things on the way to town."

"No problem. I can get a cab. Thanks for the ride. You have a newspaper around here?"

"The chain owns a magazine now and I'm running it for a while, until we get it in shape."

"A magazine?"

"Yes. You probably heard of it. *This Texas*? We bought it from the last owner's estate."

"Drayton Philby?"

"Yes, I think so."

"I grew up on that magazine," Don said. The thought of Lewis and his father-in-law in charge of *This Texas* made him want to puke.

CHAPTER SEVEN

D on stood in the bright Austin sun, waiting for his taxi. The clouds that had menaced the jet were distant shadows off to the west and any rain in them was headed for somewhere far away. The flowerbeds in front of the private terminal were graveled, with desert shrubs, a reminder to Don that Central Texas was fast becoming Phoenix. *Just as little rain and just as many Californians. Better music, though. And Tex-Mex.* His stomach growled at the thought of a plate of Pedro's *migas. Maybe I'll go back to Pedro's and confront some devils.*

He thought of calling Charlton and sharing the bad news, but he couldn't decide what to say. There had to be a way. *Maybe we could get a good jury in Velda. No, they'd show up in court with the best old boy lawyer out of Amarillo, probably Max Kilgore himself and a staff of Yankees, and beat him to a pulp. When they finished with poor Charlton, he would be as sympathetic as a Catholic priest child molester.*

Where is that taxi? He thought of calling again, when what had to be the oldest cab in Austin limped into the drive. It was painted purple with faded gold stripes. A ten-foot Plexiglas figure of a bumblebee perched unsteadily on its roof.

An aging hippie flipped his cigarette butt out the window "You call a cab?" he asked.

Don nodded. "Are you a taxi or an exterminator?"

"You want to go, get in. Otherwise I have places I need to be."

I bet, Don thought. He threw his duffle into the back seat and climbed in after it. He hadn't been in a car that smelled of cigarette smoke and marijuana since he left town. He waited while the driver entered something in the keypad that was velcroed to the peeling dashboard. When he finished, the driver sat waiting for Don to speak.

"Latest technology, huh?" Don said.

"Yes, sir." He scratched his scruffy beard with nicotine stained fingers. "Where to?"

"The Cartwright House. Do you know where that is?"

"Nope."

"No G.P.S.?"

The driver stared at Don in the rearview mirror. "Does it look like I've got a G.P.S.?"

Don dug through his coat pockets and finally found the address. He handed the scrap of paper to the driver. "It's on Town Lake."

The driver eyed him suspiciously. "Where are you from?"

"The Panhandle," Don answered. "Why?"

"Damn Tea Partier, right?"

"Should I just get another cab?"

"It's not Town Lake. It's Lady Bird Lake, and if you don't like that, you can just get the hell out of my cab and walk to town."

"Incredible," Don said softly. "I didn't mean to insult Mrs. Johnson. I grew up here and it was always Town Lake, that's all."

The driver scowled. He read the address and mumbled to himself. "Sixty dollars," he said finally. "Cash. In advance. I do not take credit cards."

"Are you kidding me? Sixty dollars? I'll give you twenty-five."

"You won't get from here to there for less than sixty dollars." He turned around in the seat and eyed Don. "How can you live in the Panhandle and not be a Tea Partier?"

"My Austin genes, I guess. Look, Thelman," he said, reading from the driver's I.D. card, "I'm not on expense account. I'm on my way to check on my folks. Isn't there some way we can make a deal?"

Thelman took out a joint and sniffed it. "You smoke?"

"No, I don't, but thanks."

Thelman stretched his hairy arms over his head and yawned. "I've been over at the cabbie lot waiting for a fare for two hours. I'm the last indie cabbie in Austin, and every now and then they throw me a bone, just so they can tell the commission I'm competition and keep other chains out. You're my bone." He eyed Don for a second. "I'm ready to go off-shift. I really could use a toke." He opened the door and got out of the cab. "You drive. Off the meter, twenty-five dollars. Cash, no card. You drive and I'll smoke."

Don smiled, nodded his agreement, and got into the driver's seat. He sank down so far he couldn't see over the steering wheel. "You're a big man, Thelman. I need a pillow or something."

"Oh yeah," the cabbie answered. "I've worn that seat down to nothing. Just a second." He leaned in and pulled the trunk release. Don got a whiff of his unwashed body, mingled with the acrid smell of marijuana and Juicy Fruit chewing gum. He could hear Thelman as he rummaged in the trunk. He slammed the trunk lid down and re-appeared beside the driver's seat, holding a cracked plastic cushion. "Get out."

Don climbed up out of the cab and watched as the big man fussed with the pillow. "There," Thelman said. "Be sure and adjust the mirrors. That right one is tricky. Just fiddle with it until it catches." He stood by the car until he was sure that Don was buckled in safely then got in the front passenger seat and carefully lit his joint. Don started the car and played with the radio. "Leave that alone," Thelman barked, expelling a lungful of powerful smoke.

Don had an idea. "Thelman," he began.

The big man had closed his eyes. He ignored him.

"Thelman," he said louder.

"Just drive, man. Don't talk all the time."

"Is it all right if I go by Universe Race World?"

"Go wherever you want to go. This magic chariot is yours."

Don started slowly out of the parking lot. A man walking stiffly in cowboy boots and skinny jeans came from the terminal and waved frantically at them.

Thelman sat up. "Look at that fool. He wants a cab ride to town.

That'll be a long wait. Probably a Russian millionaire. You can tell those new boots are pinching, can't you?"

"Shouldn't we give him a lift? You could use the fare, right?"

"I'd have to drive, and I don't want to drive. That's an important difference between Old Austin and New Austin you should always remember. If I don't want to drive, I don't drive. Those other cabbies will fight for every fare. I'm a dying breed, cowboy. When I first came here, there were enough people like me to make a difference. Not any more. That Universe Race World? We could hardly get fifty people to protest when they handed out the subsidies for that motherfucker."

Don shook off the waving Russian, if that's what he was. "Off duty" he said. The Russian gave him the finger and limped back toward the terminal. "Big subsidies, huh?"

"In addition to the county building roads out there and paving everything in sight and putting in sewer and utility service, which, incidentally, the people who live out there had been without those same services forever, the sovereign State of Texas is giving them sales tax rebates of forty million dollars a year. Don't even get me started on the subject of state tax rebates."

I hadn't meant to, Don thought. "You're an educated man, Thelman. What are you doing driving a cab?"

Thelman inhaled deeply and blew smoke out the open window. "Making my way, making it pay," he said. "Every day I get to meet people and tell them my philosophy of life. I tell foreigners what Austin is really like, what it's become, how it's fucked itself. I'm talking about people who ordinarily wouldn't give me the time of day." He laughed. " Once they're in my cab and I lock the back doors, I've got a captive audience. A captive audience." He lay back in the seat and laughed again. "What's fun is getting some right-wing dingbat in my back seat and telling him the truth. Some of them squirm and fidget and ask how much longer to get to town, or beg me to shut up. They don't tip, but it's worth it."

"What did you study at the University? I'm assuming you went to U.T."

"Still do."

"Really? What are you, forty years old? A late bloomer?"

"Oh hell, no. I've been at it for twenty years. I have enough hours for a degree in economics, in history, in philosophy. But what's a degree anyway? Just a piece of paper. It's the quest for knowledge, for enlightenment, that's what's important."

"Isn't there some kind of time limit?"

Thelman pulled out an old leather wallet, stuffed with clippings and cardboard discount cards. He found a dog-eared card. "My University I.D. All this bullshit about in or out in six years doesn't apply to me. I'm grandfathered."

"You could be a grandfather."

"Hell, I may be."

A freshly washed Yellow Cab pulled up beside them. Don stopped and the driver yelled, "Hey, Thelman. I'm looking for some foreigner, needs a ride to town. Have you seen him?"

"That would be this man," Thelman said, pointing at Don. "I'm teaching him to drive American style."

"Thelman, are you high again? You could lose your license, letting him drive your cab."

Thelman laughed. "You won't say anything, Buddy. Meet me at Woodrow's later. I've got some really good African."

They watched the other cab make a U-turn out of the parking lot, too soon for the driver to see the Russian hopping out of the terminal barefoot, carrying his lizard cowboy boots.

Don roused Thelman enough from time to time to help him find his way. They drove down newly paved roads, past old farmhouses with poorly tended yards to the racetrack.

"Folks rent out their front yards on big race days. Capitalist oppression of the poor man. Rich shits from all over the world, in their leather coats and gold jewelry, jetting in and going to the race here, then Rio or Monaco or God knows where. All the time poor old Elmer over there has to scratch out a living renting out his front yard to poor fools who pay a month's rent money to come here and gawk. It's a fucking crime, that's what it is. Talk about the one percent." He lit another stubby joint and stared belligerently at Don.

Don smiled. "You're not a fan of Universe Race World?"

"No, I am not. It's not Austin, you know."

Don stopped the Bumblebee at the entrance to the track, drawing stares from people waiting to go inside. Some took photos of the taxi. Thelman ignored them. Don could see the grandstands and the tower. Cars were coming and going. The parking lot was half full.

"What's going on out here today? Is it a race?"

"Oh, there's always something. Concert of some sort. Some Nashville shit. They can't be bothered with Austin talent." Thelman fumbled in the glove compartment and came out with a sack of *Lupe's* donuts. He offered one to Don, who shook his head. "Try one man. Lupe's been making these things forever. Lot's better than that franchised shit they sell all over town."

"I know *Lupe's*. Later, maybe." He watched Thelman devour his second donut. He doubted there would be any left for later.

"It's all about land. Land and money," the old hippie complained. "Take *Austin City Limits*. It used to be, a regular person, such as myself, could go over to the office and get a ticket and go watch them tape it. Good music, good beer, good weed. Then they moved downtown, sold their name to a developer, got this new space, that I have never been inside of, by they way, and probably never will be. Now, its how much money did you give the goddamn classical radio station that whored itself to the land developers. *Austin City Limits*? It never was supposed to be a fucking money machine. At least in my book. It's just not right."

Thelman folded the empty donut bag neatly and dropped it on the floorboard. "My recycling can," he said. "Every bag gets re-used. I take it back to Lupe and she refills it for me."

"Admirable."

"I'll ignore the sarcasm."

Don checked a location on his phone. "There's a place near here called *Austin Next*. Do you know where it is?"

Thelman laughed. "I do happen to know where *Austin Next* is. Turn around and head south." Don backed up. "Careful for that foreigner," Thelman said. "Don't create an international incident."

The road was paved all the way to *Austin Next*, a four-lane parkway with scrawny live oak saplings dying in the median. Don stopped the cab in front of a large wooden barricade on which there was a sign that read "Absolutely No Trespassing." Various legal notices flapping in the light breeze were tacked to the No Trespassing sign. Beyond the barricade, an even wider version of the boulevard stretched into the distance, an asphalt snake crawling in the middle of what looked like a war zone. All around the road was evidence of unfinished work. Mounds of dirt beside foundations. Piles of gravel. The skeleton of an eight-story building. A partially finished helicopter pad.

"This is it?"

"Yes. You are sitting in the middle of the famous *Road to Nowhere*."

Don got out of the car. He took photos of the scene. The notices tacked to the No Trespassing sign were foreclosure notices. He took photos of them as well. "This is all that's left of *Austin Next?*"

Thelman stood beside the taxi, stretching and smoking another joint. "Another in a long list of Austin land scams. A politician tried to get rich, went broke, and now the banks own it. They'll finish it when the government makes it worth their while. In the meantime, it sits here and rots."

"They finished the road?"

"More or less. They had enough bond money for that, before they went belly-up. But the road's unusable. The interchange with the Interstate, over that way," he said, pointing west, "hasn't been started, and there's an unfinished bridge over Tonkawa Creek, down that way, where they found the burial grounds."

"Tonkawa burial grounds?"

"Indeed. It's an interesting story."

Don looked at his watch. "Jesus. I need to get to town. My momma will be sure I died in a plane crash. Let me do something and you can tell me about the burial ground on the way to town." He texted Faye to check on the status of foreclosure proceedings and attached the photos. He asked her to send him the names of the lawyers representing the banks. He saw ahead a legal free-for-all, with banks fighting each other for preferred position while the carcass was picked clean.

Don found his way back to the main highway without Thelman's help, which was fortunate because the big hippie was asleep, leaning against the passenger door and snoring softly. Once they were headed toward Austin, Don poked him on the shoulder. "Thelman, tell me about the burial grounds."

He took off his aviator shades and rubbed his eyes. "Where are we? Oh, I see. You know your way to wherever you're going?"

"Sure. The Tonkawa burial grounds?"

"The what? Oh, right. It's an interesting story."

"And I'd love to hear it." A kid in a Camaro passed him on the right side and cut sharply in front of him. Don resisted the urge to brake, and instead goosed the old cab and rode the Camaro's bumper.

"Careful," Thelman warned. "This cab is not paid for."

"You have got to be kidding me," Don said, slowing down and backing off the Camaro. "The Tonkawas?"

"The Tonkawas were the first Austin land grab, did you know that?"

Don stayed in the right lane as he navigated the flyover, high above the Interstate. He glanced to his right at the downtown skyline. Cranes and new buildings rose all along the both sides of the lake, almost blocking out the landmarks he knew well, the Icicle Tower and the old hotels; even the capitol building, on its hill looking down on Congress Avenue, was barely visible. He turned his attention back to the highway just in time to avoid the Camaro, which had apparently been hanging back to cut him off again. This time Don slammed on his brakes and grimaced as the young driver sped away. "Asshole," he said.

"People think it was the Comanche, and it's true that most of the fights were with them. But this was Tonkawa country, and the Texans just took it away from them."

Don barely managed to merge into the right lane for the exit to Capitol of Texas Highway. The traffic was heavy and going fast and the old cab roared in complaint as Don tried to keep up with the flow of traffic.

"The story is that Stephen Austin himself negotiated a treaty with the Tonkawa tribe to buy several thousand acres on the river. Personally, I think that's bullshit, but it makes us Anglos feel better."

"Under the Treaty Oak, right? Is it still alive or did the poisoning kill it?"

"It's hanging on. Imagine. It lived five hundred years, that giant oak. Before some nutcase poisoned it. It's produced some acorns, so that's a good sign. There were fourteen of the big oaks. The tribes called them the Council Oaks. They were sacred, Treaty Oak in particular. It had a one hundred twenty seven foot spread, the finest example of a mature oak in the world. Over the years the Council Oaks were cut down one by one to clear property or to use for lumber until only Treaty Oak remained. It would have been cut down too if the city hadn't bought it, sometime in the 1930's." He shifted his big body in his seat. "In fact some settlers got here before Stephen Austin and started the town of Waterloo. That was in the 1830s. The Tonkawas were more easy-going than the Comanche or they would have run the settlers out. I bet they wished to hell they had." Don squeezed into the long line of cars turning onto MoPac, the only north-south expressway on the west side of Austin. *Not very express*, he thought. He knew much of Thelman's story, of course. Before he wandered off into the law, Don had expected to be a history professor, with an emphasis on Texas-Mexican relations. He had a master's degree and at one time, before all the trouble, before Wesley screwed him over, he had a good chance at a slot in the doctorate program. *Oh, well. Listening to Thelman's mishmash of Texas history was the price of learning about the Tonkawa burial grounds.* He turned north onto MoPac, merged into the speeding traffic on his left and settled into the middle lane, toward Town Lake. *Oops, Lady Bird Lake.* Thelman leaned closer and shouted in a raspy voice over the road noise. "Texas has always been about land, you know that, don't you?"

Don nodded. "So you mentioned."

"The settlers came for the land, which they took away from the Mexicans, who had taken it away from the Indians."

A bit of an oversimplification, Don thought, but he didn't say anything.

"The Mexicans actually respected the Indians' claims to some extent, but when the Anglos got here, they finished the job. They made treaties, broke treaties, anything to get all the land that was left. What the settlers didn't get, the Republic of Texas just proclaimed it was public land. How about that? Just took it."

Don was still too pedantic to let that alone. "I think Spain claimed the land by right of conquest, and treaties with the native tribes. Mexico got it from Spain by revolution and Texas got it by treaty."

Thelman snorted. "Isn't that what I just said?"

No, it isn't. "The burial grounds?"

"Why do you think Mirabeau Lamar wanted Texas' capital to be here?"

Don knew the answer to that one. "To insure the westward expansion of Texas?"

"Bingo. Hey, didn't you want the Fifth Street exit? Go up and look at the old Treaty Oak?"

"It would break my heart. And, there's something I want to look at first, up by the University. Go ahead with your story."

"Well, I do need this trip to end someday. I have a gig tonight at Cotton Eye Mary's."

"Don't tell me. You write songs and play the guitar."

"You've heard about my group? *Thelboy and the Playmen?*"

"Who hasn't?"

Don took the Enfield exit through the half-cloverleaf interchange to Lamar Boulevard. It all looked familiar now. He took a right turn up the old Nineteenth Street hill. The old cab strained as he downshifted, crawling up the hill. Impatient students in BMWs passed him on both sides, staring disdainfully at the Bumblebee. *Frat boys. Still no sense of humor.* "So what happened to *Austin Next*? They found an old Tonkawa burial ground and that killed the project?"

"Oh, *Austin Next* was terminal before that. Cost overruns, labor problems. But when they stumbled on the old burial ground, they had to report it and the feds said they would have to do a study of them and that it might take two years. The investors stopped sending money and the banks shut the place down."

"You say, labor problems? Governor Braeswood was a plaintiff's lawyer. He had labor problems?"

"Bob Braeswood was a Democrat governor. I'm a Democrat…"

"Really? You're not just saying that?"

"Do you want to hear this or not? Anyhow, I had hopes. But once Braeswood got in office, he wasn't any better than that old wavy-haired boy we had before him. I don't know what happened to him. As soon as he was out of office, he was running around buying tech start-ups and talking about how *Austin Next* was the greatest thing since peach salsa."

"You never know." Don maneuvered the old cab down the shady streets of West Campus. He stopped where the Haven Hotel once stood. It was now a construction site. A large sign announced "Coming Soon! Exclusive Apartments! Now Leasing!"

"Jesus. It's gone."

"Lena's? Gone the way of all Austin. Land in this neighborhood is too valuable for a funky old hotel and cafe."

They got out of the cab and walked to the construction fence. All that was left of his boyhood home was the old oak tree. It was fenced off by yellow tape. It looked like an unwilling witness being detained at a crime scene. "At least they saved Lena's favorite tree. I used to sit under it and wait for the bus."

"You're welcome."

"What?"

"*We* made the city council pass a tree ordinance. Trees more than twelve inches in circumference, you need a special permit to cut a big one down. I worked hard for that ordinance. So you're welcome. Otherwise your tree would be gone."

Don put out his hand. "Well thank you, man."

"No problem."

Don felt his eyes well up with tears, not so much for the old hotel, which he had advised Dorrie Louise to sell, and which was no memorable structure even when he lived there. *It was tacky, actually*, he admitted to himself. No, he was tearful for Lena, the chain smoking, plain talking woman who took him and his mother in when Dorrie Louise had nowhere else to go. When she did find someone to marry, it was Lena who persuaded Dorrie Louise to leave Donnie Ray behind. It was Lena and her poet husband Ralph Rothschild, Papa, who stood by Donnie Ray through all his troubles. *Dammit, I owe it to Lena to protect Papa and Dorrie Louise now.*

He blew his nose and wiped his eyes.

Thelman patted him on the shoulder awkwardly. "You really must love that tree."

Don laughed. "I grew up here. My room was where that dozer is digging right now."

"You were lucky, man. Lena was the coolest. And that meatloaf."

"Every Monday, as long as I can remember."

"Right. What was on Thursday?"

Don smiled. "You know. Thursday was enchiladas."

"Right." Thelman hooted. "I could use a plate of those right now. Want to go out to Pedro's and get some? And a tall Shiner Bock? Let's do it. Have a beer for old Lena!"

Don took one last look at the construction site, trying to implant in his memory the Haven as it was. "I'd like to, Thelman. I really would. But I've got somewhere I need to be."

"Your loss, man."

"That's right. It's my loss."

CHAPTER EIGHT

Dorrie Louise met Don at the door of her apartment. "Oh, Donnie Ray! Where have you been? I must have called Montibello twenty times, asking if you had come in. He probably thinks I've lost my mind."

Don smiled and kissed his mother. Montibello, the large, muscular black security guard had insisted on taking Don's duffel bag and had personally escorted him to the apartment door. "He was really glad to see me. I'm sorry I'm late."

Papa's chair was by the window, empty. "Where's Papa?"

"Oh, he's down in our fitness center, doing his exercises."

"Exercises? Papa?"

Dorrie Louise's eyes sparkled. "He's completely energized. He says he has to keep his strength up for the Hieronymus Parcel fight. I swear, he has the energy of a man twenty years younger."

"What fight?"

"Sit down. Let me get you a nice glass of iced tea." She pushed him down on the couch. "You look tired, Donnie Ray." She ran her hand over his forehead. "A nice glass of iced tea. Are you working too hard?"

"You know me, Mama. Work, work, work. I've always thrived on it."

The small woman took goblets from the cupboard and opened the refrigerator door. "I remember your poor study habits. So if it isn't work, it must be Bridget leaving." She poured the tea, sliced a lemon, squeezed the lemon into the tea, and handed it to him. "Just the way you like it. Do you talk to her?"

"No, Mama, I don't. We decided to break it off. She's moved from

Velda and she's started a new life in New Orleans. But it's not work or Bridget that's got me worried. It's you and Papa letting Wesley Bird cheat you out of your money."

"I'm sure it's all a mistake," she said. She took the tea pitcher into the kitchen and put it down on the dark faux-marble counter. "When the project gets back on schedule, everything will be all right. Meantime, we'll just tighten our belts a little. We'll be fine. And of course, we have the Hungarian gold coins."

"The what?"

She settled beside Don on the old leather sofa. "Didn't I tell you? It could have saved you a trip down here." She patted his cheek. "Wesley came up here to explain. He didn't have to do that, did he? He met with all the investors in the Cartwright conference room. He explained that the project was running late and that they had to slow down to protect Indian burial grounds they discovered on the property. Professor Tankersley, the archeologist. He knew about the burial grounds. He explained it all to us." She smiled. "Lord, did he ever explain it. Anyway, it ended up that everybody agreed that is was very important that they do all they could to protect that sacred place. Everybody was willing to wait on their dividends if it meant saving something as special as that. We were right, weren't we? To want to save sacred burial grounds? I know I'd feel that way if it was my ancestors' graves."

"Mama..."

"But he didn't want us to worry, so as extra security, he gave us certificates for Hungarian gold coins. He signed receipts for them right there in the conference room, and the certificates were delivered by messenger the next day. It made everybody feel much better; especially some people who had been complaining. Not Papa and me, of course. I've never had any doubt."

"I was just out to *Austin Next*, Mama. It's shut down."

"I know, but Wesley says it's only temporary."

"It's not temporary. It's in foreclosure."

"They can't foreclose on the governor, Donnie Ray. They can't do that, can they?" She sat down. "Oh, my."

66

"They already have. *Austin Next* is posted for sale. I'm not sure, but I suspect that your investment is worthless."

"But the certificates! We have the certificates for the gold coins." She ran to Lena's old desk and searched through a stack of papers. "Here," she said. "They're for twice our investment. Twice."

Don took the gilt edged documents and thumbed through them. They were certificates, executed by the Bank of Hungary, guaranteeing redemption in gold coins of the Republic of Hungary, dated in the 1920s. "I'll research them to make sure, Mama, but I think I'll find that these certificates are worthless." Don looked at the last sheet of paper. It was a receipt for five thousand dollars. "Mama, did you give Wesley more money, for these certificates?"

She looked down and twisted her ring. "Well, there were transfer fees."

"My God. Mama, listen to me. Wesley is a crook. He's defrauded you and he ought to be in jail."

"Oh, my." She fanned herself. "Oh, I hate to tell Papa. He's been so busy, fighting to keep the Hieronymus Parcel from being sold." She looked up at Don. "You're sure? You're absolutely sure?

"I'm sure, Mama."

❪❪❪❪❪

Don and Papa walked from his and Dorrie Louise's apartment to the garage where Dorrie Louise kept her car. Don had agreed to drive Papa to the home of Judge Dockery Ashley. "Why must you see him, Papa?"

"To ask him to delay the sale of the Hieronymus Parcel until STC's study is completed."

"Do you think he will?"

"If not, we will have to file a lawsuit. Dean Berkeley has agreed to handle the litigation. I hope that Judge Ashley will listen to reason."

Cartwright House had been built in stages as it evolved over the years from a retirement home for retired Methodist clergy and their widows to its position as the foremost senior living facility in the city. The result was a confusion of hallways and sealed off corridors. "It's deliberate I think," Papa said. "Its exercise for our mental facilities to recall how to get somewhere in this establishment. The elevator to the garage was in the "B" building. They walked down the halls of the "C" building, the newest building, where Papa and Dorrie Louise shared an apartment. Leaving the "C" building, they passed an elevator with warning tape across the door and a sign that read "Out of Order." Papa looked annoyed. "If they would just finish repairs on that elevator, we could go directly to the garage, rather than walking over to "B" and then back."

"Has it been a long time?"

"Everything at Cartwright House takes a long time. They delayed the elevator while they remodel some more apartments." Remodeling of apartments was a way of life at Cartwright House. The oldest units were half the size of the newest ones. When residents died or left, if their apartments were suitably situated they were combined into larger units. Minerva Wisconsin's penthouse apartment was in the original building and comprised four of the original units.

Papa went on. "I will probably die before that elevator is repaired." He squared his shoulders. "Oh, well, the exercise is good for my heart." With that, he increased the pace.

Don walked fast to keep up with the old man.

A man pushing a walker with tennis balls on the front legs looked up when they passed him. "Hello, Professor," he said. "I saw it again this morning, by the apartment they're remodeling on the fourth floor. " He pointed in the direction they had come.

"That's interesting, Paul," he said. "Did it speak?"

"No, no, it never says anything, just smiles at me, then disappears."

"Then no harm done, right, Paul? Do you know your way home?"

"Yes, yes, thank you, Professor." He reached into the basket of his walker. "Nice bananas today. Would you like one?"

"That is very kind of you but I have eaten."

The man pushed his walker down the hall. When he was out of earshot, Papa turned to Don. "A former student. Brilliant mind. Now he is convinced there is a ghost haunting the building. He has several others convinced also. There are sightings every week. They have even named it. They call it Rufus." He sighed. "Can you imagine? A student of mine. I am really old. Sometimes I even think I see Rufus myself. A dark spot, in the periphery of my vision. Cataracts, I suppose." He pointed to a narrow corridor to their left. "This way. I think. It's confusing."

"Do you like it here, Papa?"

"What do you mean?"

"Being around people like Paul. Do you like it here?"

They stopped. "Let's sit here for a minute," the professor said. "I do not want to tire you."

"I hope that's a joke," Don said.

They sat down on a couch in an alcove looking out over the courtyard. Men and women were strolling under the leafy trees, sitting beside a splashing fountain, reading books. "It seems pleasant enough."

Papa took off his glasses and cleaned them with a starched cotton handkerchief. "It is pleasant. Do I like it? No, I suppose I do not. However, at this stage in my life, I prefer it to the alternatives. I worry about your mother. She is one of the youngest residents here, however, she is determined to stay and look after me."

"She's a willful women, isn't she?"

Papa laughed. "Yes, God bless her." He replaced his glasses on his Roman nose. "They are good to us here, Don. They try to anticipate our needs. They feed us well, exercise us, entertain us. I am told it is like being on a cruise ship."

"That sounds good."

"But the cruise ship only stops when someone dies and they need to disembark the body."

"Oh."

"Professor Lindemann is a very gregarious man. Unlike me, he makes friends easily. He knows everyone who lives at Cartwright House. He said to me at dinner the other night that the hardest part of living here is watching so many of your friends die."

"I'm sure that's true," Don answered.

Papa stood, flexed his knee, and pulled his pant legs straight, then sat back down. "We live in what they refer to as 'Independent Living.' But of course, it is not that. When you elect to reside here, you lose a measure of independence. Oh, our minders minimize that. They stress how free we are in our choices, how much influence we have on what happens here. There are dozens of committees, surveys, meetings; everything to reinforce the impression that we have influence, have power. In truth, though, we do not. We have made a pact, in which we traded a large part of our independence for the promise they will look after us for the rest of our lives, come what may."

Don looked around. On the opposite wall, a "You Are Here" sign told the reader that he was in the north wing of the "B" building. The carpet was the same design as that in the "C" building, but it was worn from years of shuffling feet and walkers. The handrail smelled of disinfectant. A sign warned residents of a flu epidemic.

"Is that a bad pact, do you think?" He smiled. "Do you believe that you have made a pact with the devil?"

"No. Quite the contrary. We have made a pact with the angels."

Don sat silently, waiting for him to continue.

Papa sighed and looked down at his highly polished tan brogues, the same style of shoes that Papa had worn all Don's life.

"And this pact you made with the angels decreases the choices you can make, is that what you are saying?"

"It is." He rested his hand on Don's knee. "Have you ever thought what Heaven would be like?"

"I can't say that I have, Papa. Tell me."

"It would be horrific, my boy. Imagine. Not a single decision to be made. Not an iota of free will. Inertia. Boredom. Who would choose that?"

Don laughed. "Do you suppose there are committees in Heaven, Papa, so people can believe they're making decisions?"

Papa chuckled. "Probably. Most of us here are accustomed to determining basic matters for ourselves."

"Such as what?"

"All the trivia of daily life, I suppose. What time do I get up? What do I wear? What might I have for lunch? Who cleans my apartment? Who are the people I choose to see every day? When can I no longer care for myself and have to move to assisted living or nursing care?"

"Come on, Papa. You never worried about those things. Lena took care of all that."

"Yes, she did. She did it so I could write. She did it out of love. This is different. She never saw me as a child."

"And they do that here, see you as a child, I mean?"

"Perhaps. Maybe more as teenagers, aging backward into infancy. They prefer we act as responsible teenagers, and many of us do. Some of us are rebellious middle-schoolers. In the end, though, the people to whom we have entrusted our lives, know where we will end up. They know, and they care for us today in the context of what we will become."

"We see ourselves as what we once were, robust and independent, using our free will with impunity. The angels see us as what we will become, helpless and completely in their care, lucky to be in Heaven on Earth. The power is with the angels. We will die and Cartwright House will not. And that is the way it should be, I reckon."

He stood carefully. "We are late. We must leave Heaven and go visit the Honorable Judge Dockery Ashley, a man who is certainly living in Hell on Earth. That poor soul has seen his power drained away by age and the rise of a new generation. He clings to what little he has left. The H.H. Company? How pitiful is that? And wealth? He has squandered all his wife's fortune and is now misusing the benefice of Hiram Hieronymus."

《《《《《

Judge Dockery Ashley's colonnaded white brick mansion, with a circular drive and a lushly watered green lawn, sprawled on five acres in the middle of Austin's very best old neighborhood. His wife's maternal great-grand-father had married the daughter of a Texas governor, who had the house built as a wedding gift by Abner Cook, the architect of the state capital. Flowerbeds with lush plantings bordered the walk to the front door. Its ebony black sparkled in the sunlight, dappled by the overhanging red oak trees.

Papa had called ahead and Ashley's wife had assured him that the Judge would see them. "I hope she spoke to him," Papa said. "She's a bit unreliable."

Papa had shown no emotion when Don told him about the *Austin Next* foreclosure. "I'm an old man, Donnie Ray. Nothing surprises me any longer." No emotion, only the insistence that he needed to see Ashley at once.

Wilda Ashley met them at the door, the ice tinkling in her tightly clinched Bloody Mary. She swayed a little. "He's in there," she said. She pointed toward a doorway and turned back to the open bar, a black lacquered Japanese affair with numerous doors and cubbyholes. "Toddy?" she asked Don. "You are…?"

"Don Cuinn, Mrs. Ashley," Don replied. "Professor Rothschild's stepson." It was easier than explaining their relationship.

"Not Jewish, though, are you?" She ran her hand down the sleeve of Don's corduroy jacket. "Would you care to join a lady in a drink while the Professor talks business with Judge Ashley?"

Don resisted the urge to laugh. "Very tempting, ma'am, but I need to be in their meeting."

"Go on, then." She drained her glass and refilled it immediately.

Dockery Ashley, the one-time county judge, and for decades one of the most powerful men in the state, was stretched out on a yoga mat. He was dressed in exercise pants. Don was surprised to see that his round body was muscular, with very little body fat. He was also hairless, both his skull and his barrel chest. He lifted his body off the mat with one arm in a one-arm side plank and stared at them with cold cobalt eyes. "Well, Ralph, to what do I owe the honor?" He steadied himself in an angular position above the mat.

"This is my stepson, Judge. Don Cuinn. He drove me over. I do not drive, myself." Don could tell that Papa was nervous. That was unusual.

Ashley glanced at Don but didn't speak to him. "Get to the point, Ralph. I have an appointment and I'd like to finish my workout." He lowered himself slowly and with a quick turn and roll assumed a sitting position on the mat. He held his chin in his cupped hands waiting for Papa to speak.

"Judge, is it true that you mean to put the Hieronymus Parcel up for sale, for commercial development?"

"I can't discuss H.H. Company business with you."

"We are readying our own proposal, Judge. Surely you can delay a sale until you receive it."

Ashley stood and put on a silk kimono. He slipped his feet into a pair of red slippers. He confronted Papa and Don like an angry samurai warrior. "Who is this 'we,' Ralph? The same group of retired ivory tower professors who tried to make us close the Primate Preserve?"

"We did more than 'try,' Judge. We forced you to close that barbarous establishment."

Ashley scoffed. "You give yourself far too much credit. Those monkeys were going away as soon as the federal government withdrew the funding. Those spineless Washington bureaucrats caved at the first claim of *cruelty* to animals. Never mind the cruelty to humans, who have been deprived of invaluable research that could prevent horrific diseases."

"We differ on that, Judge," Papa said. "The monkeys are gone. Now you have the opportunity to put that wonderful land to a noble public purpose such as Hiram Hieronymus intended: build parks and trails and public water access. We will bring you a master plan creating priceless parkland for generations to come. Surely as a public charity you will consider the greater public good before you decide to sell this land. Surely you will consider what Hiram Hieronymus would have wanted done with his gift? Do not force us to go to court to uphold his intent."

"Don't bother sending us any proposals, Ralph. The H.H. Company funds charities all over this county. Its income has been reduced by the loss of the government grants. Responsible commercial development, done in compliance with the strictest possible oversight by the city, will allow the

H.H. Company to benefit the needy, rather than a few of you liberals who oppose all development."

Don spoke up, "I suppose a sale would also allow the H.H. Company to continue to pay its officers generous salaries."

Papa frowned and motioned for Don to be still. Ashley seemed to take notice of Don for the first time. "I remember you, Cuinn. You're the one who stirred up that trouble with the attorney general. Payne was a friend of mine. It's a shame what you did to him." He pointed to the door. "I don't owe you any explanation, but the salaries I and the other two directors draw for managing the H.H. Company are well earned." He turned to Papa. "If you mean to sue us, you'll have to do better than this." He cocked his large head in Don's direction.

Don flushed. *You bastard.*

Papa smiled thinly. "We will sue, Judge. Dean St. Livermore Berkeley himself has agreed to handle our case, and he says we have a good one."

Ashley laughed. "Lili-livered Berkeley? Has he ever even been inside a courtroom? Maybe Cuinn here would be better after all." He pointed to the door. "Now if you will excuse me."

They left the room. Ashley followed them into the hall. "Oh, by the way, Ralph, I understand that a number of Cartwright residents invested in the *Austin Next* project and their investments are lost. That's Wesley Bird's project, I believe. A special friend of yours, Cuinn. Interesting man, Wesley Bird. I've talked with his former mother-in-law, Anne Morgan, and she tells me the family has washed its hands of him. 'A lost cause' she called him." He turned to Papa and said, "Ralph, you and your son have a long relationship with Bird. You invited him to Cartwright House. You introduced him to fellow residents. In fact, you vouched for him."

"Now, wait a minute," Don said.

Ashley ignored him. "You vouched for him, Ralph. If Wesley Bird concocted a fraudulent scheme and your friends lose their money, who do they have to blame?"

Papa flinched. "I assure you I feel remorse about that."

"Papa, don't." Don said. "You're not to blame for Wesley Bird being a con man."

Ashley stared coldly at Papa. "The next time you advise your neighbors about something, let's say, about the Hieronymus Parcel, remember the grave mistake you made. Perhaps you may want to stay your hand, and leave such matters to people who know what they are doing."

"What are you getting at, Judge?" Don asked.

"Ralph knows very well what the honorable course is here," Ashley said, "and it's not attacking me." He turned and left them standing in the hall.

Don led Papa outside. "Are you all right?"

"Yes, I'm fine." He looked at the surveillance camera over the front door and stood up straighter. He adjusted his tie. "Later. We'll talk later, when we get home. I need to think."

⟨⟨⟨⟨⟨

They returned to Cartwright House without speaking. When they got out of the car, Papa said, "I know a place where we can talk. I do not want to disturb your mother." He led Don down a long service driveway. When they reached the front of the Cartwright House grounds, he pointed across the street. "Over there. That's the Hieronymus Parcel. There is a bench under a large oak where I sit and contemplate the human race and its peculiarities."

They made their way carefully across the busy street. A city transit bus was parked at the bus stop. Donnie Ray recognized the dress and casual manner of grad students as they stepped off the bus and headed toward the waterfront. The old oaks shaded them as they walked.

"This place hasn't changed."

Papa pointed to a wooden bench and they sat down. "This bench was here when I came to Austin the first time, an undergraduate with a thick accent and a love of the English language."

"How old were you?"

"Barely sixteen. Only ten years after my father sent us to Cuba to escape the Nazis." He looked up. "This tree was large even then. It must be two hundred years old. I fear it will not make three hundred."

"Maybe it will. It looks healthy."

Papa shook his head. "Not when Dockery Ashley gets done. There will be a parking lot where we are sitting."

"A parking lot? Really?"

"Oh, yes. And the Monkey House and those wooded play areas, where the monkeys used to play and the children play now, those will be replaced by condominiums and retail shops. The entire tract, given in trust by Hiram Hieronymus, will be razed and made into another mixed-use development. Oh, they will preserve a token tree or two. Maybe even this one, but this…" He stretched out his arms, "…this will all be history."

"That SOB Ashley is a man who is accustomed to having his way."

"Do not call him that. It is disrespectful."

"I'm sorry, Papa, but I think I disrespect him."

Papa shook his head. "Lena always said I had no common sense."

Mama *should never have let Papa get into this mess*, Don thought.

"What did you do, Papa? For Wesley, I mean?"

"I made some calls, I had friends come to a meeting. Many of them live at Cartwright House. We agreed that the STC group should organize the community to oppose the sale of the Hieronymus Parcel." He turned to Don and drew himself up straighter. "Quite prominent people. Knowledgeable people. They were kind enough to elect me chair. We started a campaign. We have been at the public meetings to protest the sale of the Parcel. I believe we are making headway." He paused. "Or at least we were. But now, this investment debacle changes everything."

"Wait a second, Papa. What can Ashley really do? These are your friends. They'll understand, won't they?"

They stood up. "No, it is you who does not understand. I encouraged that same group to invest with Wesley. Many of them put their savings into his . . . fraud. It is my fault." He took Don by the shoulders. "Help me, Don. Help me get their money back."

He thought, *If you had just called me, this would never have happened.* But what he said was, "I will, Papa. I'll find a way. If I had the money, I'd give it to you. I don't have it, but I'll find a way." *But how?*

"Thank you, son. You must. And I will not rest until this wrong is righted. In the meantime, I need to inform my friends what has happened to their investment." He sighed. "Then, I will resign from STC."

"Think about it, Papa, before you do that."

Papa looked at the placid surroundings. "No. I must. The Hieronymus Parcel will have to be saved without me."

They made their way slowly back to Cartwright House. Papa seemed more stooped and walked less steadily than he had earlier. They waited at the elevator.

When the door opened two women got out. One smiled at Papa and said loudly, "Oh, Professor Rothschild, when will you agree to do a reading at our book club? I can promise you an attentive audience."

Papa shook his head. "My next book, perhaps."

"When will that be, do you think?"

"Oh, any day now." he said. He bowed slightly and stood aside for the women to pass. When he and Don were alone in the elevator, he said, "Two of my former friends, I fear."

CHAPTER NINE

Jungle Java was on Burnet Road, halfway between the Broken Omelet and the Frisco Shop, a local restaurant that had survived only because it moved when threatened by encroaching fast food restaurant chains. Don remembered its "real" location on the Drag. It was mid-afternoon and the coffee shop's parking lot was full, as were the bike racks. Don finally found a place for Dorrie Louise's old Honda between the bike racks and a sagging clothesline. *It looks right at home.* The bikes were chained well. *Not everything is the same,* he thought. In addition to an apparent wave of bike thefts, Burnet Road itself had changed. Jungle Java was new since Don left Austin. He tried to remember what was there before, but except for a couple of burger joints, all he could remember were car repair shops and a Greek bakery. Now it boasted restaurants with cute names and newly opened apartment/condo buildings. He had passed three coffee shops, not to mention a Starbucks, before he got to Jungle Java. *God, if Burnet Road can be gentrified, what's next? South Lamar?* he wondered.

He got out of the car, thought about locking it, and then decided not to bother. The Honda was worth more stolen than not, but even one of the roadside panhandlers on MoPac had better taste than that. He made his way across the broken asphalt. Whoever owned the Jungle Java wasn't spending any money on maintenance. Why would he? The next owner would raze the place and build another six-story mixed-use building, like the one across the street. He stared at it for a minute. *God, if I could somehow move the Hansro Building to Austin I'd be a wealthy man. It could be marketed as mid-twentieth century chic, probably get a historical preservation designation, not have to pay property taxes.* Actually, it looked as good as the building across the road. Wood and stone and red brick running in no known pattern, with the obligatory Tuscan towers on the ends of the crazy-quilt building, and a big parking garage at the back.

Wesley had picked Java Jungle because, as he told Don, he lived in the complex across from the coffee shop. Don surmised it was a stark change from the Timeless, the luxury condo by the lake where Wesley stayed when he worked for Sawbucks Banjo. *How the mighty have fallen,* he thought.

He stepped inside, out of the bright afternoon sun, and waited for his eyes to adjust to the darkness. There was a line at the service bar and all the tables seemed to be filled with young people staring at their smart phones or working on their laptops. An attractive girl with bright eyes glanced up from heating a panini and saw Don looking around. "You want Wesley? He said to send you back. He's over there." She pointed to the back of the shop.

"Thanks," Don said. Wesley's taste in women always had been impeccable.

"Donnie Ray, back here." The familiar deep voice rang across the room but no one looked up. He squinted and saw Wesley's big form swallowing a small bistro table. Wesley waved for him to come back. No one looked up from their screens. A Hispanic barista, clearing a table, smiled at Don. "That's Wesley Bird back there, right? He's famous or something isn't he? You know what, man? He comes in here all the time. Sets up office at that table."

He whistled.

"You a friend of his? He has your latte."

"*Gracias,*" Don said. He maneuvered his way through the crowded room to the private spot in the corner that Wesley had staked out.

Wesley closed his phone and scooted a chair back from the table with a booted foot. "Sit, D.Ray. Sit and tell me what the hell's going on." He extended a hand as if to shake Don's but Don ignored the offer. "My God," Wesley said, "you look terrible."

Don sat down. "I wonder why? Can you think of any reason why I might look bad?"

Wesley pointed at a large earth-friendly paper cup in front of Don. "Maybe you need your morning coffee. Or maybe you just need to get laid. I got you your favorite: latte grande with two extra shots. It's not as good as Starbucks, but what the hell, it is what it is."

Don looked at the latte. He hated to admit it, but it did look good. He missed Starbucks. Sometimes he would drive to Amarillo to have a latte grande. He'd thought about trying to get a Starbucks franchise for Velda, but the cowboys wouldn't drink anything but their Folgers re-boiled six times. He took a sip, then a larger one. It was all he could do not to sigh. "Very thoughtful of you, Wesley. You remembered what kind of coffee I like, but you couldn't stop yourself from cheating my folks out of their savings. You are a kind and generous man."

Wesley grinned. "Don't go hard ass on me, Donnie Ray. I've got important things on my mind."

Don leaned over the table and hissed, "You don't have anything more important in your life than getting them their money back."

"Easy, son. It was business. I told them there was risk. Deals go bad. Hell, I lost a lot more than they did."

"Come on. You didn't put any money in that deal."

"Money, no, that's true. But the DA is after me, Donnie Ray. I may have to go to the pen."

Maybe there is justice in this world. "Oh, you'll figure a way out of that. You always do. It's other people who get hurt."

"You still have a stick up your ass because of the San Jacinto deal? I thought we put all that behind us the last time we talked."

Don swirled the foamy cream into the smoky coffee. "I remember. How long after that did you swindle Papa and Dorrie Louise?"

Wesley looked down, then raised his eyes and stared directly into Don's eyes. "There were people waiting in line to get into *Austin Next.* Everybody wanted a piece of it."

"Bullshit. If that was so, why take money from them? You swindled them and you swindled their friends. Why? Why the hell did you do that, Wesley?"

The one-time All-American tight end shifted his bulk in the little chair. "I really believed I was doing them a favor, getting them in at the ground level."

"Get real, man. I've read the documents. They're three levels from ground level. You promoted the hell out of them."

Wesley shifted again and smiled. "You read the documents? Shit, I never did that. But you're a lawyer now, aren't you? Anyhow, they stood to make a ton of money when the project got finished. Nobody wanted that to happen more than me. If it hadn't been for those dead Indians…"

"The Tonkawa burial ground."

"That's right." He drained his espresso and looked at the empty cup. "Let's have some more coffee." He got up and went to the front counter. Don watched him standing under the cartoon cutouts of Tarzan and Jane that hung over the coffee machines. Wesley's large shoulders slumped, then Don could see him catch himself and straighten up and stand erectly. He handed the cute girl a ten-dollar bill and waved off the change. *That's Papa's money,* Don thought.

He accepted the coffee. "You were saying?"

"All right. Here's the deal." He took a deep breath and placed both hands on the table. "The real deal. It was all going so well. The permanent financing was almost in place." He gritted his teeth. "I had to have my share of the equity, Donnie Ray. I had to, or I would just be a hired hand, you know? Cindy's folks turned me down flat. I guess they could tell the marriage was going down the tubes. I took investors wherever I could find them. Bob Braeswood had his part of the equity. From the cough drop settlement."

"Oh, yeah. Cough Drop Braeswood." Braeswood had been a plaintiff's lawyer who got into politics after his one big killing, a class action suit against the cough drop companies, claiming that one of the ingredients in cough drops caused impotence in rats. Impotent men from all over the country answered the Braeswood law firm's television ads, eager to blame their performance anxiety on cough drops. "That made Braeswood a fortune. Why did he want to build *Austin Next* anyway?"

"Well, that's the thing. Cough drops wasn't like tobacco, or asbestos. He made some money, sure, but he was never *rich*, not like in *big rich*. Bob wanted to play with the big boys. Hell, he wanted to run for president. To do that, he needed to make some real money. This was real money. Plus, it was just one of a dozen things we were doing: start-ups, venture capital, oil deals. Anything that had a big jackpot, Bob wanted in. It seemed like the banks couldn't wait to back him. He was supposed to be so smart, you know. Really, he knew less about business than I did."

"Did any of the deals work?"

Wesley shook his head and grinned sheepishly. "Not many. Bob's about to declare bankruptcy. But he's got friends in the right places. No criminal charges for Cough Drop. That's reserved for yours truly. Bob had good lawyers putting together our deals, Donnie Ray. Anything even close to the line, he left for me to do. You know, financing statements that weren't quite accurate; assets that were overvalued or weren't there at all. Things like that—go ahead, sign it. I thought, 'When *Austin Next* is finished we'll be rich and all that stuff won't matter.' Well, it matters now. Damn Indians. And I was too stupid to see it. I drank the Kool-Aid. I believed my own bullshit. Isn't that something?"

Don remembered the countless evenings after they had taken their dates home and decided to have one last beer, long nights when he and Wesley shared their life stories. He had told this man everything: his dreams, his fears, and he thought Wesley had done the same. Now, he wondered just what had been true back then, or if Wesley even knew the difference between the truth and his lies. "But the Hungarian gold coins, Wesley. For God's sake, you went back for a second bite and you sold them worthless certificates for some fucking Hungarian gold coins?"

"Do you want some? I have some more."

"You son of a bitch." He rose out of his chair, ready to leave.

"Just kidding D. Ray, just kidding. I bought those certificates from an ex-quarterback with the Tampa Bay Buccaneers. A tenth of a penny on the dollar, but still a lot of money. I bought a hundred million dollars worth. Cost me ten thousand dollars."

"Are there any coins?"

"Sure. At least that's what I was told. They're in a government vault in Buda. Or is it Pest? One of those places. All we have to do is win this case at the World Court that my guy and his buddies are gonna file."

"Jesus. You are going to jail."

"I needed the money. I had to have the money. Braeswood's paying my lawyer fees, but only if I take the fall. Not a word about his involvement. He was just a poor innocent investor, like everybody else."

"Why would you do that?"

"He hired Brave Tipps for me. Brave tells me that he'll do his best to get a good jury, all University football fans. He hopes we can rescue victory from the jaws of defeat."

"Just like the Nebraska game."

Wesley grinned. "Wasn't I something? A ninety-yard catch and run. Conference champs, Rose Bowl, National champs." He shook his head. "I know it's a long shot. If I could afford to fire Brave and hire Lot Mercury from Houston, I'd rat Braeswood in a *mofo* minute. Otherwise, it's just a crapshoot. Does an Austin jury want to send its favorite All-American to prison?" He thought for a minute. "What I really need is for Cindy's family to decide that they don't want their ex-son-in-law in prison. They could make it happen. But I'm not expecting that. Cindy's mom is a real bitch."

"And the wealthiest woman in Texas, as I recall."

"Right. That's my, my, uh, what?"

"Your conundrum?"

Wesley snapped his fingers in the old familiar way. "Exactly." He looked up and waved at someone. "I do have one friend left though."

"You don't mean me, do you?"

"No. I mean her."

A pair of strong hands gripped Don's shoulders, kneading them in a familiar way. He might have guessed who it was from the massage, but he didn't have to guess. He knew immediately from her scent when she brushed the side of his face with hers.

"Hey, Anna Kaye," Wesley said. "I believe you know Lawyer Cuinn.

Anna Kaye Nordstrom, former outside hitter on the University's champion volleyball team, turned Don's head in her hands and kissed him full on the lips. "Hello, Lover. Have you missed me?"

Don tasted the sweet lipstick, breathed in the familiar perfume, and caught his breath. "Hello."

She pulled over a chair from the next table and swung her tall body into it. Her short skirt rode up her legs and Don decided yes, he had missed her. She touched him lightly on the arm. "Donnie Ray, aren't you worried about your reputation, being seen with Public Enemy Number One?"

Don smiled. "What about your reputation?"

"A professional arrangement. Every real estate developer needs a good public relations consultant."

"That would be you? Don't take your fee in gold coins."

Wesley cleared his throat. "I'm sitting right here, you know. Anna Kaye is a loyal friend, more than I can say for some people. She's handling my P.R. *Pro bono. In toto.*"

"And doing a bang-up job of it, I'm sure."

"Get me a decaf cappuccino, Sweetie, will you?" she said to Wesley.

The big man jumped to his feet and hurried to the counter.

"I never thought I'd see Wesley jump on command," Don said.

"Me either. Kind of sad. I liked the old Wesley better."

She watched Wesley placing the order, then turned back to Don. "You look awful, darling." When Don didn't answer, she said, "I'm not working for free. Wesley doesn't know it, and Cindy swore me to secrecy, but she's paying for me. She still loves the worthless SOB, but she can't possibly stay married to him."

Don smiled, remembering a night when he and Anna Kaye were naked in a canoe on Lady Bird Lake. Like a klutz, he capsized it, and they spent the evening in a blanket on the shore.

"I warned her not to marry him," Anna Kaye said. "Everybody did. But he conned her and he conned her family."

"Did you know he took money from Papa and Dorrie Louise?"

"Oh, Baby. I'm so sorry."

"And you're trying to get him off."

She shrugged. "It's just a job, Donnie Ray." She whispered as Wesley came near, carrying a large cappuccino. "Don't tell Cindy, but it's wasted money. I'm not doing any good."

Wesley sat down. "So tell me? Did you convince the drunk to reduce the charges?"

She took a sip of her coffee and blotted her lipstick carefully. "The thing is, Wesley, the District Attorney doesn't like you."

"Doesn't like me? That cocksucker! They stopped him for drunk driving! The DA! They showed videos of him fighting with the deputies in the county jail!" Wesley told Don.

"That even made the news in Velda," Don said.

District Attorney Vernon Lakey earned his reputation by prosecuting state officials accused of corruption. He had made a career of bringing down midlevel politicians, and once, even the lieutenant governor. Don had watched the stocky DA, smirking on T.V. while he proclaimed that, "Stealing from the citizens of this great state will not be tolerated while I am District Attorney." State officials quailed at the thought of Lakey's investigators invading their offices looking for, and even worse, finding evidence of bribes taken or influence sold.

Now they were treated to videos of the prosecutor being arrested on Ben White Boulevard at three in the morning, an empty bottle of bourbon on the front seat of his county-owned Suburban. The police video, somehow leaked to the media, showed Lakey screaming at the deputies. "Do you know who I am? Call the sheriff. Call Mike Tyball and tell him you have the fucking District Attorney by the side of the road, interfering with his official duties! Do it, goddammit!" The reports, shown over and over, cut to the lockup where Lakey was put into restraints, still yelling and slobbering, until in front of a friendly judge, he pled guilty and was sentenced to a weekend in jail and six months' probation.

"What does he want, for me to give him a blow job? That slimy SOB."

Anna Kaye smiled. "Wesley, talking like that may be why he doesn't like you." She finished her coffee. "Besides, no one's proved Vernon Lakey is gay."

Wesley sputtered. "I don't even know the man. And yes, I would blow him if it would keep me out of jail." He turned to Don. "Wouldn't you?"

"Haven't faced that decision yet."

Wesley went on. "No, it isn't that he doesn't like me. It's that the fix is in. Our distinguished governor gets a pass, and I get a ticket to the pen." He turned back to Anna Kaye. "How do we fix this?"

"I'm doing my best. You're Wesley Bird. Nobody in his right mind wants to send the University's All-American to prison. Not even Mr. District Attorney."

"That pussy!"

❝❝❝❝❝

Don waited for Anna Kaye in the parking lot. She hugged Wesley and pointed him toward his apartment across the street. "I'll call," she shouted over the traffic. They watched Wesley shuffle across the street, head down, shoulders slumped.

"It'd be a blessing if a car hit him," she said. "Put him out of his misery. He's not going to like prison life."

"Don't underestimate Wesley Bird. By the time he gets out, he'll have the meth concession, system-wide."

She laughed. "Don't be bitter."

"I am bitter. Is there a chance in hell of my folks getting their money back?"

"From Wesley? From the banks? What do you think?"

Don sighed. "Yeah." He opened the car door. "I better go tell them the bad news." They hugged and he kissed her on the cheek. She held the hug for an extra second, cocked her head, and looked at him.

"Where are you staying, Donnie Ray?" she asked.

He thought for a minute. *Is this going where I think it is?* "I've got a room at some hotel near Dorrie Louise and Papa's apartment."

She laughed. "Do you remember the last night we were together?"

He smiled. "I do, but I'd be surprised if you do. We were out drinking and you spent the night in an empty guest room at the Haven."

"All I remember is waking up in a strange nightgown."

"That was Dorrie Louise's doing. She undressed you and put you in one of Lena's."

She touched his cheek. "Come stay at my place, why don't you?"

He reddened at her touch. "You have an extra bed?"

"No, I don't," she said. "Donnie Ray, I do believe you're blushing."

"Anna Kaye," he said. "I'm no good at relationships. I'm screwed up, ever since I lost Cecilia."

"Who said anything about a relationship? Come stay with me, we'll have a good time, and you can go back to Wyoming or wherever it is you live."

He hesitated.

"For old times sake." She lowered her voice. "After all, we never did get that last night together you promised me."

He remembered her athletic body and her bawdy ways and nodded agreement. *This is not a good idea,* he thought. Even so, he heard himself saying, "I do try to pay my debts." *I'm a weak person*, he admitted to himself. "Where do you live?"

"A new place. You'll love the neighborhood." She kissed him on the cheek and ruffled his hair. "I'll pick you up at the Cartwright House about six."

CHAPTER TEN

Papa listened quietly as Don told him about his meeting with Wesley. "Mama needs to hear this too. Where is she?" Don asked.

"At the meditation class in the courtyard. They are all down there in their leotards, seeking peace for their inner selves."

Don said, "She'll need all the inner peace she can get, when she hears the news."

Papa stood up erectly. "Don't underestimate your mother." He picked up a small leather bag. "Come walk with me. It's time for my swim."

"Your swim?"

"Every day. Twenty laps. It clears some of the elder fog. It kept me off a walker."

The old man strode purposefully through the maze of hallways, carefully avoiding the statuettes and artificial flowers with which the residents had decorated the doors of their apartments. "Cartwright art," Papa said. "Oh well, if it makes them happy."

The old man's a snob, Don realized.

Papa steadied himself occasionally on the handrail that ran down one side of the halls. "I am not concerned about our money, Don. Your mother and I have enough. I have a generous pension; she has her social security. We will survive."

"Even so, Papa. It's a lot of money."

"Money. What good is it if you have all that you need? I did not remember that when Wesley came calling and I should have. I became greedy, and I have only myself to blame."

"You probably were thinking of helping Mama, maybe even me."

"Whatever the reason, I was wrong and I can accept the consequences of my actions. But my friends, those people I led into this. We must find a way to repay them."

But how?

"The word is out. I have written a letter to my fellow investors telling them of the foreclosure. I have also resigned as the chair of STC." He waited while an attendant wearing a Cartwright jumpsuit passed them before he continued. He spoke softly, "Who will lead the fight to save the Hieronymus Parcel now?"

They walked on in silence.

He sighed. "Here we are." He pointed at large double doors. He jangled his key chain until he found the access fob. He passed it over a pad beside the door and the doors sprung open, revealing a lap pool. The room was enclosed with high windowed walls and a slanted roof, diffusing the afternoon sun. Lounge chairs and striped towels gave the space the appearance of an upscale resort.

They were alone except for one woman who sat on the pool's edge, dangling her toes. She was small and compact, with the figure of a young woman and the face of a well-preserved matron. It was Minerva Wisconsin. "Hello, Ralph," she called. "Please tell me the water will be warmer when I get in."

"Hello, Minerva," Papa answered. "This is my...uh...adopted son, Don Cuinn."

She nodded brightly at Don. "I'm Minerva Wisconsin," she said, waving bright red fingernails in his direction.

Don waved back.

"And yes," Papa said, "the water will be warmer when you get it in."

"Oh, Professor. You're so wise. Please join me."

Papa turned to Don. "Go find your mother and have that talk. I will join you later." He disappeared into the men's locker room and left Don with Minerva Wisconsin.

She smiled again. "Not joining us?"

"I didn't bring a suit."

"Pity," she said. She slipped into the water and began a perfect Australian crawl with all the signs of having had excellent swimming instruction as a girl.

❮❮❮❮❮

Dorrie Louise took Don's news just as Papa had predicted. Her face was radiant in the sunlight. *Meditation class agrees with her,* Don observed.

"Oh, it'll all be fine, I'm sure," she sad. "Why should I worry? The two smartest men in the world are working on it." She rummaged in the refrigerator and came out with the pitcher of iced tea. She poured two glasses full and handed him one.

Don took the tea and sat at the old dining table he remembered from the owner's apartment at the Haven. He rubbed his hand across the burn marks, made by cigarettes that Lena had forgotten to put out. *Lena would have known what to do. No, Lena would never have given Wesley any money in the first place.* "What two men?"

"You and Papa, of course. Where is Papa, anyway?"

"Having a swim. With Minerva Wisconsin."

His mother laughed. "That'll never work out."

"What do you mean?"

She put two spoons full of sugar in her tea and plunked a lemon slice into the tawny liquid. "Papa has this idea that he can convince Minerva to buy the Hieronymus Parcel and donate it to the city."

"And that won't work out?"

"Papa has no sense of money, Donnie Ray. It's thirty million dollars."

"She's not worth that much?"

"Oh, she might be." She brushed a lock of graying hair back from her forehead with a gesture that Don recognized from his earliest memories. "What they say, Donnie Ray, is that her money comes from her first husband, and that as hard as she worked to get it, she's very careful about what she spends it on."

90

"You're saying that she's frugal?"

"Yes. And they say she is used to getting her own way. Including every decision that's made around here. So they say."

"Who's 'they', Mama?" Donnie Ray asked.

"Who's what?" She looked confused for a minute and then said with a giggle, "You mean, who told me? One of the women here. A woman who used to be her friend."

"Former friends are the best sources."

"Well, this one is. She was Minerva's best friend until Minerva tried to steal her husband."

"But she failed?"

"He died."

"I never figured you for a gossip, Mama."

"That's the number one activity here, Donnie Ray. Only outranked by going to dinner. Anyway, Minerva Wisconsin has had a very exciting life, if you know what I mean."

"I don't know what you mean. I believe I'll switch to beer." He was glad he had brought a six-pack. He got a beer out of the refrigerator and opened it. "So tell me about Minerva Wisconsin. You're dying to, aren't you?"

"I may have another glass of iced tea. My throat is so dry."

"Gossiping does that."

She swatted at him with the back of her hand. "Show some respect, you little devil."

She poured her tea, stirred in the sugar, and sat back down. "Thank goodness Papa isn't here. He hates gossip."

Don smiled. "Are you going to tell me or not?"

"When Minerva Pacett was at UT, her sorority sister was a girl named Mary Bagg. You know—the wealthy Bagg family—descendants of Senator Bagg? The Pacetts were from Hillsboro, somewhere up there. The father was a drinking lawyer, the mother a piano teacher. Somehow, they managed to send Minerva to the university, got her in Pi Phi, but they weren't rich. Minerva never had the clothes or the car, or the trips like the other girls in her sorority. What Minerva did have, though, was beauty. They say she was drop-dead gorgeous. You can tell that, even today."

"Yes, you can," Don said. "I've seen her in her bathing suit." He finished his beer and sat it carefully on the floor between his feet. "Go on."

"One Thanksgiving, Mary Bagg invited Minerva to spend the holiday at her house—the Bagg mansion—over in Old Enfield. You can imagine how impressed Minerva was: a little Hillsboro girl in the finest house in Austin. The family took her in and treated her like she was Mary Bagg's sister. They loved her—especially Mary's father, Raymond. Pretty soon Raymond Bagg was driving the girls everywhere, taking them on outings and driving them to Dallas to shop at Niemans."

"I think I know where this is going," Don said. "I need another beer." From the kitchen, Don heard Dorrie Louise as she bustled around the living room, tidying up, shuffling newspapers and magazines.

When he came back and settled again at the old table, Dorrie Louise smiled. "Ready?"

"You may proceed."

"Thank you, Your Honor. As you probably guessed, before long, Raymond was looking after Minerva even when Mary was busy. No one thought much about it, but then someone saw him parked around the corner from the Pi Phi house, and then, sure enough, here comes Minerva out the back door and she gets in his car. At night."

"Damn those 'someones.'"

"Nobody is sure what Raymond thought was happening, but he probably never expected to divorce the woman he'd been married to for thirty years and run off with a co-ed the same age as his daughter."

"But that's what happened."

"Yes, it is. That is exactly what happened. The first Mrs. Bagg got the big house and some money, I imagine, and Raymond Bagg got a twenty-year-old bride. He was approaching sixty."

"Wow!"

"I'd say. By the time Mary Bagg got her B.A. degree in Art History, she had two new half-sisters and one new half-brother. She went from being her daddy's only little girl, to one of four children—and the other three were adorable infants. She never had a chance."

"What happened to her mother?"

"The first Mrs. Bagg? Raymond said he wanted to be completely fair, so in his will, he set up trusts, leaving a one-fourth interest in his estate to each of the four children. The mothers got the income off their children's interest for their lifetime."

Don finished his beer and smiled. "I'm sure Minerva liked that, but it probably didn't sit well with the first wife."

Dorrie Louise took Don's empty beer bottles and washed them out before putting them in the blue recycling bin. "It didn't help that Minerva was the trustee of all the trusts, including Mary Bagg's."

"Boy, he must have really hated his first wife."

"I think he was wicked mean. He did it just for the heck of it."

"What happened?"

"You don't need another beer, Donnie Ray. Sit back down." She waited until he was seated again. "There were lawsuits, of course, and Minerva ended up buying out Mary's mother, who got the house and some oil properties and enough money to make her comfortable, but Minerva and her children got everything else."

"And everything else was a whole lot?"

"You know all that development out the old Dallas Highway, from Austin to Georgetown?"

"Where Build You-A-Computer's headquarters is?"

"All that was the Bagg Ranch. Minerva's made a fortune off of it, and she has a lot of land left."

"Land. It's always about land."

"What?"

"Just something a taxi driver told me." Don got up and stretched. He sneaked a look at his watch. It was almost time to tell his mother that he was spending the night with her least favorite female friend of his, Anna Kaye Nordstrom. He still remembered the look on Dorrie Louise's face when she took the blond girl, passed out in his apartment, and bedded her down in an empty guest room at the Haven Hotel. No, Dorrie Louise would not have forgotten.

Should I lie? Forget it; that never worked. Dorrie Louise could detect a lie before it was out of his mouth. Not knowing what to do, he played for time. "Go on with the story, Mama. What happened next? Is that when Minerva married Coach Wisconsin?"

"Oh goodness, no. First, there was Cordell Achieson."

"Achieson. That's a familiar name."

"Papa can tell you all about him. He and his brother, Marshall, were architects. They designed some new library building at the University. Papa was on the faculty committee that reviewed the plans. That's how he got to know Cordell Achieson. He says Achieson was a brilliant architect. 'What a waste,' he told me. Achieson had drawn up the plans for the new house that Raymond built for Minerva when they were first married. It's a big castle-like place, near the Racquet Club."

"I remember that place. That's Minerva's house?"

"Yes, Raymond took Minerva to Europe and when she came back, she was a different person, sophisticated, you know? Anyway, she had photos of chalets and country houses she had seen in Europe and she insisted that the architect take her favorite parts from all of them and design her new house. Papa says that Cordell Achieson hated every minute of that commission, but Minerva knew exactly what she wanted."

"I really do need that beer, Mama," Don said.

"Bring me one too, Donnie Ray."

Don found the last of the beers. "This is a first, Mama. When did you start drinking?"

"Oh, Donnie Ray, there's lots of things about me that you don't know. Anyway, talking about Minerva Wisconsin makes me need alcohol."

He opened the beer, poured half in a glass for his mother, and took the half-full bottle for himself. "What happened next?"

She took a sip from the glass and made a face. "I'll never be an alcoholic, I'm afraid."

"It takes practice."

"He wasn't happy married to Minerva?"

"He must have been crazy about her. After Raymond Bagg died, Cordell Achieson left his wife and his children for Minerva. The rumor at the time was that he was the real father of Minerva's children."

"Probably spread by the first wife."

"I'm sure. That doesn't make it untrue, though."

"You really don't like Minerva, do you?"

Mama held out her glass for more beer. "And the boy, Raymond III, is Cordell's spitting image." She took a sip from her glass. "Beer is awful stuff." She took another sip. "Anyhow, Minerva knew firsthand how close an architect and a young wife could get, so she insisted he stop taking clients and devote himself entirely to her businesses, designing office buildings for her new developments and the like. By all accounts, he had a miserable ten years, married to Minerva."

"Twice widowed?"

"She was when she set her cap for Coach 'One-Eye' Jack Wisconsin."

Don smiled. "The most famous football coach in NFL history. His Detroit team was undefeated two seasons in a row."

"Minerva met him at a charity affair. People there said she spotted him, latched on to him, and never turned him loose. He didn't have a chance."

"As a player, he was very illusive. I guess his juke moves failed him."

"If you say so. He was a widower with no children."

"So, relatively painless by Minerva's standards. No broken homes or abandoned children."

"She worked at it, I'll say that for her. She hired a University ex-quarterback to teach her about football. She learned all the terms, the strategy, and the history. She's a walking encyclopedia of football!"

"All for the sake of love."

"Coach Wisconsin died last year, so Minerva's on the prowl again."

She took his empty bottle, washed it, and put it in recycling with the others, then turned to him. "Why do you think I've learned all this? I'm not interested in gossip."

"What do you mean?"

"You need to know your enemy, and Minerva is mine. She means to marry Papa. She's had a sugar daddy and an architect and a coach. Now she wants a poet!"

Don remembered the smiling woman on the side of the pool. "Papa?"

"He'll be putty in that conniving bitch's hands."

He smiled. "First beer, now swearing. It can only end one place. You're going straight to Hell, Mama."

"Minerva Pacett Bagg Achieson Wisconsin will do that to you."

They sat and stared at each other. Don tried to get his mind around the thought of Papa and Minerva coupling, but his imagination refused to go there. It was time to leave. He hesitated, then said, "I need to go, Mama. I have a friend coming by to pick me up, Mama."

"That's nice, Donnie Ray. Who is he? Do I know him?"

"It's not a 'him', Mama...and you do know her."

A frown creased Dorrie Louise's face. "Don't tell me it's that wild one, that gymnast?"

"Anna Kaye was a volleyball player." *She was also pretty acrobatic,* Donnie Ray recalled.

"You know I never liked that girl. She tried to come between you and Cecilia, I know that for a fact."

"Cecilia's gone, Mama."

"This girl's a bad influence, Donnie Ray Cuinn. I can't believe you broke up with that perfectly nice red-headed girl, and now you're taking up with this one."

"I'm not taking up with her, Mama. We're going out for dinner and a drink."

Dorrie Louise shook her head. "Do you plan to spend the night with her?"

Don grinned. *This is worse than high school.* "I'm a grown man, Mama."

"Then act like one. Men! It's bad enough that I have Papa to worry about. Now I have to worry about you, too."

CHAPTER ELEVEN

Anna Kaye was waiting for him in the driveway of the Cartwright House behind the wheel of a bright yellow Fiat 500. He peered through the window. "Is there room for both of us in there?"

"Get in the car, Donnie," she said.

He tossed his duffle bag in the back seat and settled into the passenger seat. It was roomier than it looked from the outside.

"Like it?" she asked. She gunned the Fiat out of the drive and laughed as two attendants, smoking cigarettes, jumped out of the way. "Quit smoking!" she yelled at them. One replied with a good-natured obscene gesture.

"Let me guess," Don said. "You bought a girl's car to squash recurring questions about your sexual preference."

"Very funny." She looked over at him and the Fiat bumped against the curb.

"Watch it. This thing's not crash-worthy."

"I may prove you wrong on that," she said. She hit the accelerator again, and they careened crazily down the boulevard, heading toward downtown.

"Driving never was your strong suit."

"Shut up."

She took the cut-off to Cesar Chavez and drove along Lady Bird Lake past groves of dogwood and cherry blossom trees. They passed the multi-million dollar pedestrian bridge. He admired the young girls in short shorts and skimpy tees jogging determinedly on the path beside the road.

"Where are we going?"

"For a drink, then dinner. But first, to the old power plant."

He looked to his left and saw the one-time eyesore. Construction equipment surrounded it and the entire block was fenced off. "What's going on?"

"P2P." She pulled into the worksite and stopped in front of the entrance. A worker in a hardhat smiled and waved her through. "Public-private partnership."

"There seems to be a lot of that going around. They know you here?"

She parked the car next to a trailer and hopped out. "Come on. I'll show you around."

They walked carefully throughout the construction detritus and into the massive main hall. The plant had been there as long as Don could remember, but he couldn't recall ever having a conscious thought about it. It was just there. Now that he was inside, he was stunned. "This place is huge!"

Anna Kaye led him to a protected area beside a construction trailer where they could watch the work in progress. "It was built in the 1950s," she said. "It supplied electricity to Austin for forty years. It operated as a power source until 1989. The city council argued about what to do with it for ten years after that."

"That sounds familiar."

"Finally, council approved a plan to repurpose the buildings into retail, residential, and outdoor spaces."

Don looked up. "It's an amazing space."

Anna Kaye smiled and took a pamphlet from her shoulder bag. She read, "This is one of the few remaining examples of Art Deco municipal architecture. The project will preserve its unique architecture. There'll be office, retail, and event space. The ground floor will include a courtyard and be open to the public."

"And you're its principal flack?"

"Be nice," she said. She grabbed him around the neck and kissed him. He heard a rapping on glass and turned to see two men looking at them through the window of their construction trailer. The men smiled and one made a thumbs-up gesture.

"I do believe you're blushing again, Donnie Ray Cuinn," she said.

She patted him on his rear and led him by the hand out of the building. Once outside, she pointed to the east. "The power plant gets all the attention, but the real money is up there. Almost one hundred acres of prime downtown, waterfront property. This used to be on the edge of downtown. After it's developed, there will be shops and businesses and condos all the way to Lamar Boulevard, way over there." She swung an arm back toward the west.

Her blouse rode up over her midriff and he got a quick glimpse. *Still in great shape.* He felt a familiar stirring and forced himself to look away.

"Several of the major projects are already underway," he heard her saying. "Look up there." She stood behind him and pointed back to the north where cranes were hovering over the framework of a large structure. She pressed against his back. "That's going to be a thirty-story residential tower. Three hundred luxury condos—a million and a half each. There's already a two-year wait list."

"Affordable housing," he said. He turned and took her in his arms. "I'm impressed."

"By the project?"

"That, too," he said. He held her close and memories of their nights together washed over him. "So what is your part in all of this?"

"I represent one of the developers. I help them answer questions from the environmentalists, get their message out to the media, print media and social media, that sort of thing."

"Is their message a good one?"

"Who knows? There's some public space set aside in the project. Is there enough? I for one do not know." She picked up a loose piece of paper, crumpled it and tossed it in a trashcan. "It's Austin. The developers say the city is screwing them and the 'greenies' say the developers are getting away with murder."

"And you don't care who's right?"

She smiled. "My client is always right. A girl's got to make a living. Come on. I'll buy you a drink."

They got back in the yellow Fiat. Don looked at her, her bright red lips, her golden blonde hair with its cinnamon scent, her short skirt riding above her knees, offering a glimpse of her long legs and marvelous body. He didn't know what came over him. Actually, he knew exactly what came over him. It was lust, plain and simple lust for her. "Pull over there," he ordered. "Behind those trees."

"What?" she said.

He grabbed the wheel and steered the car toward the shadows behind the old power plant. She braked to a halt and turned to him with an expression of surprise. "Donnie?"

He wasn't sure what actually came next. All he could remember was clothes flying off, seats being reclined, knobs and gearshifts punching him in odd places, and her body atop his, as they made frantic love. She was as agile as he remembered.

Later, she lay curled in his lap. She said, "Donnie, I never knew you to be so aggressive."

"Hmm," he answered contentedly.

"I like it." She rose up and kissed him. "You know, this is the first time I've made love in public since you left town."

"Me, too." He felt for her. "Again?"

"I must be getting old, but I think a bed would be nice, don't you?"

"I do," he said. "Or you need to buy a larger model car." He reached into the back seat and retrieved their clothes.

She assembled herself so that she was almost properly dressed. He sat and watched her. He rubbed his bruised hip and thought about putting on his pants, but he felt too good to move. She found a Kleenex, wet it with her mouth, and scrubbed her lipstick off his cheek.

He looked down. "You missed a spot."

She started the car. "Shut up and get dressed. We're going to have some marvelous food now."

After he dressed, she steered the Fiat out of the construction site and waved at the flagman, who grinned.

Did he see us? he wondered. *Oh well, if he did, he's jealous as hell.*

100

He leaned back and watched Austin at play. When they stopped at the red light on Lamar Boulevard, she gave a voice command to her phone "Call All the Pig."

A male voice answered. "All the Pig."

"Porter, it's Anna."

"Anna, sweetheart. What's up?"

"Porter, a very good friend of mine just flew in. We need the table by the corner window. We're on our way."

"It's promised to a councilman. Where are you?"

The light turned green. She gunned the little Fiat. "We've been screwing around up at the old power plant." She winked at Don. "D&P Construction is a client and I'm bringing their president to dinner next week…with his investors from the big city. Sweetie, I really do want that table."

"You're irresistible, Anna. The councilman canceled on me last week anyway."

"So screw him. You've already got your permit to add the deck. See you in ten. Please have Dirty Martinis on the table—ice cold." She pushed the off button. "You'll love Porter."

"I love him already. Can he cook?"

She turned onto the Lamar Avenue Bridge and now they were in South Austin. "You'll love what Porter's done. It was a taco stand and now it's *the place* to go in Austin."

"On South Lamar?" He looked up at an apartment building where a hamburger joint used to be.

She changed lanes suddenly, cutting off a woman in an SUV who honked vigorously. "Sorry, you California bitch," she muttered, swinging back into the other lane and speeding through the light at Barton Springs Road just before it turned red.

"Still the longest light in Austin?" He released his grip on the seat and tried to relax. She seemed to know what she was doing.

"They're all long now, Sweetie. You would not believe—." She changed lanes again, cut in front of two gesturing bikers, almost ran down a jogger with a German Shepherd on its leash, and stopped in a flurry of dust and gravel in front of a broken down building painted with red and orange stripes, barely missing a long line of people, mostly young, waiting by the entrance. She tossed the keys to a valet attendant in a red and orange striped Polo shirt and khaki shorts.

"Miss Nordstrom, hi! Porter said to tell you that your drinks are on the table. The corner table."

"Call me 'Anna,' honey," she said. She hugged him and planted a wet kiss on his cheek.

"Anna, I'm in love," he said with a grin.

She strode passed the long wait line and into the crowded restaurant like a film star. Next to the flat-bellied girls with boyish figures, she was Rubenesque. Don could hear the other diners ask each other, "Who is that?" Everyone assumed she was a celebrity. If anyone noticed him at all, it was probably to wonder what he was doing there, with her. He thought about their time in the car, just a few minutes before, and smiled. He was happy to be anonymous.

They sat down and Don looked around. The designer of the restaurant had retained much of the decor of the tire and battery shop, which had been there when Don was a student. "Wasn't this Garcia's? I bought my used tires here."

"It's possible, dear. I never came over here, never crossed the lake if I could help it, and now I live on South Lamar." She shook the stainless cocktail shaker and poured them each a glassful of the foamy mixture.

"Dirty Ms are still your drink of choice?" They clinked the ice-cold glasses and he took a long sip, savoring the bite of the olive juice.

"You won't catch me drinking artisanal beer, like our fellow diners." She motioned at the diners sitting at the two long communal tables in the center of the room. Theirs was one of only a few tables for two in the place.

She looked up at the waiter, who was waiting expectantly, and, Don suspected, looking down Anna Kaye's blouse. He smiled at the waiter, feeling generous. *Look all you want.*

"Sweetie, bring us the plate that has all the little pieces, you know what I mean?"

"Porter's Plate of the Day? Today it's—"

"It'll be wonderful." Here she lowered her voice. "And there's no need to tell my out-of-town friend what he's eating, is there?"

The waiter leaned over Anna Kaye's shoulder to take the menu, took one last look and winked at Don.

"So what are we eating?" Don asked. He topped off their large glasses with the rest of the martini.

"I'll give you a clue. The name of the place is "All the Pig.""

"And therefore—?"

"Austin is very locovore. Porter only uses locally raised pigs, and nothing goes to waste."

Don thought a second. "Pigs have tails. And snouts. And feet."

"Despite the name, it's not just pigs. It's all animals." She sipped her drink and patted his arm. "I've really missed you. When are you moving back?"

"And do what? Practice law?"

"You'd be a natural at real estate development. We could find you some backers. Everyone wants a piece of Austin."

He looked around for the waiter. He was starving. "You're kidding. I could never do that."

"Beneath you, is that it?"

Before he could answer, the waiter appeared. She grabbed the plate from the waiter's hands and thrust it in front of Don. "Try this." When he hesitated, she said, "Don't ask. Just try it."

He opened his mouth and she fed him a spoonful of a meat and curd mixture. He swallowed it.

"Well?" she asked.

"Not bad. In fact, pretty tasty."

"And that, lover, is what rabbit innards with chickpeas tastes like."

He gagged and felt the food coming back up. She handed him a piece of crisp pork skin. He nodded thankfully and chewed it rapidly. "Whew. I need another drink."

"Really, darling. You can't be happy way up there, wherever it is you live."

He hesitated and then took a piece of unidentifiable meat. "You know me. I'm not happy anywhere, but I have a life there. I have a law practice. The bank and I own the tallest office building in Velda." *I need to call Faye and see how many more tenants I've lost,* he reminded himself.

The waiter hovered nearby with another dish. It was a plate of salad greens with a piece of animal bone placed artfully atop dandelions and watercress. Three small radishes decorated the plate. She handed him a skinny marrow fork. "Like this," she said, picking up the bone with one hand and pulling bone marrow out with the fork. "This is the best thing you will ever eat in your life. " She offered a bite to Don.

He took it carefully. "Now that is good," he said. Don had another piece of crackling and then picked up his bone. "Not much of it though." He examined it carefully. He looked up at the waiter, who had appeared with another pitcher of dirty martinis. "What animal is this from?"

"That would be veal," the waiter said. Don took a bite of the greens and then attacked the bone, searching for a second bite of the elusive marrow. Don looked around. "What are they having?"

The waiter answered, "Well, the tall man is having the pig trotter with mashed potatoes, and his partner is having pig cheek and tongue. Then at that table there," he said, pointing to a group of loud men eating gustily, "tongue and beef, and tripe and onions."

"What's he cooking special tonight?" Anna Kaye asked.

"There are several choices: the veal liver with turnips and bacon. It's wonderful." He looked at Don. "If you like liver."

"Oh, he's game for anything."

"Except maybe liver," Don said.

"I see," the waiter said. "Then how would you feel about pigeons with braised chutney? Or, we can always do braised artichokes and butter beans, if you aren't a carnivore."

"Hey, I'm as much a carnivore as anyone in here. Any beef?"

"Not tonight. We're doing veal. It was slaughtered on the property, and we pride ourselves on it." He thought for a second, then said,

"As you are Anna's friend, I could ask the chef to sauté some veal in sourdough bread crumbs, perhaps with green beans and anchovies."

"Bring it on," Don said.

Anna Kaye ordered the pigeon, deviled kidneys, and salted duck legs.

They drank, talked about the old times, and wondered about Wesley's chances, until the food finally came.

"What do you think?" she asked between bites.

"He makes a living out of this?"

"Porter is very opportune. He's always in the vanguard. He had the first upscale sushi place when sushi was all the rage. He sold that and opened a French bistro on the far east side, where people lined up to get in and hoped their car would be there when they finished. Now it's nose-to-tail eating. People in Austin feel guilty about eating animals, so he lets them satisfy their craving for meat and not feel bad about it because he only buys locally from farmers who raise the animals humanely and he slaughters them himself, and, as the waiter said, he uses every single part of the animal."

"And Austin is eating it up."

"So to speak."

Don leaned back in his chair. "So something in Austin hasn't changed."

"What's that, sweetie?"

Don looked around. The line outside was longer than when they arrived. "They're still suckers for the latest fad."

"Austin's not unique. These fad's are everywhere."

"They may be, but Austin is different. People believe their own hype here. Austin is the greatest, the best, the weirdest, the most fun, the fastest growing, the greenest, the fittest, the happiest, the smartest, the hippest."

"And aren't we?"

"No, you're not. You can eat the whole pig, but pig intestines are still full of shit, however you dress them up." He thought a minute. "And that' s why I'm not moving back."

She laughed. "You really miss it, don't you?"

"Yes," he admitted. "I love Austin."

When they finished, she handed her credit card to the waiter, waving off Don's attempt to pay. "Tomorrow, you can pay. We'll go out to Pedro's and get some *migas*. That hasn't changed." She scribbled her name on the waiter's mobile card reader.

The same valet had the yellow Fiat ready. He handed Anna Kaye a card. "Remember me to any casting directors you know, Anna."

"An actor? You're ravishing, sweetie. The camera will eat you up." She swung her long legs into the driver's seat. "Give the man a tip, Donnie Ray."

He reached into his pocket and retrieved a couple of ones.

"Ten," she said. "Give the actor a ten."

She careened out South Lamar. There was enough daylight for Don to look for familiar landmarks, but he did not find many. Where he remembered an auto repair shop and a seedy beer joint, he now saw an Irish pub and a ramen house. A used car lot had been displaced by a six-story apartment building with a Starbucks on the first floor. "Where did everything go?"

"Progress," she answered. "But you don't like progress, do you?"

"You nailed it," he answered. "I want Austin to be like it was when I was a grad student." *Before Wesley Bird sold me down the river.*

"You and everybody else, darling. Never was and never will be."

He stared at a throng outside the door of a club. They held beer bottles and their perspiring young faces and toned arms shone in the blinking strobe lights. He could hear the thump of the bass playing inside the club. "Progress."

`She kept on South Lamar, past the hacienda style Mexican restaurant that had been one of the first to relocate to the area, thirty years earlier. The cavernous parking lot was nearly empty. "That's a tear-down now. As soon as the family lets go and stops believing they can still compete, there'll be condos there."

"Progress," he muttered again

"But Donnie, that's where you and I could make a fortune…places like that. Put the deals together. We know the people." She grinned at him. "With your looks and my brains, we'd be unstoppable. Just think about it."

I flunked being a history professor. I have a small town law practice. I'll probably be filing bankruptcy when I get back to Velda. My former best friend is a con man. The man who raised me is a pariah poet. And I'm the bastard son of a father I've never met. Yes, I have all the qualifications to be in the real estate development business in Austin.

"Just think about it, Sweetie." When he didn't answer, she patted him on the knee. "Say you'll think about it, and I'll do that thing you like so much." She patted him again, but higher on the leg this time. "Will you just think about it?"

I'm a bastard all right. "Sure. I'll think about it," he said, covering her hand with his own.

As it happened, Anna Kaye's condo was in a ten-story building next door to the most famous honky tonk in Austin: The Purple Spur. He remembered late nights with Wesley at the Spur, drinking beer until closing time, and then drinking in the parking lot until dawn. The condo loomed over the old beer joint. "I'll bet that you can't see the sunrise from the Spur anymore," he ventured.

"They kept the Spur, that's the main thing," she answered. She stopped at the gate to the garage behind the condo. "And they kept the bus."

He looked and there in the shadows, he could see the famous tour bus, dating back to Jacky Jaxson's early road tours. Jacky had given the bus to Paulie Prinkett, who opened it for guided tours. On occasion, if he was high enough, Jacky even escorted out-of-town tourists on the ten-dollar tour that let them walk through the old bus, touching the bunk bed where Jacky had once slept. Jacky had been known to light up a joint and offer puffs to the prettiest girl or the oldest, just to hear them giggle.

"Does Paulie still sell tours through the bus?"

"Probably, but to be honest, I haven't been over there in years, and I live next door. Of course, it's crowded on football weekends, and they still have the chicken fried steak, but the action has moved on."

"Progress."

"We don't go there, but no one wants to lose it. There was such an outcry when the Atlanta people bought the property. At first, they were going to demolish the Spur. Instead, they built around it, and promised to keep it open. Paulie is still there."

"So maybe Paulie doesn't have to do bus tours."

"If I know Paulie, as long as there's a buck in it, the bus tours will go on."

《《《《《

Anna Kaye's apartment was furnished with chrome and glass and leather. "Very nice," Don said.

"International Style," she said.

She had a view of the capitol building, thanks to one of the sight corridors the state legislature had imposed on Austin, which one lobbyist, a former speaker of the house, was adept at getting waived. Office towers flanked the capitol. On the left side of the capitol building, the University tower was lighted in the school's color, celebrating the victory of the women's softball team.

Later, after leaving her bed, they sat next to each other on the balcony, partially clothed, sipping iced coffee. She turned to him and asked, "Have you thought about what I said?"

She had kept her word and he owed her an answer. "It wouldn't work, Anna Kaye."

"Why not? Too much change for your taste? Or, you don't want to get your hands dirty?"

He hesitated, choosing his words. "It's not that. I wouldn't be any good at it. I just have a very low tolerance for bullshit. Ever since Wesley double-crossed me, I've become very cynical. I believe the worst about everyone. How could I sell something, or promote something, when I suspect everybody I deal with of being a cheat?"

"There are honest developers."

"Of course there are." He sat down the coffee and put his arm around her. "But with my track record, I'd never meet one."

They sat quietly in the darkness. He felt her stir. "Are you awake?"

"Hmm," he said.

"It's her, isn't it? Cecelia, I mean. You can't come back because you're in love with her memory."

He sat up. "I do love her memory, you're right about that. She was the love of my life. Something happens to you when you lose the love of your life. Something shrivels up inside."

"I know," she said. "I lost the love of my life too."

"You did? Really?"

"Really. The only difference is, I have a chance to get my love back." She stretched out her arms and pulled him close. "Come here."

Later, back in her bed, he rolled over and faced her. "I always felt you and I were playmates. I never thought for a minute that you would want to marry me. I was sure you'd have a rich husband by now, and be raising young Amazons in River Oaks or Highland Park."

"So did I, until you left. I knew then, but it was too late."

He got out of bed and pulled on his pants. He thought for a minute and then put on a shirt and his shoes. "I'm going for a walk."

He waved at the night guard in the lobby and went out to the front drive of the condo building. Next door, the Spur was quiet, but its lights were still on. He walked across the dimly lit parking lot, passed the Jaxson bus and into the familiar front entrance. Pictures of country music stars from decades past decorated the small vestibule. A fake palm drooped beside the counter that still displayed Purple Spur T-Shirts and koozies. He stepped into the main room. A couple in their fifties, both wearing worn jeans and scuffed boots, were slow dancing to a Jaxson oldie playing softly through giant speakers. They had the dance floor to themselves and the tables on either side of the dance floor were empty. At Paulie Prinkett's table in the back, next to the kitchen, Paulie was bent over a ledger. His black wig was perched perilously on his head. He was seriously overweight, and despite the ceiling fan rotating above him, his face glistened with sweat. He looked up at Don and nodded. "Hello, Bubba," he said. He picked up his beer bottle and waved it toward Don. "The regular?" he asked.

Don smiled. Paulie called every customer Bubba, but he remembered which beer each one drank.

"Thanks, Paulie. I believe I will."

Paulie shifted his large frame and the old wood chair creaked ominously. "Jorge," he yelled, "bring Bubba a Tecate." He closed the ledger and motioned for Don to sit with him. "Long time. Where've you been?"

"The Panhandle. Velda. You ever hear of it?"

Paulie watched as Jorge, his white apron draped over his skinny body, set the sweating bottle on the table in front of Don. "Velda? Yes, I've heard of it. Used to play there, when I was touring with the Sons of the Doughboys." Paulie had played a wicked acoustical guitar, and was still known to pitch in on occasion, if some punk kid was too stoned to remember to show up for one of the Spur's weekend live music nights. He grinned at Don. "Asshole of the world, as I remember it."

"It's not so bad, once you get used to it."

"Why in God's name would you want to get used to it?"

"Good question." Don looked around. The middle-aged couple was still hanging on to each other, shuffling around the plank dance floor. "Paulie, may I ask you something?"

"You want a Jacky Jaxson story? That'll cost you more than one beer, Bubba."

"No. In fact, please don't tell me a Jacky story."

"Then what?"

"Is it too late to get a chicken fried? My girl dragged me to some place where they serve you pig intestines. I'm starved."

Paulie laughed. "Fucking nouvelle cuisine," he said with a surprisingly good French accent. "Never too late for chicken fried here, you know that." He leaned around the kitchen door. "Jorge, fix Bubba a fried platter. And bring him another beer. And while you're at it…"

Jorge appeared at once. "Here you are, Señor Paulie," he said, handing Paulie a Shiner Bock and Don another Tecate. Paulie grunted his approval and Jorge scurried back to the kitchen. Don heard the grill pop on.

They drank silently and waited for Don's fried platter, chicken fried steak, cream gravy, mashed potatoes and Texas toast. Don remembered that sex with Anna Kaye had always given him an appetite. When the platter came, it was sizzling; the steak batter was crusty and brown; the cream gravy was lump-free and heavily peppered. Just like he remembered. And there was not a pig intestine or a green vegetable anywhere in sight. He attacked the meat ferociously.

Paulie returned to his ledger.

Finally Don burped and pushed the empty plate aside. "Thank God, some things never change."

Paulie sighed and closed the ledger again. "Yeah, they do. Ever since Atlanta bought the property, seems like all I get in here are Bubbas like you, in town for a visit, or Yankees wanting to see where Jacky got his start, or fucking jetsetters here for Formula One soaking up the local color. They'll pay twenty bucks for a fried platter and seven bucks for a beer. But my regular Bubbas, they're leaving me. I hate it, but what can I do?"

"At those prices?"

"Oh yeah, the new owners are making money, but it's no fun running a goddam tourist trap." He blinked and looked at the ceiling fan. He said, "You know, Bubba, when I agreed to sell this place to the Atlanta boys, I sent my then present wife to Rockport and told her to fix up the cabin. 'We're moving to the coast,' I told her. My plan was to take my share of the money, a shitload of money, and live out my days fishing and my nights pickin' at the Coral Garden."

Don wiped the grease off his chin and said, "Why didn't you? In fact, why don't you now?"

"Well," Paulie said, shaking his head, "it ain't that easy. This here is an Austin institution, and apparently, I have got to run it until I drop dead. And even then, they'll probably stuff me and prop up my corpse by the gift counter."

"I don't understand."

"If you'd been here for the demonstrations, you'd understand."

"The demonstrations? Here?"

"Damn right. Everybody from a bunch of seventy-year-old hippies to the Visitors' Bureau were out here, protesting the sale. 'The Purple Spur is an Austin institution,' they said. The hippies remembered coming here fifty years ago, and the convention people said it would hurt tourism. And then the damn magazine got involved, you know the one, *This Texas*, claiming that the Atlanta boys were greasing some palms down at the permits department."

"So you made a deal?"

"I didn't make any deal. Jacky made the deal."

"Jacky Jaxson?"

"He owns a majority of this place. So he cut a deal where the condos were built all around the Spur, the Atlanta people own the place, and I operate it for at least ten years. Jacky sold me into slavery for ten years, and all he has to do is play two concerts a year here. We got our money, or at least Jacky got his. Mine is paid out over the ten years. They sold the deal to the council, and the protests just died away."

"And goodbye, Rockport."

"The wife stayed down there, married Siter Change. You know Siter?"

"I'm afraid not."

"Siter's the best fishing guide in Rockport. So I lost my money, I lost my wife, and Siter won't take me out in the Gulf anymore. It's a trifecta disaster."

"The Perfect Storm."

Paulie stood up, leaning on the table, which groaned under his weight. He began to clear Don's dirty dishes. "Speaking of that magazine—wasn't that you that did the number on the attorney general? What was his name?"

Don put two twenty-dollar bills on top of the check. "Eban Payne. Yes, that was me."

"I thought you looked familiar. That *This Texas* bunch, you don't want to mess with them."

"There's a new owner. The magazine's politics may have changed."

"Too late for me," Paulie said, pocketing the twenties and not offering Don any change.

⪻⪻⪻⪻⪻

When he got back to the apartment, Anna Kaye was in bed, snoring softly. He undressed and climbed into bed beside her. She rolled over and they lay close. It was nice. He wondered how she would like Velda. He knew Velda would like her. *She'd take the place by storm.* He wasn't coming back to Austin; he knew that. He also suspected that Anna Kaye Nordstrom would never leave, even if she was telling the truth when she said he was the love of her life.

He was right. Over an Einstein bagel the next morning, she even refused a sightseeing trip to see where Don lived and worked. "I'm too busy, sweetie," she said. "The power plant presentation to the security analysts is next week."

In a way, he was relieved.

"And of course, I promised Cindy I would try to help keep Wesley from incarceration."

"What's going to happen to Wesley?"

"He's going to jail, darling. His name is on every one of those fraudulent documents."

"No sign of Braeswood?"

"Governor Braeswood signed nothing. It was all Wesley. Besides, Braeswood appointed the DA. It would be very ungrateful of him to indict Braeswood. He's no longer governor, but he has a lot of powerful friends."

"And then there's the Hungarian gold coins."

"The what?"

He told her how Wesley had made a second pass through the Cartwright House, selling certificates for Hungarian gold coins to the seniors.

"Jesus Christ," she said. "That's worse than lying to the banks."

"Papa is devastated. He introduced his friends to Wesley. But you know what's bothering him the most?"

"What?"

"He's the head of a group that's fighting the sale of the Hieronymus

Parcel for development. Now he's too ashamed to show his face, and the protest may just fizzle out."

She finished dressing. "Tell the professor that trying to save the Hieronymus Parcel is a hopeless cause. Judge Ashley has decided to take the money. The developers are lined up. The city is on board. The sale will definitely go through."

Don thought a minute. "Isn't that what people thought about the Spur? Suppose *This Texas* investigated the sale of the Hieronymus Parcel. Would they find anything?"

She picked up her sunglasses and perched them on her head. "There's always something. I have heard some rumors. But it's too late."

"The fix is in?"

"In Austin, we prefer to say that the necessary prerequisites have been met and the various stakeholders are in agreement."

He picked up his duffel and walked out of the apartment with her. "You can drop me off at the *This Texas* office. I need to talk to the new publisher. Dave Lewis."

"I know Dave."

"How so?"

"We ran the Central Texas 10K race together. He's amazing. Can you imagine running a 10K on artificial legs? I've been showing him around. We've had coffee a few times."

He felt a twinge of jealousy. *There's a surprise. Let a girl tell you she loves you, and it changes everything.*

CHAPTER TWELVE

He had only been gone from Velda for a few days, but as always when he returned to the Panhandle, the endless horizon and the bright sky startled him.

Faye sent Bobby Bill McCathey, the gimpy ex-cowpoke, Don had inherited from Jake, to pick him up at the Amarillo airport. Faye had Bobby Bill bring Don the mail for him to read on the drive to Velda.

When Don had protested that he didn't need a driver, process server, general or in Bob Bill's Case, errand man, Jake had insisted. "He's free. You can't just cut Bobby Bill loose. The Pervoys would never forgive you." Then Jake confided how the cowboy had been kicked in the head when he worked on the Pervoy Ranch; how Jake had gotten Bobby Bill to waive any claim against the Pervoys by giving him a job at the law firm; and how he billed all of the cowboy's wages to the Pervoy Ranch. "It's all perfectly reasonable," he'd said. The Pervoys got to deduct the legal expenses (they couldn't have deducted a personal injury settlement); Jake got a driver to take him to Amarillo to the airport, to make courthouse runs, to repossess cars, and serve divorce papers. "Best of all," he'd said with a grin, "it's free!" So, Bobby Bill had a job. And, with his cracked skull and his stiff left leg, he was no use to anybody as a cowpuncher.

Don listened, finally agreed, and then instructed Faye to stop billing the Pervoys. Bobby Bill was overhead to the law firm, just like Faye was. "Treat him that way," he told Faye.

"You can't afford it," she had argued, but he told her to do it anyway. Faye had frowned her tight-lip grimace and Don knew she disagreed.

"Just do it, Faye. If this law firm can't pay for Bobby Bill, we're going under anyway."

Don opened a folder with GFC's answer to Wiley's race discrimination lawsuit. As Don had expected, the Swiss company had pulled out all the stops. The biggest law firm in Houston, and the best corporate defense lawyer in Amarillo. *Take no prisoners,* he thought. *For the first time, Don felt some optimism about this case. If the notice of a claim got this kind of response, imagine the fun when we haul their CEO's fat ass all the way from Zurich to Velda for a deposition.*

"Uh, Don," he heard Bobby Bill say. The driver was glancing sideways at Don. "Can I ask you something? Something personal?"

Don put the papers on the console. Bobby Bill didn't talk much. When he asked for help, he usually needed it: a cousin in jail in Muleshoe; a sister run off to Vegas with a bass player; his mother's small estate and no will. "Shoot," he said, turning in the seat to face the driver.

Bobby Bill stuttered. "Thing is…you…you know, out at Pervoys'…there's this…this…really nice woman name of Reba who works at the dude ranch."

Don smiled. After Eugene Pervoy's brother died and his widow hurried back to Oklahoma, Eugene and his wife Ginelle, turned the huge contemporary house the former sister-in-law had built into a very expensive resort, complete with riding, hunting, rodeo exhibitions, gourmet food, and Napa wines. "Are you thinking of getting hitched?"

"Well, yes, I…I…am." He giggled a little. "She says she'll have me. Big dadgum surprise to me, I tell you."

"Any woman's lucky to have you, Bobby Bill. Congratulations. Have you set a date?"

"Right away. We're going to go over to the courthouse and get it done. Don't want her to change her mind."

"That's good. Listen, the Hansard Trust owns a nice cabin overlooking Palo Duro Canyon. I'll get it for you, for the honeymoon."

"You will? Well thank you; thank you very much." He looked at Don again. The car swerved in front of an on-coming truck.

"Watch it, Bobby Bill!" Don shouted.

"Sorry," he said, swinging the car back into the right lane. He slowed down and then said, "There's something…something else."

Is Bobby Bill going to ask for a raise? How should I handle that? I'm already deep into the last of my cash reserves.

"The thing is, Ginelle says if me and Ruby get married, I ought'n to work in town. She says she has plenty I can do out there, picking up guests, showing kids how to rope, I don't know what all."

"Ginelle wants you to quit the law firm and go back to the ranch?"

"Yes, sir, she…she does." A white SUV swung around them, horn blaring. Bobby Bill had slowed the car down to walking speed. "What do you think?"

He tried to imagine the firm without the cowboy, eager for the next job, no matter how insignificant. "I think it's just fine, if that's what you want."

The cowboy pressed on the gas, bringing the car back to normal speed. "I think it is. Now Ginelle said when I told you, for you to call her."

"There's no reason for me to call Ginelle. I think it's a fine idea. We'll miss you, but we'll manage."

Before Bobby Bill could answer, Don's cell phone chimed the musical line "Where the Deer and the Antelope Play" from "Home on the Range." "Don Cuinn," he said.

"Don Cuinn, this is Ginelle."

He looked over at Bobby Bill and smiled. "The bridegroom and I were just talking about you, Ginelle. You're stealing my cowboy?"

"He told you about Ruby?"

"He did. And you approve?"

"I do, but they need to be together. He doesn't need to be driving into Velda every day."

"O.K."

"Besides, like I told Faye, we're paying for him anyway. We might as well have the full use of him, don't you think?"

"Well, yeah," Don said, "I know how Jake set it up. And why."

She interrupted before he could tell her he had instructed Faye to stop billing the ranch for Bobby Bill. "I told Faye the other day, that charging us for Bobby Bill is a bunch of horse manure. I would have told you too, but you were down in Austin or somewhere. It wasn't right when Jake Rosen set it up and it isn't right now. You should know that, Don Cuinn."

Damn Faye! "That was in this month's statement?"

"Yes, of course. I stopped in on my way to Amarillo last Friday."

Ginelle was working on an associate's degree in accounting at Amarillo College and Faye said she had a better business sense than any of the Pervoys, living or dead. She had honed in on the billing for Bobby Bill, and she was right. "Listen, Ginelle, we probably owe you an adjustment. I'm in the car right now, but I'll call you as soon as I get to the office."

"Oh, honey, you don't owe us anything. You've done more for this family than we can ever repay you for. But I don't like all this play-acting. I've had enough tax courses to know that the IRS will eat us up if they find this. This was Jake's doing. Jake always had to make everything complicated. He loved that. Let's just keep it simple, O.K. honey?"

"You've got it, Ginelle. I love you. Bye."

Bobby Bill had kept his eyes on the road the entire time Don and Giselle were talking. Now he said, "Everything o...o...okay...Don?"

"Abso-blooming-lutely fine. Ginelle is a good woman. You pay attention to what she tells you, and you'll do fine."

"Do you want me to try to find you a new driver? It'll be hard, with the shale drilling, everybody's short of help. But I may can find somebody."

Don settled back in the seat and closed his eyes. "Thanks, but no need. We'll cover it."

"How? Who's going to make the courthouse runs and serve summons and go get supplies and all that?"

"Faye will be doing that."

"Faye? Faye? Are you talking about the same Faye I know?"

"Yes, indeed. The same Faye." He smiled. *How long did she think it would be before I found out she was still billing the Pervoys for Bobby Bill's wages? Of course, I'm totally incompetent when it comes to the accounts, so maybe forever. This should be fun.*

❆❆❆❆❆

Don sat in his car in front of Charlton Denning's neat red brick house, waiting for the unemployed journalist and his partner to come home. "We have to go to Amarillo to shop," Charlton had explained when Faye called him to set up the meeting. "Mr. Particular simply will not have it any other way." Faye reported the conversation brusquely, still simmering from Don's announcement that there would be no replacement for Bobby Bill.

"You told me yourself we couldn't afford him, Faye, remember? When we stopped billing the Pervoys?"

"But who will do Bobby Bill's work?"

"We'll all have to pitch in, you and me and Wiley." He picked up a stack of pleadings he had signed on the way back from Amarillo. "By the way, on your lunch hour, will you take these to the clerk's office, then deliver copies to opposing counsel?"

He turned away and shut his office door before she could protest. *How long will it take her to find a way we can afford a replacement for Bobby Bill? A week? Two? She's a stubborn old girl.*

Charlton's house was on Carnation, one of the flower streets, easy enough to find because the developer had named them in alphabetical order. The streets stopped at Gardenia, the last street opened up before the developer ran out of money and left town. The streets were carved out of caliche hills and gullies enough years ago that the trees had some height. Each house on Carnation Street boasted a bright green lawn of Kentucky bluegrass, nurtured with fertilizer and an abundance of water that ignored the probability that the town would ever run short of water. Of course, it was already short, but green lawns were important in a Panhandle town and city officials knew better than hint at restrictions on lawn watering.

Denning's front lawn, however, was lush even by Veldanian standards. Blooming hedges, flowering shrubs and seasonal plantings converged on a tile pond with crystal clear water and floating water lilies of a luminous pink color. Honeysuckle in bloom entwined itself on a redwood arbor that enwrapped the front door. "You'll find it easy enough," Faye had told him. "They've won the best front yard contest the last four years. Pity the person who buys that house, having to maintain it. And they say the backyard has twice as much upkeep."

"Charlton's a gardener?"

"Oh, I don't think so. It's his…what do they call them now?"

"Partner?"

"*Yes.* His *partner.* He *is* an officer in the Women's Garden Club. They say when he entertains the garden club, the food is wonderful." She sniffed. "Of course, I wouldn't know. I've never been invited."

"You don't garden anyway, do you, Faye?" Dead plants still languished on the deck outside his apartment, not watered since Bridget left.

"I do not," Faye replied. "Still, it would be nice to be invited."

Don checked the time on his phone. Velda's Odd Couple were late. He rehearsed silently his pitch to Charlton.

First, Lewis has agreed to give you a one-year contract to do investigative reporting for This Texas, with no decrease in salary. Also, he's promised to make the job permanent if you do well.

Lewis had been easier to deal with than he expected. He was just in from a run. He sat on an exercise bench and took off his prostheses. Don watched unhappily as Lewis massaged the bruised stumps. For a second, he imagined those muscular calves entwined around Anna Kaye's naked body. *You bastard. Using your injury to seduce the woman who loves me.*

"I owe you an apology," Lewis said. "I checked with my office, and you were right. It was a one-man delegation that called on K.L. It was that discount store guy you mentioned who was demanding Charlton Denning's resignation."

"Bert Martin?"

"Right. K.L. sent me down to be the hatchet man. None of the others are willing to get their hands dirty."

"The others?"

"There are three Lehrer daughters. They're all married, and the husbands work at the paper. The other two don't like doing actual newspaper work. So that left me. To make matters worse, they lied to me about the situation. They told me the town was up in arms, readers and advertisers, all demanding we get rid of the guy."

"What about your father-in-law?"

Lewis opened a bottle of lotion, squirted some in his palm and rubbed it into the stumps. "K.L. hasn't been to a paper in twenty years." He propped his legs onto a stool between the two of them. Don tore his eyes away from the angry scars and looked Lewis in the eyes.

"Where does that leave us?"

"I can tell you this," Lewis said, "because we're going to settle this thing today. Kingston Lehrer has no room in his universe for homosexuals."

Don cleared his throat. "A free-lancer. Charlton would make an excellent investigative reporter, here in Austin. Writing for this magazine."

Lewis thought for a minute. He braced himself on the bench and then used his powerful arms and shoulders to swing his torso into the waiting desk chair. "Maybe we can do that." He scooted his chair behind a plain oak desk and opened a gray folder. Lewis thumbed through the documents.

As he waited, Don looked around the large room. All traces of Drayton Philby, the deceased blind publisher of *This Texas,* were gone. The oriental rugs, the leather chairs, the walnut bookcases with leather-bound volumes had been replaced by an old-fashioned oak desk and mismatched chairs that might have come from a warehouse somewhere. *Probably where KL furniture goes to die when they close down a newspaper.*

Lewis closed the folder. "Here's what I can do. I'll take Denning on as an investigative reporter for this magazine for a year. If he produces, it'll be permanent. Same salary and benefits."

"Your father-in-law won't object?"

"Why do you care?"

"Well, the offer of a permanent job isn't worth much when the boss man hates gays and my client is one."

Lewis frowned. "I really shouldn't go into family business with you." He paused, thinking. "But…I guess you have a point." He turned in the chair and pointed to the enclosed garden, visible through large glass doors. "See the woman out there? The one doing the stretching exercises?"

Don stood up and looked over Lewis' shoulder. A woman with long black hair pulled back into a ponytail knelt over a workout bench, stretching her glutes. Her behind was gorgeous, and when she stood up and faced the window, he saw that she was beautiful, tall, and regal, with a boyish figure. A smaller, compact woman stood beside her.

"The magazine belongs to her. That's Cordelia Lehrer. My wife. The other one is her coach."

"I'm confused," Don confessed. "*This Texas* belongs to your wife?"

Lewis laughed and turned back to face him.

Reluctantly, Don took his eyes off Lewis' wife.

"I understand your confusion," Lewis said. "When I heard that this magazine was for sale, I knew that the KL chain would never buy it. Liberal. In Austin. A magazine. But Delie and I talked it over. Her Daddy will do anything for her. He even let her marry me, a poor reporter with missing parts. After a certain amount of wheedling and pouting by his favorite daughter, he told her trustees to buy the damn thing. As long as he doesn't have to read it, and it makes money, I can do just about anything I want with *This Texas*."

"That's why you're here?"

"To make sure it does well. And, Delie loves Austin, Hell, she's down here more than she's in Akron. As you can imagine, I don't like to be away from her too long."

Sorry, Anna Kaye, Don thought, happily. *I believe Lewis already has all the woman he could possibly need.*

A car drove fast down Carnation Street, interrupting Don's musings. It wasn't Charlton Denning. He opened his briefcase and made sure he had the contract; Lewis had already signed it. *Let's see. What's the other reason Charlton should agree, although Don couldn't see why he would need a second reason. Oh, yes.*

Second, Austin is a great place, especially for a gay couple. That needs to be implied, not said out loud. Just in case, Faye had found several Austin gay websites and downloaded the links for Don.

Alongside those was the third reason: one that Don was sure would be irresistible to any reporter worth his salt: a copy of Papa's file on the proposed sale of the Hieronymus Parcel.

When Charlton and his partner finally arrived, the portly ex-editor ushered Don in. "I'm so sorry," he said. He breathed heavily. Beads of sweat covered his red forehead. "Come in, and please excuse the house. We've been gone all day. Mr. Particular couldn't find the correct brand of paper towels." He pointed to his partner. "Oh excuse me, have you two not met? Graff, this is Mr. Don R. Cuinn, Esquire, who is representing us in our massive lawsuit against the K.L. newspaper chain and all that it stands for."

The tall, thin man, dressed in a tight fitting athletic shirt, skinny Bermuda shorts and barefoot sandals, extended his hand. "Hello, again. I'm Graff Madison. We met at the community concert last fall, remember?"

"Yes, right." He shook the hand, which was surprisingly firm and strong. *All that gardening.* He did recall the couple, dressed in matching pale blue tuxedo jackets and pale blue color coordinated patent leather shoes. How could he forget? He remembered Bridget whispering to him, "Play nice," when he had joked about them as they made their way to front row seats. "Opposites do attract," Bridget had said. Graff was the exact physical opposite of Charlton Denning, rail thin where Charlton was plump, scowling where Charlton was bubbly friendly, suspicious acting where Charlton was open and accepting. *If there's going to be a problem, it'll be Graff,* Don thought.

Charlton seated him on the tufted couch and insisted on Graff making coffee. "Unless you'd rather have wine?" he asked.

"Thanks, no," Don answered, adjusting the doily he had accidentally wrinkled. "Coffee will be just fine."

"Well," Graff said, taking the doily from him, "I'll have a glass of Pinot if you two don't mind. You go right ahead and talk your business. I'll be in the kitchen, tending to my duties, out of the way."

"Oh, Graff," Charlton said with a sigh. "We won't talk a word of business until you get back."

Don used the time to tell Charlton about the marvels of Austin. "Oh goodness, yes," Charlton said, "we've been there many times. It's our favorite place in the world to visit."

Graff returned with espresso in demitasse cups on an antique china tray decorated with green ivy and blue flowers. Don took a sip and wished for a cup. "This is really good."

Graff almost smiled. "Specially ordered beans. From Nicaragua."

"Ah," Don said. "It's worth it." He didn't dare to ask for a second small cup of the exotic, no doubt very expensive, brew. "Well," he said, reaching for the papers in his briefcase, "I met with Lewis when I was in Austin, and I have some very good news."

Graff sat beside Charlton on the loveseat and they read the agreement together. "Hmm," Charlton said. "Hmm, I see."

"What does it mean, Char? I don't understand a word of it? Are they taking you back?"

"Well, not exactly, sweetheart," he said, patting Graff on the leg. "They're offering me a job on a magazine they bought, in Austin."

"In Austin? In Austin? Move to Austin? Leave all my friends? Go to a strange place?"

"Austin isn't strange," Don offered. "It's weird."

Graff let out a long cry.

Charlton frowned at Don.

"Not a good time for a joke, I guess. Sorry," Don said.

"Sweetheart, Austin is wonderful. You love Austin, remember?"

"To visit! To visit! Not to live there! You promised, Charlton Denning! You promised me we would never leave Velda." With that, he stormed from the house.

Don heard a car door slam. He looked at Charlton. "Is he O.K.?"

"Let's have a glass of that Pinot." Don watched him tidy up the coffee service and followed him into the kitchen. "He always does that," Charlton said.

"Goes for a drive?"

"No, not really. I don't know why not, now that you mention it, except that he doesn't like to drive. Whenever we have a little spat, he locks himself in the car and won't come out until I apologize. It's quite a regular event on Carnation Street, I assure you."

He poured them both a large glass of the red wine. "However, I will say that this is more than your ordinary domestic quarrel."

Don took a gulp of the wine, then another. Charlton did the same and then poured them each another glassful. Don retrieved his briefcase from the living room and handed Charlton the material Faye had gathered about the gay lifestyle in Austin. "It's not San Francisco," he said, "but surely it's more accepting of gay couples than Velda."

Charlton leafed through the material. "I think that's what's bothering Graff."

"Really? I'd think he'd welcome that."

Charlton perched his large bottom on the chrome barstool. "I've thought about it a lot," he said. "We're exotic here. People are kind, for the most part. There's always a Bert Martin. But by and large, people like us. They think we're fun. They love it when we're outrageous. *What will those boys do next?* they probably ask themselves. We can act like the campiest old queens you can imagine, if we want to, just for kicks. But it's more than that. People in Velda value us for who we are. People believe I'm a good newspaperman, or as good as K.L. will let me be. The women in the neighborhood absolutely believe Graff is one of them. And he is. You should hear him on the phone, gossiping about some woman's dress, or which dentist's wife is running around on her husband." He swiveled on the stool, remarkably agile for a fat man. "We're the big gay fish in the little Velda pond. But in Austin, in any big city, we won't be exotic any more. There will be people queerer than us, a better people person than me, a better house husband than Graff."

Don looked at the dregs of red wine and walked to the sink. He rinsed the glass and set it on the quarried stone counter. "Do you want the job, Charlton? I hope you do, because I think it's a great opportunity for you."

Charlton nodded. "I do want it, Don. It's something I would really like to do." He scribbled his name on the employment agreement and handed it to Don. "Thank you so much for making it happen."

"You're welcome, Charlton. And now, I have a great story for you." He handed him Papa's file on the Hieronymus land deal. "Look that over and we'll talk."

Charlton walked him to the front door. Graff sat erectly in the car, smoking a cigarette. "Shit," Charlton said. "He knows how much I hate the smell of cigarette smoke in the car. He only does that when he's really upset." He smiled grimly at Don. "Actually, he doesn't smoke. He doesn't even inhale. He keeps his cigarettes in the freezer."

Don patted Charlton on the shoulder. "You have your work cut out for you. How are you going to convince him?"

"I have one thing going for me."

"What's that?"

"The little fag loves me."

CHAPTER THIRTEEN

The next month, Don and Anna Kaye sat in Assistant District Attorney June Fennel's small office, next to the grand jury waiting room. The cubicle, and a number of others like it, opened to a bullpen where assistants to the assistant district attorneys were busy dealing with the reams of paperwork that accompany law enforcement. There were large offices at one end of the room, where the district attorney and his first assistants worked behind closed doors.

Don and Anna Kaye were waiting for Papa, who was testifying before the Wesley Bird grand jury. Papa was the first witness. The other Cartwright House investors, some of who had already gathered in the waiting room, would follow him.

"The DA is claiming that Wesley dreamed up all these complex fraudulent transactions. Wesley's not that smart," Anna Kaye said. "So he wants to soften up the grand jury by parading all the old people who've lost their savings, bring them in first, before hearing from the bankers and accountants about the technical stuff. That way, the grand jury will be ready to hang Wesley, whether they understand the *Austin Next* financing or not."

"Also," Papa had said, on the way to the courthouse, "he wants to get our testimony on the record before we die."

"You're more likely to die of boredom, waiting around," Anna Kaye had said. "I was here for four hours last week, when they brought Wesley in, and all he did was take the Fifth."

"I guess he was smart enough to do that," Don said.

June Fennel, in whose office they were waiting, was a nice looking young assistant district attorney, dressed in a black pinstripe suit. She and Anna Kaye were neighbors in the same South Lamar apartment building. The women shared complaints about the management and maintenance problems that kept recurring in the newly built condo.

"It's the same all over town," June said. "Too much built too fast." She laughed. "We hear about it, believe me. Irate tenants want us to put their landlords in jail."

"I'd vote for that," Anna Kaye said.

Don stood up and stretched. "This is taking a long time."

"It always does," the young lawyer said. "Prentice Hall is presenting." She looked at Don. "You've heard of Prentice?"

"Oh, sure," Don lied. "Who hasn't?"

"He's the best prosecutor in the office, everybody says that, even Vernon Lakey. Prentice is trying out his case on the grand jury. When he's through, they'll true-bill. They always do."

"How is the district attorney?" Anna Kaye asked. "I'm available if he needs a media consultant."

"You're working for Wesley Bird," June said with a smile. "Wouldn't that be a conflict of interest?"

"You're thinking of lawyers," Anna Kaye answered. "Media consultants can have all the conflicts we want."

"How convenient." June pulled out a drawer and propped her stylish shoes on it. She looked over at Don. "You agree? Maybe we should have a drink and talk about legal ethics."

Anna Kaye held her palm out in warning. "Hands off. This one's mine."

As best as Anna Kaye had been able to find out, the grand jury was hearing evidence to decide if Wesley should be indicted for securities fraud and for money laundering. The securities fraud was misrepresentations to investors about the financial health of *Austin Next*'s various partnership and companies. The money laundering was Wesley's use of the money for his own personal use and as part of a Ponzi scheme to pay fictitious returns to investors.

"The famous ten percent dividend my mama was so proud of," Don said. The allegations were considered especially damning because many of the victims were retirees, whose pension funds and IRAs had been invested with Wesley.

"I thought the feds handled this kind of case," Don said.

June answered, "They do, but the states are getting more involved. Texas leads the nation in convictions in cases like this. About two hundred in the last three years." She looked at Anna Kaye, "You should tell your client that Texas imposes some of the harshest penalties of any state for this kind of securities fraud."

"I'm sure Brave Tipps explained all that to Wes," Anna Kaye said. "All those convictions show that the DAs are listening to their constituents' demands for vengeance, which never hurts at election time." She smiled. "Your boss could use some good publicity right about now."

June glanced at the closed door to District Attorney Veron Lakey's office at the end of the room. "The official line is that the district attorney was incapacitated that night because of alcohol and prescription pain killers, and that he deeply regrets his actions." The media firestorm about the district attorney's arrest had, in fact, died down. Lakey was even said to be considering a run for re-election.

"What kind of penalty is Wesley looking at?" Don asked.

"It's scary, isn't it, June?" Anna Kaye asked.

"Well, yes," June said. "White-collar criminals used to get off easy, with probation or a light sentence, while at the same time, black kids who stuck up a convenience store for a few hundred dollars had to do hard time. The thought was that securities fraud was a victimless crime. I mean the victims were banks and rich people, and securities fraud was certainly not as bad as armed robbery, for instance. The investors should have known better. But now...," she paused and shifted her weight in the leather chair. Her dress rode up a little and Don admired the shape of what he could see. She pulled her skirt down and winked at him, then went on. "But now, there have been so many financial frauds that the thinking is changing. These days, many Americans manage their own retirement funds.

If an unsophisticated investor gets caught up in one of these investment schemes, it can cause a lifetime of financial damage. The result is, prosecutors are throwing the book at guys like Wesley."

"He hasn't been proved guilty yet," Anna Kaye said.

"Sure," June said. "How does Professor Rothschild feel about that?"

"Wesley is guilty as hell," Don said. "How much time might he get?"

"Well, a guy down in the Valley with a non-existent fracking company conned two hundred and fifty investors out of several million dollars. He promised them big returns. He pled guilty to securities fraud and misapplication of property and he was sentenced to sixty years in state prison. He has to serve one-third of the sentence even to be considered for parole."

"Jesus," Don said. "That is harsh."

"The prosecutor in that case told us that the prison term was justified because even after he knew he was under criminal investigation, the guy continued to fleece investors. And, most of his investors were retirees."

"Like here."

"Exactly. And like in that case, Wesley Bird came back for a second round, with the Hungarian gold coin certificates, when he knew he was under investigation. So I expect we'll go for the maximum on each count. That could add up to hundreds of years."

"Wow!"

"Of course, who knows what the grand jury will do—let alone a trial jury?"

"So, you think they'll return a true-bill?"

Anna Kaye sipped her Diet Coke. The red can matched her jacket. She sat the can down on June's sleek teak desk. "What does that mean, true-bill? Does that mean Wesley will be indicted?"

June took a tissue from her desk drawer and placed it under the cola can.

"Sorry," Anna Kaye said. "Nice furniture, by the way."

"All this crap?" June waved a hand at the matching office furniture and new leather chairs and designer table lamps. "Product of a drug bust. We confiscate their cars, their electronics, and their furniture. What we can't use is auctioned. Of course, this probably came out of an office the size of a football field. Actually, I don't care for it. Is that bad? Maybe I'll learn to like it, but I'll never admit it." She smiled guiltily at Don. "I tend to obsess about things."

"Good trait in a prosecutor."

"I hope so." She turned back to Anna Kaye. "You asked about the true-bill? This is the grand jury. You know the difference?"

"Between what?"

"Between a grand jury and a petit jury."

She smiled at Don, who returned the smile.

"She doesn't," Don said. He leaned over and whispered audibly, in Anna Kaye's ear. "Shall I tell you, or are you willing to let this beautiful lawyer embarrass you?"

Anna Kaye slapped him lightly on the cheek. "You can have him," she said to June. "No, tell me. I've never been sure. What's the difference?"

Don started, "A grand jury no-bills or true-bills, that is, indicts or doesn't. A petit jury, 'twelve good men tried and true', acquits or convicts…"

An elderly man hobbled into the space outside of June's office, interrupting Don in the middle of his lecture. He leaned on his cane while a middle-aged man supported his other arm and said, "Wait here, Dad. They told us to have you here at eleven, so it shouldn't be too long."

"Why do I have to come down here, anyway? Tell me again what it's all about?"

"About the football player and the money you gave him, Dad. Remember?"

"I'm too old for this," his father answered, slowly lowering himself onto a chair.

The door flew open again. Don looked up, expecting to see Papa. Instead, a red-faced, overweight man in a dark blue suit with his red necktie flapping, stormed through the door and slammed it shut behind him. He grimaced at June and hurried past them to the door at the end of the hall. "What the hell, Vernon?" they heard him say.

June raised her eyebrows. "That was Prentice Hall."

"He seems upset," Don said.

"You think?" June answered.

The three of them sat silently, watching the door through which Hall had disappeared. Don could hear the muffled sound of angry voices. It seemed that everyone in the office, clerks, witnesses, other lawyers, everyone in fact except the elderly man, were riveted to the room at the end of the hall. The old man tugged at his son's shirtsleeve. "I told you; I need to pee." When his son didn't answer, he repeated loudly, "I said, I need to pee. Right now."

His son looked around helplessly. "The men's room?"

Don stood up. "Come on. I'll show you."

"Thanks very much," the son said. Together they ushered the father out of the district attorney's offices. Don pointed to the men's room on the other side of the stairway. "Thanks," the son repeated.

He won't be so nice when he finds out who I am, Don thought.

He got back just in time to see Prentice Hall return. His puffy cheeks were red with anger. He straightened his tie and his coat. "Send everyone home, June. Cancel the rest of the witnesses."

June sat up in her chair. "Really?" she asked.

"We've got a plea. I need to go tell the jury."

"Wesley Bird is pleading? To fraud and embezzlement? How many years?"

Hall sighed. He noticed Anna Kaye and Don for the first time. "Hello, Cuinn. What the Hell. You probably know anyway. Blondie, you certainly know." He looked angrily at Anna Kaye. "Everybody knows but me! The fraud and money laundering charges are being dropped. He's pleading to passing forged papers."

"The Hungarian certificates? But that's, what, two to five?" June looked shocked.

Hall snorted. "No years. He pleads, gets sixty days in county jail and five years probation."

"Sixty days?" Don said. "Are you kidding me?"

"For the gold certificates. The *Austin Next* deal goes away. Thanks for

132

bringing the Hungarian coins to our attention, Cuinn. That was a real fucking help. It gave our cross-dressing district attorney the cover he needed." He straightened his tie and shirt, shook his head a few times, and went back to the grand jury room.

Don looked at the others. "What just happened here?"

"Yes, tell us, June," Anna Kaye said.

June grabbed her purse and keys. "First, let me get someone to release the witnesses. Then let's get out of here. Which one of you is buying me a drink?"

They went into the hall, where people were talking confusedly. The door to the grand jury room opened and Papa came out. He saw Don. "I think I am free to go," he said.

"You are, Papa.

In the hall, they met the old man, returning with his son from the toilet. "Hello, Chippy," Papa said.

The old man looked the other way. Don couldn't tell if he recognized Papa or not, but he heard his son ask, "Was that who I think it was?" Don decided to let them find out for themselves that the grand jury hearing was over.

Papa shook his head. "So bad. It's all so bad." He stood upright, refused help from Anna Kaye or Don, and said, "I think we deserve a good lunch—and a drink. Shall we?"

"Absolutely, Papa." He introduced June to Papa and then looked at Anna Kaye "Can we all fit in the Fiat?"

"Is that a pun?" she replied. Of course we can. June may have to sit in your lap, but you won't mind that."

As it turned out, there was room in the back of the yellow car for Don and June, although June's purse had to go in the trunk. Papa struggled to get into the front passenger seat, mumbling about arthritic knees, but he seemed energized by the prospect of lunch out. "I know exactly where I want to go, and I am to be the host, is that understood?" With that he told Anna Kaye to drive to a small restaurant off Sixth Street.

"*L'Ancien Régime?*" Anna Kaye asked. "It's been here forever, hasn't it, Professor? Thank you for thinking of it." She kissed Papa on the cheek.

He smiled and said, *"C'est mon plaisir, jolie jeune femme."*

"Oh, I love to hear a man speak French," June said. "Say something in French to me, Don."

"Steak frites," Don answered.

Papa buckled his seat belt, shifted so he could see into the back seat, and asked," Now someone tell me, what in the world is going on? Is what I heard correct? Did the district attorney say I will not be testifying in Wesley's trial after all?"

"You heard right, Papa," Don said. "Wesley's pleading guilty."

"I hope his time in prison will make him a better man," Papa said.

Don looked at the others. "Bad news on that front, Papa."

Papa sighed. "What now, Don? What could be worse than sitting in that room all morning, listening to the lawyer describe each one of the documents I had signed and asking me if I had signed it, what I thought it meant, and why I had done it. Some of the grand jurors even seemed to think I should have known the finances were suspect. 'After all,' one said, 'you are a professor of English. Didn't you read the documents?'"

"What did you say?"

"What could I say? I did not read the documents. I glanced at them, that is all, because I trusted Wesley." He turned to Anna Kaye. "I always liked Wesley. Do you understand?"

She nodded. "He's very likable."

"And very convincing," Don said. *I should know.*

June spoke up. "Wesley's made a deal, Professor Rothschild. He's pleading guilty on the gold coin certificate fraud, and we are dropping the *Austin Next* charges."

Papa shook his head. "Really? They do not believe they can convict him?"

June answered. "My guess is the district attorney is convinced..." She paused and smiled at Anna Kaye,..." or was convinced by someone very persuasive, that it wouldn't be wise to try Wesley for misrepresenting

Austin Next's finances."

"Why would it not be wise?" Papa asked.

"There's too much risk that some silent partner might get dragged into it…ah…I'm not saying there was a silent partner…. But the Hungarian gold certificates were Wesley's alone. Much cleaner that way. Our district attorney works in mysterious ways, his wonders to perform. At least until the next election."

"So Wesley gets off with a slap on the wrist," Don said. He caught Anna Kaye's eyes in the rear view mirror. "You knew?"

"Well," she answered, "I knew a deal was in the works. I wasn't sure it would come together. I did my part. I earned my fee. Maybe with a bonus."

"I'm not sure I want to be in the same car with you."

She shook her blond hair and smiled at him in the mirror. "Honestly, Donnie, did you really want Wesley to do hard time?"

Papa spoke up, "I for one was conflicted. And it was my money—mine and your mother's. Sending him to prison would not get the money back, would it?"

"I know," Don admitted. "Somehow, I never really expected him to go to prison. I knew he'd find a way out. Or find somebody who'd find it for him. But it's unfair."

Anna Kaye said, "He was still your best friend, Donnie, and a good friend of mine. Remember all those good times? They count for something, don't they?"

"I suppose so. But how did you do it, really?"

"It was Anne Morgan, Wesley's ex-mother-in-law."

"The richest woman in Texas," Don and June said in unison, and laughed.

"Cindy and I convinced Anne Morgan. She's a good friend of Bob Braeswood's wife. She hates what that poor woman is going through. She feels so bad for her that she bought everything at the Braeswood bankruptcy, including the ranch, and gave it all back to them. But what if Wesley got a maximum sentence and decided to make a deal, and turn against Braeswood? Who knows how that might have ended up? Anne Morgan put aside her disgust with Wesley and used her influence with the district attorney to get this deal done."

June spoke up. "If Lakey is really going to run again, having Anne Morgan Patson on your side can't hurt."

"This is the end of it, then?" Don asked.

June said, "Unless the feds come after him, which I guess depends on who's in the White House and how they feel about going after Governor Braeswood. Otherwise, Wesley serves his ninety days in Travis County jail, with time off for good behavior, goes on probation, and eventually, if he behaves, gets it all expunged from his record."

"He might become a congressman after all," Don said.

The others burst into laughter. "Heaven help us," Papa said.

"About your friends' money, Papa. I have a few ideas," Don began.

"Later, my boy. At the moment, I do need that lunch and that drink."

They waited on the sidewalk outside *L'Ancien Régime's* dark blue front door and watched Anna Kaye maneuver the Fiat into half a parking space. She scribbled a note and stuck it into the parking fee stanchion, then walked fast to where they waited.

"What was that?" Don asked, opening the door to the restaurant.

"What?"

"The note you left. Do you need some bills?"

"No." She looked at June. "I wrote we are here on official county business and to send the bill to the district attorney's office."

June smiled. "That ought to work. The DA is well-known on Sixth Street."

There was a small waiting area just inside the restaurant entrance. Six or seven tables lined the outside wall and curtained windows looked out at flower boxes filled with blooming plants. On the wall opposite the tables a bar displayed bottles of Pastis. Behind the bar were dark, well-stocked wine racks. A woman looked up. "*Bonjour*," she began, but when she saw Papa, she dropped the papers she had been holding. "*Mon Dieu*, is it you Ralph? It's been so long." She came hurrying from behind the bar. The fifty-something woman was stylishly dressed. Papa stepped into her outstretched arms and kissed her on both cheeks. "Sylvie, Sylvie, so good to see you." He stepped back and held her at arms' length. "Vous êtes aussi belle que jamais." *(You're as beautiful as ever.)*

She replied, "*Galant, comme toujours,* Ralph." *(Galant as always, Ralph.)* She turned to the others. "Professor Rothschild and I are friends forever. We are from the same part of France."

"The Perigord," Papa said. "But you much later than I. You are so much younger. And lovely." He placed a hand on Don's arm "Sylvie, this is Don, you've heard me speak of him often. Don, this is my dear friend, Madame Sylvia Bonnard."

Sylvie offered her cheek to be kissed. "Ah, the famous attorney. I have heard so much about you." She smiled at Papa. "*Il est encore plus beau que sa photographie.*" *(He is even more handsome than his photograph.)*

Don gave her his hangdog grin. "Vous êtes beaucoup trop gentil, Madame." *(You are much too kind, Madame.)*

"Of course you speak French," she said. "Ralph' made certain of that, I am sure."

He had not used his French in years, but it came back in the presence of the Frenchwoman. All Don knew about Papa's boyhood years in the Perigord was that he and his mother had fled from there to Cuba when the Nazis came. His father died in a concentration camp, his mother died in Cuba waiting to come to the U.S., and so Ralph Rothschild had come as an orphan, adopted by family friends. Yet Papa seemed to have happy memories of his childhood in France.

Don introduced Anna Kaye and June to the smiling Frenchwoman. She quickly rearranged a table in the corner. "Sit, please. Ralph, an *aperitif* perhaps?"

Papa answered at once. "It has been a very trying day, Sylvie, a very trying day. I am in desperate need of an *Armangac*. Can that be arranged?"

Sylvie smiled. "Always, Ralph." She turned to the women. "For you, *mademoiselles*? There is a lovely white wine from the Perigord, the *Monbazillac*. It is a favorite of mine."

Both women nodded. Don spoke up, "I want to join Papa."

"A good choice, Don." Papa rubbed his eyes with a starched white handkerchief. "Bring us what you are cooking, Sylvie." He turned to the others. "Unless one of you is a vegan. In that case…"

"I want what you're having, Professor," Anna Kaye said.

June added, "So do I."

"It will be wonderful, you can be sure." He looked at Sylvie, who was waiting patiently. "It's settled then, Sylvie. And by the way, do you still have the wine book with the quotation about *Armangac.* I think the young people would enjoy it."

"I think so, Ralph. Let me look."

As they waited for their drinks, Papa said, "*Armagnac* is the oldest brandy distilled in France, well-known for its therapeutic benefits. In the 14th century, a French Cardinal, as I remember, claimed it had 40 virtues."

Sylvie appeared with a thin book, and read from it. "It was *Prior Vital Du Four*, Ralph, and he wrote about *Armangac.* She read:

It makes redness and burning of the eyes disappear, and stops them from tearing; it cures hepatitis, sober consumption adhering. It cures gout, cankers, and fistula by ingestion; restores the paralyzed member by massage; and heals wounds of the skin by application.

It enlivens the spirit, partaken in moderation, recalls the past to memory, renders men joyous, preserves youth and retards senility. And when retained in the mouth, it loosens the tongue and emboldens the wit, if someone timid from time to time himself permits.

"I'll have a bottle to go," Don said. "I can use all forty."

A waiter appeared with their glasses and Papa raised his in a toast. "To *Armangac*, may it deliver me from the likes of Wesley Bird. And to Wesley himself, our friend. May he learn from his tribulations."

They sipped their drinks and talked small talk, anything but Wesley

Bird. In a few minutes, Sylvie set a large plate of *foie gras,* gherkins and crusty bread in the center of the table. "That should remind you of home, Ralph. Some good red wine now? I have a bottle of *Percharmant* I have been saving for you." She turned to the others. "It's very hard to find outside the region."

Papa smiled slightly. "Of course, Sylvie. Thank you." He passed the bread to the others and they began to eat, feasting on the *foie gras* and washing it down with wine and brandy.

"Oh, God," Anna Kaye said, "have I died and gone to heaven?"

They ate silently and smiled at each other, then sat up eagerly when the waiter and Sylvie appeared with breast of fresh duck with figs, a truffle soufflé, grilled asparagus, and a walnut cake on a crystal stand.

When they had finished, June sipped her coffee, burped slightly, then said, "I need to get my resume ready. Right after a two hour nap."

CHAPTER FOURTEEN

Don was in the federal courthouse in Amarillo to assist Wiley in his race discrimination lawsuit against the Swiss. Don appreciated the dignified courtroom, the dark paneling, the high windows, the silence. It was different from the county courthouses where his trial work usually took him. This courtroom gave significance to the cases being tried there, suits involving federal law or, as in this case, cases where the defendant was from out of the state. It was Wiley's first time in federal court and he was perspiring already.

They were there to defend Wiley's deposition notice, which would require the chairman of *Gesellschaft für Chemische,* or GFC as all the American lawyers preferred to call it, to travel from Basel to Wiley's law office in a former country store, in Antelope City, there to tell under oath what he knew about the wrongful discharge of Jamail Jobey. "Corporate executives hate to be deposed," he said to Wiley when he suggested the deposition, "especially foreign ones. They're terrified of American lawyers. They think we aren't gentlemen."

It was the day that Wesley was to be sentenced by an Austin judge. Don had his notebook computer on, the sound muted, and he watched the media circus on streaming video. He also received intense texts from Anna Kaye as she sat in court "representing Cindy." Don could tell she was enjoying the spectacle as she reported that many "important people" were crediting her for Wesley's light sentence. "It's not completely true, but I can't go around denying everything that's not completely true."

Meanwhile, in Amarillo, the Swiss had reacted violently to Wiley's "preposterous" deposition notice. Two prestigious law firms, Hill & Dalton, an international firm out of Geneva, and Bost & Bost, the largest firm in Houston, had swamped both the court and poor Wiley with objections, motions, and counterclaims. They were aided and abetted by Thompson, Fite, the most prominent law firm in Amarillo. Max Kilgore, the firm's chief litigator, was making the actual argument before his former law partner, U.S. District Judge William Harrison Pearce.

Wiley, on the other hand, was alone except for Don and Maye Martin, Faye's twin sister, who had been called out of retirement to assist. Their client, Jamail Jobey sat at the counsel table with Don and Wiley. Jobey was not the only black face in the room. Bost & Bost had brought two black female lawyers from Houston, to add some color and gender balance to the defendants' counsel table.

"Mr. Kilgore," the judge said, peering down from his bench, "I gather from your motions that your client isn't interested in sampling Panhandle culture, especially the Velda County variety." He lifted a foot high stack of legal documents and shoved them to one side.

The GFC side of the room tittered appreciatively. Kilgore smiled at his fellow litigators, as if to say, "I told you the judge had a sense of humor. Nobody knows him better than me." He smiled sympathetically at Don and Wiley, then replied. "Your Honor, I'm sure that Mr. Sturgeon would love to visit. However, as our motions and the supporting briefs make clear, there is no legal justification for what the plaintiff is asking. If I did not know counsel better, I might think this is an abuse of process and ask the court to sanction him."

Quite a concession, considering he met Wiley for the first time this morning, Don thought.

Judge Pearce adjusted his reading glasses on his bony nose and called on Wiley to reply. "Mr. Franklin...?"

Wiley had struggled to his feet, but Don was engrossed with the video of Wesley reading a statement to the judge in Travis County and did not notice that Wiley was in trouble until Maye poked him in the ribs.

Don looked up and saw Wiley's panic. He jumped to his feet. "Your Honor, may I approach the bench?"

"All right, Mr. Cuinn," the judge said.

Don picked up his notebook computer and walked nervously to the bench. He glanced at Maye, who was whispering to Wiley. *Calm him down and remind him what he's supposed to answer,* Don tried to convey telepathically.

Judge Pearce spoke softly, "I'm warning you this had better be good. One warning is all you get in my courtroom."

Don opened the notebook and set it on the side of the bench. "Your Honor," he said softly, "you went to the University. You have to see this."

The judge muttered, "Very irregular," but looked at the screen. He looked up at Don. "My God. Is that Wesley Bird?" he whispered.

"Yes, it is, Judge. Pleading guilty to a state jail felony."

Max Kilgore interrupted their viewing. "Your Honor—?"

Pearce looked up. "Come up here, Mr. Kilgore."

Soon, the three of them were hovered around the screen, following on closed caption the University's last All-American read his statement, admit his mistake, blame it on poor legal advice, and promise never to repeat it, followed by the judge sentencing Wesley to ninety days in the county jail, five years' probation, restitution to the investors, which everyone knew would never be made, and a $20,000 fine.

The judge closed the notebook and returned it to Don. "Take your seats, gentlemen."

Don heard Max explain to the gang of lawyers around his table, "Procedural matter. Got it squared away."

"Back on the record, Madam Clerk, please. Now, where were we? Oh yes, Mr. Franklin. You've been accused of abuse of process. You seem to be outnumbered. Would you care to respond?"

Wiley squared his shoulders, gulped and then said, "Outnumbered, yes, Your Honor. I'm sure having two-dozen of Houston and Switzerland's finest attorneys and their support staffs in town will do wonders for the Amarillo economy. However, we have the advantage of having the law on our side."

Good job, Wiley! Good job, Maye! Don observed.

"I read your answer, Mr. Franklin." Judge Pearce picked up Wiley's thin brief and laid it next to the stack of papers from the other side. "Tell me why the Court should drag Mr. Sturgeon across the Atlantic? What can he possibly add to this litigation?"

Maye handed Don a worksheet; he scanned it and passed it on to Wiley. "Your Honor, this is a compilation of the defendant's work force in the European Union, Canada and the U.S. We have asked the company to provide us the ethnicity of those employees. They have refused to do so. We expect to get that information from Mr. Sturgeon when he is deposed."

Max Kilgore had been huddling with several of the lawyers.

It looks like a rugby scrum over there, Don thought, having watched a lot of rugby on ESPN 9.

Kilgore rose. "Your Honor, we declined to furnish that information because the data does not exist, and in any case, it is irrelevant to this case."

"What do you say to that, Counselor? How can they furnish it if it doesn't exist?"

Wiley was on a roll, now. The hours of prep that Maye and Don had given him were starting to pay off. "If ethnicity data doesn't exist, it is because there are no blacks in any of their European or North American operations. We expect to establish that from Mr. Sturgeon's deposition."

Kilgore rose, "Your Honor," he began, but the Judge waved him aside. "But is it relevant, Mr. Franklin?"

"Well…,Your Honor…, we expect to establish that GFC has a deliberate corporate policy in Europe and North America of discrimination against racial minorities in the workplace. Mr. Sturgeon is the chairman and is knowledgeable of that policy. That would certainly be relevant to the plaintiff's claims here."

The judge nodded. "I see—"

"But, Your Honor," Kilgore began.

"Don't interrupt me, Counselor. I was speaking." The Judge frowned at his former partner.

Kilgore turned red and sat down. "Sorry, Your Honor."

Judge Pearce let Kilgore sit for a long minute before speaking. "I was going to ask, does Mr. Sturgeon ever have occasion to visit his company's U.S. headquarters in Houston?"

Kilgore stood, his face still red. "I would have to check, Your Honor."

Faye thrust a folder into Don's hand. Don looked at it and then up at the judge. He handed it to Wiley. "Your Honor," Wiley said, "this is a newspaper account of an interview that Mr. Sturgeon gave to the Houston Chronicle last year in which he said that he visits Houston at least once every quarter."

Don handed the clipping to the clerk, who handed it to the judge. Smiling, Don gave a copy to Kilgore.

Kilgore glanced at the clipping, then dropped it on the table. "Hearsay. Not material. Not relevant. But that's all beside the point, Your Honor. Deposing the chairman of a large multinational company in some piddling little case in Velda?"

Don looked at the judge and they exchanged smiles. "This court has no piddling cases, Mr. Kilgore. Considering there are thirteen lawyers and twice that many assistants on your side of the room, the defendant doesn't consider it piddling either. Get with opposing counsel and work out a date for Mr. Sturgeon's deposition. In Houston."

"Will Houston suit you, Mr. Franklin?"

Wiley beamed. "It suits us just fine, Your Honor." Maye, Don, and Jobey embraced him in a group hug.

CHAPTER FIFTEEN

Anna Kaye finally agreed to visit Don in Velda.

Wesley was about to begin his ninety days in the Travis County jail. The city had essentially shut down as the planning and permitting departments waited for the upcoming elections, when a new council and mayor would be chosen and Austin would learn which developers had backed a winner and which green lobbies had power. "All I can do is sit and wait. It's depressing beyond belief. I may as well be up there with you," she said on the phone.

"That's a ringing endorsement," he said.

Rather than fly, Anna Kaye insisted on driving the yellow Fiat to Velda.

"You have no idea how far it is."

"I've already decided. I'll drive to Abilene and spend the night with my old volleyball coach, and then come on the next day."

"You'll regret it," Don told her.

When she finally arrived in downtown Velda, she climbed out of the car, its yellow paint splattered with mud from a sudden downpour near Childress.

"A drink, for God's sake, get me a vodka," she ordered. "Why did you let me drive? I was nearly blown off the road by the wind, I was caught in a hailstorm outside of a place called Anson, I was run off the road by a trucker near somewhere I never heard of, and I am tired. Give me a back rub, hon, will you? Do they have running water in this God-forsaken place? I need a bath. Where's that vodka?"

"You're right," Don said. "I should have warned you not to drive."

She threw her arms around him. "Give me a kiss, sweetie."

Had there been any traffic on Velda Avenue, it would have stopped at the sight of the tall blond beauty kissing the small-town lawyer, but to Don's chagrin, there wasn't a car to be seen. He led her into the Hansro lobby. "This is all mine." He pointed up at the Art Deco ceiling and the 1950's style elevator.

"It certainly is…unique," Anna Kaye said, handing him her carry-on. "Does that elevator work?"

"Sometimes." He pushed the up button and they waited. When the elevator doors finally opened, a group of GFC employees got off. They spoke to Don and smiled at Anna Kaye. "Tenants," he explained. "At least, for a while." The new woman in town would be dinner table conversation all over Velda that night.

He opened the door to his penthouse apartment and ushered her in. "Welcome to my digs."

She stepped inside and took in the large living room and the wall of glass doors opening onto the outside terrace. "My goodness, Donnie Ray. This is yours?"

"More than I need, but, yes, it is. Comes with the building. My office is across the hall."

"How convenient. And all this antique furniture…. My God, is it real?"

"So I'm told." He pointed to the hall. "Bedroom is down there, on the left. Let me get you a drink."

She smiled. "A drink, a bath, and a screw. Can you arrange that?"

He turned her around and kissed her, loving the feel of her body against his. "Does it have to be in any particular order?"

Later, they lay together on the four-poster bed in the guest bedroom. He decided that it was easier for the two of them to use the second bedroom than to try to rid the master bedroom of traces of Cecelia. He was not going to take her picture down.

That afternoon, Don watched happily as Anna Kaye and Faye squared off. They detested each other on sight, that was obvious even to as hapless a judge of the feminine mind as Don. *They're fighting over me,* he thought with pleasure, but then he decided they would have been just as prickly with each other if he'd never been born.

They were seated around the massive oak dining table in Don's apartment. Don and Anna Kaye sipped the cabernet she had brought from Austin. John, the owner of her favorite Austin wine store, had told her to take what she would want to drink, that finding a good bottle of wine in the Panhandle was, "…somewhat difficult."

"Somewhat impossible," Don agreed.

"Velda is a lovely little place," Anna Kaye offered, smiling sweetly at Faye.

"Those of us who live here like it. Of course, it can't compare with Austin, all those bars and rock bands." Don knew Faye considered Austin the Sodom of Texas. Or *was it Gomorrah?* "Which do you like most, the bars or the bands?" she asked.

"Oh, I prefer the bars with rock bands, every time."

Faye, a teetotaler, had refused the young woman's offer of wine. She watched them drink, then got up and rummaged in a drawer in the ornately carved sideboard, which occupied an entire wall of the dining room. She produced a pair of coasters from the 1999 State Fair of Texas and placed them under the wine glasses. "This table is Tudor, Sixteenth Century," she said.

"Really?" Anna Kaye said, ebbing her hand over the dark surface. "What is it doing here?"

"Major Hansard's father, Colonel Hansard, was a collector of early English furniture. He favored the style, all the carving, the heavy legs, the dark oak."

Anna Kaye looked around. The large apartment was full of the Tudor furniture. "Is all this yours, Donnie Ray?"

"I wish. No, it belongs to the Hansard Foundation. Jake, my former partner runs the foundation. He's letting me use it until he finds a museum that wants it."

"That shouldn't be hard," she answered.

Faye stood up. "There is a beautiful four-poster bed that is especially valuable in the guest room, should you happen to go in there."

Anna Kaye smiled. "I admired it this afternoon. I lay there and looked up at the canopy and that was all I thought about."

Don smiled, remembering her stretched out on that very bed.

If Faye was surprised that Anna Kaye was sleeping in the guest room, she did not show it. "One nice thing, those Tudor beds are very sturdy, very well built. You don't have to worry about that."

Don wondered if the sounds of their lovemaking earlier in the afternoon had carried down the hall to Faye's ears? He decided she had just made a lucky guess.

"So good to know," Anna Kaye answered. "You're sure you won't have a glass of wine, Faye?"

"No, thank you. I'll go have my afternoon tea and then I have to go back to work. Someone needs to go keep the law office running." She gave Don a quick, reproving glance. "Enjoy your wine."

"Thank you, Faye," Anna Kaye said. "I'll try not to keep Mr. Cuinn away from his work too long."

"That's nice of you."

Anna Kaye watched Faye leave. She held out her empty wine glass and then said, "She's been talking to your mother."

"Why do you say that?" Don re-filled their glasses.

"Why else would she hate me? I'm so lovable."

Don took her hand and stood up. "You are. Let's go examine that canopy. I didn't notice it before."

❦❦❦❦❦

Faye may have resented Anna Kaye, but Eugene Pervoy's wife, Ginelle, took to her immediately, and the consultant from Austin found an instant friend in the blowzy, wild-haired rancher's wife. The four of them went to the Greeks for steak and beer. George and Tiny Poppoppolus had remodeled the back room into a Velda version of a sports bar, and there was a

148

din of chatter and laughter that would have been hard to resist had they tried, which they didn't. Don smiled languidly at the other couple, sated with an afternoon of lovemaking. Ginelle talked happily, gossiping about famous guests from Dallas and Houston that the Pervoy Ranch Resort had attracted.

Even Eugene Pervoy, who hardly ever said anything at all, was smitten by the beautiful blond Amazon. "You are a big girl," he said.

"And you're Don's biggest client, and a real cowboy too."

Don and Eugene winked at each other. They knew all the men in the room were looking at the two women, both bigger than life, but one stylish in an upscale designer pants suit and the other thrown together, her clothes straight from the local discount store. Everybody in Velda also knew that it was Ginelle who had transformed the Pervoy Ranch into a premiere vacation destination, with exotic game hunts, sunset trail rides, barbecues, and a first-class spa for Dallas matrons recovering from substance abuse or a facelift. "Girl," she said to Anna Kaye, cutting vigorously into her sirloin steak, "we have some real characters out there. One oilman from Midland rents our biggest villa, and he and his twenty-five year old 'assistant' don't leave the place the entire time. Then he has me bill the company for a 'game hunt.'"

"Some game," Eugene offered.

"I love this steak," Anna Kaye said. "What else do they have on the menu?"

"Steak, hot dogs, and ranch chili. That's all you want to eat here," Don said. He wiped grease from his chin and sat back, satisfied.

"You can't eat that every day. Where else do you eat?"

"Well," Eugene said, "if you want a hamburger, there's the PopPop, on the Loop. Fried fish, there's Missy's, barbeque, you go to Bob's. Anything else, the Country Club. That's about it."

Ginelle added, "We have gourmet food and a wonderful chef at the ranch. We don't eat it ourselves, of course. Eugene and the kids hate it. The locals either don't like it or can't afford it."

Tiny Poppoppolus, the younger Greek brother, appeared at the table with another pitcher of beer. "Tiny, let me ask you something," Don said.

"Miss Nordstrom here misses Austin cuisine. Where would you suggest she go to get some broiled pig snout and goat intestines?"

Tiny smiled. "That the rage downstate?"

"It seems to be," Don said. He had his arm around Anna Kaye's shoulder and he gave her a squeeze. "Tell him about that place, Anna Kaye. What's its name? *All the Pig*?"

"Have your fun," she said, "but I think you'd appreciate it, Tiny. You know food. Unlike this man with his uneducated palate."

Tiny smiled. "The nearest thing is Ginelle and Eugene's place," he said. "They whip up some strange dishes out there."

Eugene shook his head. "Goat guts? Do they really eat goat guts in Austin?"

Yes," Don said.

"Accounts for a lot, I guess," Eugene said, then took a long swallow of his beer.

Tiny brought the check. His brother George ignored Don when they came in, although he shook hands with Eugene and hugged Ginelle. Don was used to it. George hated Don, first because Bridget O'Neill had chosen Don over him, and then, when Don and Bridget broke up, he apparently blamed Don for breaking Bridget's heart, and for Bridget leaving town. Don had given up trying to heal the breach. He had enough personal problems of his own without trying to solve George's.

Outside, Eugene settled into the passenger's seat of their new Lincoln sedan and opened a bottle of beer. Ginelle put on her seat belt and started the engine. "Seat belt, Eugene," she said. Eugene lowered his window and looked up at the two of them standing by the car. "She's my full time driver," Eugene said. "When're you going to get me off of probation, so I can drive again?"

"Soon, soon," Don answered, winking at Ginelle. Neither of them wanted Eugene on the highway. His days of weekend stays at the county jail were over, but old habits die-hard and Ginelle took no risks.

She smiled at Anna Kaye. "We'll see you tomorrow night. I'll save you our best villa. That client from Midland I was telling about has gone home.

"With his assistant?" Don asked.

"You should have seen her," Eugene said, swigging his beer. "In that little bitty swimming suit."

"Drink your beer and shut up," Ginelle said.

Don and Anna Kaye walked the empty two blocks back to the Hansro Building. Their footsteps echoed off the brick sidewalks and closed storefronts. There had been a mini-renaissance in downtown Velda with the shale oil boom, but other than The Greeks and Bob's Bar and Barbeque, the stores were dark and the sidewalk was empty. They stopped on a corner and looked at the full moon, so big it seemed to fill the sky. "Look up. Have you ever seen so many stars?"

The sky was clear, the air was brisk, and the heavens were filled with twinkling stars surrounding the brightly glowing moon. "Never," she answered. "It is beautiful. But still, I can't imagine living here."

"If you gave it a try, you would change your mind. Within a year."

"Oh, sweetie. I'd never last a year."

ⅭⅭⅭⅭⅭ

The next day, they drove around Velda in his truck and looked at his favorite places. "I wish we had time to go down to the Palo Dura Canyon."

"I need to start back in a couple of days. One of the city council candidates needs a quick image lift."

Don stopped trying to convince her to move to Velda. It was hopeless, and anyway, the more she was in the apartment, the more she threatened his memory of Cecilia, so much so that some mornings he couldn't recall Cecilia's face, exactly. Then, making sure Anna Kaye was asleep, he went quietly into his bedroom and gazed for a few minutes at Cecilia's picture on his wall. It reminded him how beautiful she was, but it also reminded him why he was unhappy and why he had so little to offer Anna Kaye.

So, he became her tour guide. He drove her through the old residential neighborhoods and told her stories of the old days and how the original streets were named after Colonel Hansard and his wife. He told her about their son, the height-challenged major. He showed her the table at the Country Club where Major Hansard had lunch every day. He drove by the entrance to the Evergreen Plant and told her a sanitized version of the water rights story and how his first clients, the Thorpes, divorced, remarried, re-divorced and finally remarried for keeps. Taking Don's advice, they sold their water rights for a handsome fee, which earned him his largest fee, and enough money to buy out Jake Rosen.

They ended in Antelope City, in front of the country store law office, where he had sought refuge and started his law practice with no clients except friends and relatives of the Thorpes. Wiley was waiting for them, along with his pretty assistant. "Wiley, Beata," Don said. "Meet Anna Kaye Nordstrom, our visitor from the big city."

The Polish girl smiled prettily and did a half-curtsey. Anna Kaye kissed Wiley on the cheek and took Beata in her arms for an exuberant hug. She looked around at the converted office. "My goodness, look at this."

"It was Elmer Thorpe's store, back in the old days," Wiley said. He was excited with the visit and was chattering nervously. "There's some pictures of it then on the wall. Come in. Sit down. Beata brought kielbasa."

They gathered in the conference room, where Beata had set the table. Don had warned Anna Kaye not to eat breakfast. "Those Polish girls know how to cook," he told her.

"The salad is wonderful," she said, helping herself to another helping of the cucumbers and sour cream. "What do you call it?"

"The salad is mizeria," Beata answered. "I think the dill makes it special. And of course, the kielbasa is smoked pork. My great-grandmother brought the recipe from the old country."

"I had no idea there was a Polish community up here. How did that happen?"

"There were Polish settlements along the Texas coast, even before the Civil War. My people came here around 1900, looking for good farm land."

Don poured them more of the dark iced tea. "They did very well, very prosperous. Jake always complained he couldn't get their law business. They naturally preferred Jerry Adamcyk, who was Polish."

"My uncle." Her eyes were deep blue and her cheeks were cream. "He passed a few years ago."

Wiley could contain himself no longer. "Beata and I are getting married. Next month."

Don clapped Wiley on the shoulder. "She accepted you? You lucky dog." He smiled at Beata. "What's a pretty girl like you want with this no-account? I guess he has qualities I wasn't aware of."

She blushed.

The last time Don had made an unscheduled early evening visit to the office, he happened to notice that the bed in Wiley's living quarters was unmade. Fortunately, he had just caught himself before he said something about it and really embarrassed the poor girl.

"I'm very happy for the two of you." He turned to Wiley. "Maybe we can get some Polish law business now."

"As you say, we Poles like to keep business in the family," Beata said. "Wiley will do very well. I've already told my father and his brothers they must all have new wills."

The women cleared the table and Don and Wiley sat in Wiley's office, going over files. Wiley put down a folder. "Chief, have you thought about the deposition?"

"The deposition?"

"Sturgeon? Jamail Jobey's case?"

Don exhaled. "No," he admitted. "I've been busy with other matters." He nodded his head toward the kitchen.

"So have I," he admitted. "It wasn't easy getting Beata's papa to accept me, I tell you. I'm over there losing at checkers to that old man every night."

"Worth it though, isn't it?"

"Absolutely! But we have to get married before she starts showing. Her family is old-fashioned. Will you be my best man?"

"I would be honored."

Wiley sighed. "Good. Good. Now, the deposition? We've agreed on a date, and darn if it isn't right after the wedding."

"Don't sweat it, Wiley. Enjoy your honeymoon. The deposition will be just fine. I'll handle it." What he meant was that Maye would prep it for him. *Who, me worry?*

They drove away in Don's truck, waving at the happy couple, who stood together on the front porch of the old store. Don pulled over in the square to show Anna Kaye the statue of the antelope, restored with Thorpe money. "I'll bet if we drove back to the office, we'd find them in bed already."

"They could hardly wait for us to leave," Anna Kaye said. "Young love."

At the same time, they said, "She's pregnant!"

They laughed.

"He told you?"

"Yes. She told you?"

"Yes! Young love," she said again, wistfully this time.

CHAPTER SIXTEEN

When they got to the Pervoy Ranch, they found that Bobby Bill had opened the gate and was waiting in his pick-up for them to arrive. Don remembered when he came to help Eugene's brother, Trey, with his drug problems. That day, there was an armed guard at the gate. Today all was calm and peaceful. Bobby Bill smiled shyly at Anna Kaye. "Howdy, ma'am. Don, Ginelle said for you to go on up to Trey's Place. You know the way?"

"I believe I do, Bobby Bill. This is Miss Nordstrom, my friend from Austin."

"Hi there," she said. " Are you a real cowboy?"

Bobby Bill blushed. "Well, I used to be. Now all I do is guide folks that can't ride to places they can't get hurt and kill any rattlers that get in the way." He thought a minute. "And keep them away from the oil wells."

"How's married life treating you?" Don asked.

"Just fine. It's treating me just fine. We moved into the dugout, did you know that?"

"Good for you. Eugene always said that was the best house on the place."

"That's for sure. Ginelle's got Eugene and the kids living in Mama's House, since Mrs. Mary Marie moved back to Longview."

"I never thought I'd see that," Don said.

"Me neither," Bobby Bill said. "Good for me and Ruby, though." He tipped his hat and closed the gate behind them.

Don drove up the ranch road toward the top of the cliff. There had been rain and the flat land in between the dry creeks and caliche cliffs were full of grass and wildflowers.

"They live in a dugout?"

Don slowed down and drove slowly across a cattle guard. "They call it a dugout because it was where George Pervoy lived when he put the ranch together, years ago. He raised his family there. He built his ranch house over the old dugout, and they used it for a storm shelter when the tornados came."

At the next fork in the road, Don pointed to his right. "There it is, over there."

The adobe house was built into the side of a cliff, protected from the north wind in the winter, while getting the southwest wind the rest of the year. Large cottonwood trees shaded the big front porch.

"It's beautiful," Anna Kaye said. "It blends right in with the land."

"It does, doesn't it? When Trey was alive and running things, Eugene and Ginelle lived there. Trey and Eugene's mother, that's Mary Marie, built a big plantation-style house when she married their daddy and moved here from East Texas. That's what they call 'Mama's House.' It's hard for me to imagine Eugene and Ginelle and their batch of kids in that house." He pointed to the south. "Over there is the main oil field. That's where most of the Pervoy money comes from."

"My God, would you look at that," Anna Kaye said.

Wellheads and neatly painted tanks and lease equipment, each with its own chain link fence, dotted the landscape as far as they could see. Between the well sites, stocky white-faced cattle grazed quietly.

"What kind of cattle are those, Donnie?"

Don grinned. "You're asking the wrong cowboy, sweetheart. But hold on. You ain't seen nothing yet."

He drove up the next hill and stopped the truck. Across the canyon, they were almost blinded by the sun's reflection from a glass house and its Olympic size swimming pool.

"What in the world?"

"That's Trey's Place. He built it for his wife, and trying to pay for it was the start of his troubles." They drove across a stone dam that formed a clear pond, shaded by cottonwoods. A running stream fed the pond. The water was

156

pumped back up the hill and fed back into the stream. Eugene had shown him the pump, powered by free natural gas provided by the oil company that operated the Pervoy wells. More free gas fueled the large compressors that kept the glass house warm, or cold, in season, and heated the swimming pool all year round. Thanks to Don's negotiations when some Pervoy leases were up for renewal, the entire ranch was off the grid. "Their father Gorge III gave Trey the ranch to manage and he damn near lost it."

"What happened?"

"Gambling, then drugs, then bad business associates. Eugene managed to bail him out, but Trey couldn't stand the disgrace. He took some pills and flew his plane into the ground."

"That's awful."

"It's ancient history now. Eugene and Ginelle, mostly Ginelle, have turned Trey's Place into a really successful business." He pulled into the circular drive. "Speaking of whom, there she is."

Ginelle, dressed in a large smock over denim pants, was standing in the doorway, shielding her eyes from the sun. She waved at them.

They parked and walked over the crushed granite driveway to the house: a sprawling glass cube. The distant horizon was visible through glass walls that enveloped the house. It perched on the edge of a deep canyon, like some prehistoric bird ready to fly. They stepped inside and Ginelle hugged them. Don looked around the Frank Lloyd Wright Studio designed house. The large Klee was gone from the entrance wall, replaced by a Salinas bluebonnet painting. Comfortable looking stuffed furniture had replaced the stark Scandinavian pieces Trey's wife and her New York decorator had chosen for the massive interior spaces. Otherwise, it looked the same.

"Come on in. I'm sorry it's so bright in here, but there's nothing you can do with all that glass." She pointed at the massive wall of glass in front of them.

"The view is just stunning," Anna Kaye said, walking to the edge of the glass wall and looking down. "Can I take a picture?"

"Sure, go ahead. That's the first thing our guests want to do, take a picture out that window and send it home. The view is O.K., I guess, but when we built the new villas, we decided people who come all the way out here want some privacy, so the villas are different."

"Don told me that Frank Lloyd Wright studio designed the house. Did they do the villas too?"

"Oh hell, no, hon. No way I was going to pay them. Besides, I imagine they wouldn't have done what I wanted. I got me a good architect professor from Texas Tech, and he designed the villas. He says, I can't remember exactly, but it's like, 'The villas are consistent with the philosophy of the main house, but not slavish to it.'"

They laughed.

"In other words, he did what the client wanted," Don said.

"Exactly," Ginelle said. "So, we have the six bedrooms in this house, plus the three villas. They're named San Francisco, Dallas, and Kansas City. K.C. is the biggest, but it's taken by a Houston couple. Personally, I like San Francisco best. It's got a view without any oil wells and its own private pool. Our honeymoon couples love it. That's where I put you."

"Interesting names. Were those cities special to you?"

Ginelle winked at Don, who was daydreaming about a moonlight dip with Anna Kaye in the private pool. "Real special. Get Don to explain it to you." She looked out the entrance. "Bobby Bill will take your things over to San Francisco. Don, the bar's in Trey's old office. You know where that is? Fix yourself something to drink, look around, make yourself at home. I need to go shove a broomstick up that lazy chef's behind. Excuse me."

With that, she flew off down the hall. "Ruby," she called, "tell Chef I need to see him, right away. He's way over budget! And what the hell is black abalone?"

They sat on the back patio of the big house, watching the sunset. Anna was sipping her vodka martini and Don was on his second Coors. He didn't ask what she was thinking about, but his mind was on a quick dinner and then some quality naked time in San Francisco's private pool. He was explaining to Anna Kaye that San Francisco, Dallas and Kansas City were the names of Eugene and Ginelle's children, proudly named by Eugene after the cities where they were conceived. He was interrupted by footsteps and looked up. A large, stocky man staggered out of the shadows toward them. A middle aged, dark-haired woman with a matronly figure was having difficulty supporting him. Just as they reached Don and Anna Kaye, he started to fall. Don jumped from his chair, grabbed the man with one hand, and with the other, caught the man's glass tumbler in midair.

"Easy, easy," Don said, lowering the man onto his chair. He handed the tumbler, half full of whiskey, to the woman.

"Thank you," she said. "He was just too heavy for me."

"Are you all right, man?" Don asked.

The man raised his head off his chest, opened his eyes, blinked at Don and said, "Hello, Donnie. How's it hanging?"

"Phil? Is it really you, Phil?" Don asked.

"Oh my God," Anna Kaye said. "This is amazing."

Not so amazing, really, Don thought, *to run into Wesley Bird's ex-father-in-law, and Anna Kaye's best friend's father, on the arm of a woman who was not his wife at a hideaway in the Texas Panhandle. Actually, it's fucking amazing.*

"Oh, hi, Anna Kaye," Phil Patson said. "How you doing?" He looked up at the woman hovering anxiously over him. He took his whiskey glass out of her hand and drank it all. "Get me another, Millie, will you darlin'?"

"Phil, I don't think you…"

"Just get it, Millie. Then you and me and these young folks are going to have some dinner." He looked up at Don and Anna Kaye "Kids, do you know Millie Stein? Millie, these are a couple of old friends."

By the time they had another round of drinks, went in to dinner, ordered and finished their *gazpacho,* Phil was back to his old self. He put his hand on Anna Kaye's bare shoulder and said, "My God, girl, you always were the best looking girl of any of Cindy's friends."

Anna Kaye put her hand on Phil's. "And you could always sweet-talk better than any man I ever met." She kissed him on the cheek.

"What'd they call you, the Acrobat?"

"Sometimes." She looked over at Don, who smiled, remembering why he had called the uber-flexible girl that name, back in the day. *Truth be told, she's still pretty acrobatic.*

Phil turned to Millie, who seemed to find the encounter amusing. "This girl was an All-American volleyball player." He rubbed her shoulder. "Do you still play, Anna Kaye? You look like it, doesn't she, Donnie?"

Don nodded. "Still a player."

Anna Kaye removed Phil's hand from her shoulder and straightened the strap to her dress. "I could probably lay out if I had to."

"I'll bet you could."

Millie wiped his chin with her napkin. "Eat some of your lamb, Phil. It's cooked just like you like it. And the mint jelly. I think they make it themselves."

Phil took a bite, then pushed the plate away. "Yes, ma'am." He motioned at Anna Kaye with his fork. "This girl was always as sweet as mint jelly." He raised his glass to Don. "You're a lucky man."

Don returned the toast. He remembered the pool party at the Patson home in River Oaks, Cindy and Wes, Anna Kaye and Donnie. The party started in the afternoon. He remembered Anne Morgan in her bikini, her body wafer-thin and perfectly sculpted by the best plastic surgeon in L.A.; he looked at Cindy and could see what Anne Morgan must have looked like when she was in college. Cindy was fuller-figured, not yet the River Oaks matron who lives on grapefruit juice diets and weeks at the spa and daily sessions with a personal trainer. He wondered if Wes had realized Cindy would look like Anne Morgan one day, or if he had cared. He remembered Phil then, in his terry cloth cabana set, handsome, hair razor cut, the perfect host, the perfect rich oil man, giving Don the keys to his Jag and asking him to go over to the country club and pick up a box of cigars the manager had waiting; the joy of driving that Jag. After Phil and Anne Morgan went in, the party went on and on until Anne Morgan finally sent the houseboy down to tell them to shut it down. Then Wes and Don retired to the guesthouse and waited for Cindy and Anna Kaye to sneak out of the house.

He wondered if Anne Morgan sneaked out of her parents' house to meet Phil. She had watched them with an unforgiving eye, sizing up the

All-American as marital material. Was she once full of fun, like Cindy? He remembered the knowing look Phil gave the four of them the next morning.

It had grown quiet in the dining room. All the other guests had gone to bed. They ate in silence. Finally Phil spoke up. "You probably are wondering what Millie and I are doing here."

Not wondering at all, Phil, although I would have expected a bimbo instead of this nice lady.

"Millie is the land manager for Patson Energy Properties. PatProp, we call it."

"PatProp? I like it," Don said. "That must be interesting work, Millie."

Millie looked at Phil nervously. "The family has a lot of mineral interests in the Panhandle and PatProp manages them."

"It's all right, Millie. These are old friends. We're getting ready to make a big shale play in Velda County. A big play."

"Interesting," Don said. "My firm represents a lot of the ranchers. We'll probably be running into each other."

"Your firm? What firm?"

"My law firm. I practice law in Velda. The Rosen and Cuinn law firm."

"I'll be damned. Well, at least you aren't down in Austin going to jail with my ex son-in-law, your best bud."

"No, I'm not."

Hank took another whiskey from the waitress and held it up to the light." You and Wesley Bird aren't tight anymore?"

Don shook his head.

"So what happened? You two were joined at the hip."

Don frowned and sighed. "He stole money from my family."

"I'll be damned. Stole from them? How'd you let that happen?"

"Nobody asked me. Wesley charmed them, I suppose."

"He has charm, that's for sure. But I think Wesley may have got hit in the head on the football field a few too many times. Can you believe, he tried to get me to help him with that Austin land deal—the one that he's in such trouble about? He's in the family, married to Cindy, and here he comes, asking me to convince Anne Morgan to invest in his deal. He ought of known Anne Morgan makes all those decisions and doesn't take advice from me. He kept saying that Governor Braeswood was his silent partner. All I could think was, for every silent partner there's a fall guy. That was Wesley. He was too full of himself to see it coming. But he is charming."

He got up, drained his glass, and stretched. "Millie, honey, would you get somebody to run you down to the villa, get that bottle of brandy and a box of Cubans, and bring them up here. We'll be out back, looking at the stars."

She stood up and looked at the others questioningly.

"Don't worry, Millie," Anna Kaye said, "we'll keep Phil company. He'll be all right."

Phil got up. "I'll meet you outside in a minute." He made a detour to the men's room, walking steadily now, and then rejoined them on the patio with another whiskey. "You like cigars, Donnie Ray?"

Anna Kaye broke in. "We both do, Phil. I especially like Cuban cigars and some good brandy."

He put his arm around her shoulder. "You're my kind of girl, sweetheart. Give an old man a hand."

Anna Kaye helped him into a chaise lounge and he pulled her down and gave her a long kiss. "Yes, you're a lucky man," he said to Don. He put his booted feet up and sighed contentedly. "This is the life—clear skies, good friends, good whiskey, a Cuban coming, the love of a good woman."

"Millie seems nice," Anna Kaye said. She snuggled against Don on the outdoor sofa opposite Phil. The night air was cooling fast.

"I think Anne Morgan resents her more than she did the models or the hookers."

"Phil—" Don said, "you don't need to talk about all that."

"Aw, Donnie, everybody knows I've always screwed around. Funny thing, there I was, a petroleum engineer with my own company, small, but growing, a good group of investors, some good leases in inventory. Then along comes this beautiful young woman who happens to be the richest woman in Texas, maybe the country, and takes a liking to me." He looked at the sky. "Shooting star," he said, pointing up. He paused for a long minute, then said, "Of course I fell in love with her. When we first married, she even put family money in a couple of PatProp deals. Then she decided it would be good to have all the family oil dealings in one place. She put all the Morgan oil properties in PatProp. She seemed happy how the company was growing. I don't know, but after a while, everything seemed to change. She sent in her accountants, making me justify anything I wanted to do. It didn't take long for me to figure out that my job wasn't to build anything on my own. I'm around to look after the family oil interests."

"That's important too, I'd think," Don said.

Phil grunted. "Hell, I don't even own my own company anymore. The Morgan Family Trust owns it, just like the Morgan family owns me."

Millie appeared with a bottle of brandy and a box of cigars. She poured them each a glass of brandy and passed around the cigar box and a cigar cutter. Anna Kaye, Don, and Phil wet their cigars in the brandy. Millie took his lighter from Phil and held the flame, which flickered in the cool evening breeze, for each of them. They sat quietly, smoking. The cigar, flavored by the brandy, was dark and sweet tasting. No one spoke.

After a bit, Millie stood up, brushed her dress and said, "Come on, Phil. Let's go in."

Phil smiled at her. "You go on, Millie. I want to visit some more with Donnie. A legal question."

Anna Kaye put down her cigar, and drained her brandy glass. "I'll go in too." She kissed Phil on the cheek. "Take care of yourself, Phil," she said. She ruffled Don's hair and said, "Don't stay up all night."

"Hmm," Don said.

They sat in the dim candlelight. Finally, Don said, "Legal question? You know, Phil, I don't like to give legal advice when I'm half-tight."

"Most of the legal advice I ever got must have come from drunk lawyers."

"It was that bad, huh?"

"Nobody in Houston wants to cross Anne Morgan. So, what they usually tell me is, 'Phil, you're a lucky man. Why should you be killing yourself when you've already got it made? You made it when you married

Anne Morgan. So, just sign whatever her people put in front of you and enjoy yourself. Go marlin fishing, or pheasant shooting, or whatever you want to do. Show up for her charity balls, give her a kid or two, sleep with her when she wants to, otherwise stay out of her way. Just don't embarrass her socially or mess up anything in the family business. It's that simple.'"

"But it isn't that simple?"

"No." He reached in his pocket and took out a flash drive. He handed the little storage device to Don. "I need some legal work. It's a good thing I ran into you, because I don't have to worry about you talking to Anne Morgan. That's right, isn't it?"

Don nodded, the legal equivalent of crossing his fingers.

"On there is a copy of a deed to partial interests in sixty-four leases PatProp owns in Velda County with old wells on them. They're good shale prospects."

"With horizontal drilling and massive fracking?"

"Well, of course. What I'm getting at is, Anne Morgan's Houston lawyers drew it up, and I signed it. I need you to draw me up a second deed exactly like that one, but with a different company getting the lease interests. Draw it up so I can sign it. Then I want you to keep it until I tell you to put it on record. You understand?" He pulled a piece of paper out of his shirt pocket and handed it to Don. "The deed is to go to that company."

"FAL, a Bermuda corporation?"

"Free at last!" he answered with a laugh.

"Why don't you get the Houston lawyers to do it?"

"Because I don't want to, Goddamn it!"

Don sat silently, waiting for Phil to calm himself. In a minute, Phil said, "Sorry. This is hard. I'm the president of PatProp. I can do this. It's just that I don't want Anne Morgan to know." He smiled. "At least not while I'm alive."

Don waited.

"Okay, okay," Phil finally said. "Millie owns FAL."

"Millie? You're giving leases to Millie?"

"Not leases. Small interests in leases. A sixty-fourth interest in sixty-four leases. Carried working interests. That means…"

"I know what a carried working interest is. Millie doesn't pay any drilling costs but gets revenues after the wells pay out."

"Right. A sixty-fourth interest in sixty-four wells. That comes out to about a full well."

"You're doing this without your board knowing about it?"

"I do things all the God damned time without my board knowing about it." He shifted nervously in his chair and dropped his cigar butt in the brandy glass. "All right. Here's the deal. Anne Morgan has been after me to fire Millie. It was all I could do to get her to let me transfer Millie up here. By the way, Millie's damn fine at what she does."

She must be, Don thought.

As if he could read Don's mind, or maybe Don let himself smile a little before he caught himself, Phil said, "No, no. Not that. She's done the land work for the Morgan family since before Anne Morgan's Daddy died. She's an expert at it."

Phil leaned forward and lowered his voice. "As you can see, Millie and I have become close. Very close. She's the one I turn to when things with Anne Morgan get bad. She understands me. In a lot of ways, we're like an old married couple. Sometimes I think she's my wife and Anne Morgan is the one I've got on the side." He sighed. "I wish she was my wife. But Millie's embarrassing to Anne Morgan. As long as I ran around with some Vegas show girl or New York model, she could just shake her head and say, 'Men.' Those women aren't competition; they're just what rich men do when they get the itch. And," he said with a rueful smile, "it gives her an excuse to sleep with her personal trainer."

"Really? Her trainer?"

"Oh shit, yes. They run marathons. But if Anne Morgan's friends find out about me and Millie, the talk around town will be, 'Can you imagine Phil leaving Anne Morgan for Millie Stein? What in the world is going on?"

"Very déclassé."

"Is that what you call it?"

Don looked at the flash drive. The flickering candlelight reflected off its plastic case. "You love Millie, so you're giving her Morgan property?"

Phil laughed. "I'm not giving her anything. I'm giving it to us, to her and me. FAL is our annuity, in case Anne Morgan isn't satisfied with me moving Millie up here."

"Phil, she'll find out, won't she? Some day?"

"So?"

"When she does, she'll turn those lawyers loose on you and Millie. Fraud. Corporate malfeasance. Bad stuff."

Phil laughed, his first genuine laugh since sunset. "I don't think so."

"No? Why not?"

"The deed on that flash drive?" He motioned at the small storage device. "It's also to a Bermuda corporation, name of Barbary Coast."

"Who owns that?"

"I asked the same question when the lawyer from Bost & Bost brought it over for me to sign. He was a young guy and he probably thought I knew what was going on. When I asked what it was, he said, 'This is part of the property deal in Austin. Compensation for advisory work. Barbary Coast is the guy's offshore company.'"

"What guy?"

"Anne Morgan's big buddy in Austin. Dockery Ashley."

"Judge Ashley? Are we talking about the Hieronymus Parcel? Is Anne Morgan buying it?"

"It sure looks like it, doesn't it? You can bet that Anne Morgan wouldn't want it on Channel Two that she gave Ashley an oil well, free of charge, at the same time he's deciding if she's the successful bidder."

He stood up and stretched. "Of course, I could end up the patsy, just like Wesley has. But Anne Morgan wouldn't want that. It would represent a considerable failure on her part. However, whatever happens, Millie and I will have our little nest egg to start over with."

Don handed the flash drive back to Phil. "Phil, I can't help you steal from the company."

"You can't, huh? Well, Millie won't do it either. I hate people with principles. Do you know another lawyer maybe without so many principles?"

"I'm sorry, Phil. I don't. But I do own some office space I'd like to talk to you about. It comes with a penthouse apartment and a great view of downtown Velda."

The next morning, he left Anna Kaye sleeping soundly, and went into the kitchen and made coffee. While it was brewing, he called Austin.

A sleepy voice answered. "This is Charlton Denning, and it's early, and I'm in bed, so this had better be important."

"It's Don Cuinn, Charlton, and it is important."

"Just a minute," Charlton said. "Graff, bring me some juice, please." There was muffled conversation on the other end of the phone. Finally, Charlton returned to the line. "He's a bundle of joy early in the morning."

"How is life in Austin?"

"Well, the work is fun. I like Dave Lewis, even if he is married to a Lehrer and you never forget it."

"How about Graff? Is he settling in?"

Charlton lowered his voice. "Let me shut the door." When he returned, he said, "It'll be all right, I think. We found a nice duplex in the Hyde Park area. Do you know it?"

"North of the University."

"Yes, convenient to an organic grocery, walking distance to the campus. Lots of things going on. He's grieving about his garden and his friends in Velda. But that's not why you called at this ungodly hour."

"No. I have some information for you, on the Hieronymus Parcel sale."

"I could use some." Don heard the door open. "Graff, is there any tea? And a butter cookie." Don heard the phone drop, but finally Charlton said, "I'm back. I was going to say, I went through all the material in the professor's file. So far, all it looks like is a typical developer dispute with the neighbors who don't want their green neighborhood urbanized. I doubt if there's a story there."

"You may think different when you hear what I found out. Do you know who the Morgan family is?"

"The oil people?"

"Yes. Well, I think that Anne Morgan Patson made a gift of some valuable oil interests to a Bermuda corporation called Barbary Coast, Inc."

"So?"

"So, my source tells me that the owner of Barbary Coast is Judge Dockery Ashley."

"Judge Ashley? The president of the H.H. Company?"

"The very same. Now I wonder why Anne Morgan would do that? Do you think it might be related to the rumor that she's going to bid on the Hieroymus Parcel?"

"Let me make some notes." Don heard him turn on his computer. "Can we prove that Judge Ashley owns Barbary Coast?"

"I can't. I'm hoping you can. You're the ace investigative reporter."

"Did you say it was a Bermuda company?"

"That's what my source told me."

"You're not going to tell me who that is, are you?"

"No. My source had too much to drink and talked too much. We'll have to run this down ourselves."

Charlton chewed loudly. "In San Diego a county official tried to hide money in Bermuda. There's an investigator we used down there. He was able to get me the owners' names. He even got access to the company records."

"Judge Ashley is clever. It may take some digging."

"Sometimes, people think they're so smart they forget to be clever. This is great, Don. I'll take it to Lewis and see if he'll pay for the investigator."

Don blew a kiss to the sleepy eyed Anna Kaye, who stood naked in the doorway. "Got to go, Charlton. Just thinking, but do you reckon Lewis would spring for you to go down to Bermuda and meet this investigator in person? And you would probably need someone along to help."

"Graff loves the water."

"And yet he misses Velda."

⊰⊰⊰⊰⊰

Later that morning, Don's phone rang.

"For God's sake, Donnie, let it ring."

He had already taken three calls from the office that morning.

He disentangled himself from Anna Kaye and picked up his cell. "It's my mother," he said.

Anna Kaye pulled the sheet over her breasts. "I told you she hates me," she said.

"Good morning, Mama," Don said. He grinned at the naked girl and pulled the sheet down. "Anna Kaye sends her love."

His mother cried, "Oh, Donnie Ray, something awful has happened!"

He sat up. "What's wrong, Mama? What is it."

"It's Papa," she said. "He's…he's…"

"Papa?" His heart dropped. "What about Papa? What's happened to him?"

"Oh, Donnie Ray, Lena will rise out of her grave and strike me down. I promised her I would always look after Papa, and now…. Oh, Donnie Ray, What are we going to do?"

"Mama, You have to calm down and tell me exactly what's wrong."

"Papa…. You'll never believe this…but…"

"Just tell me, Mama. Is Papa sick?"

"It's much worse than that."

"You don't mean that Papa has died?"

"Oh, Donnie Ray, Papa's not dead. No. Papa has eloped!"

"What do you mean, he's eloped?"

"Papa and that woman."

"What woman?"

"That woman. The one who's been after him."

You mean Minerva Wisconsin?"

"Yes. Papa and Minerva Wisconsin have eloped. They are in France on their honeymoon. Donnie Ray Cuinn, you are a lawyer. You have to get that marriage annulled."

CHAPTER SEVENTEEN

D on needed time in the office after Anna Kaye returned to Austin. Faye kept reminding him that he needed to take care of business. "This law firm's cash flow problem will not solve itself." However, every time he tried to deal with a client's problem, he had another call from Austin. Dorrie Louise's three daughters, Don's half-sisters, had flocked to Austin. Besides comforting their mother, they took turns calling Don, demanding that he do something. No one had ever seen Dorrie Louise so upset.

For Don, it was a complete change of temperament in her. His mother had always been a cheerful person, even in the darkest of times. Now she kept sobbing, "I let Lena down. I could have stopped him."

"There's nothing I can do," Don explained again and again. "I can't reach Papa. He's in France and he doesn't answer his phone. He's a grown man, a perfectly competent man. Maybe by the time they get back they'll have had enough of each other and they can get a quickie divorce."

"She's already killed three husbands, Donnie Ray. Papa is next, I know it."

After the latest call from Austin, Don received a note from France. It was written in pen and ink in the fine cursive handwriting that Don knew well.

My Boy,
You will have heard by now that Minerva and I have married. She is an extraordinary woman and was kind enough to suggest we mark our new relationship by visiting my childhood home in the

Perigord. We are at an auberge near Bergerac. I am not sure when we will return, but when we do, I will need you to assist me in adjusting my living arrangements at Cartwright House and some other business matters about which I will tell you then.

I hope that with time that your mother will forgive me, and Minerva

Your devoted Papa,

Ralph Rothschild

He re-folded the letter and put it in his desk drawer. He heard footsteps, looked up and saw Phil Patson in the doorway.

"Got a minute, Donnie?" he asked.

"Sure, Phil. Have a seat."

Phil and Millie had come to look at office space, as well as the penthouse. When Don told Faye, she was surprised. "What would you do? Move out of the penthouse? I thought you liked it."

"I like money better. The bank will like it too."

"I imagine they will. Well, we can find you a nice apartment, over on the Gulch."

"No need to do that, Faye. I think I'll move back to the store."

"In Antelope City? Whatever for?"

"Wiley and his new bride will be moving to New Warsaw. He's been after me to move downtown. He deserves it, especially with the good work he's done on the Jamail case. And besides, I like that old store."

Faye sniffed and expressed her disapproval, but she met Phil and Millie and gave them a tour of the building.

Phil sat down and propped his ostrich boots on the coffee table. "Do you like being in the real estate business?"

"Real estate business? You mean this building? I had to buy out Jake Rosen to get the law practice. No. I do not enjoy it. Thank God for Faye."

"Yeah, she seems to know what she's doing. She's damn proud of that apartment on the top floor."

Don propped his own boots, bought on sale at Academy ten years earlier, up on his desk. "We call that the penthouse."

"I tell you what, Lawyer Cuinn. I'll buy this dump, take it off your hands."

Don sat up. This was the best news he'd had in a year. "Hmm. It's a cash cow."

Phil laughed. "That's bullshit. The Swiss are moving out. The place'll be empty by the end of the year."

"Faye has prospects."

"I'm the best prospect she's got, and I'm not renting. I'm buying. How much?"

Don opened his file drawer and pulled out a folder. "Here's what I owe the bank. I need that taken care of, plus something for my time and trouble."

Phil looked at the figures. "I'll pay off the bank. Zero for your time and trouble."

God, I want to sell this place. "I need a ten year lease on the space for my law firm and some room to expand," *How unlikely is that?* "I'll pay half what the Swiss are paying. Do that and you've got a deal."

Phil smiled. "Shake on it." He extended his calloused hand and shook Don's hand. "Your new landlord will be FAL."

"A Bermuda corporation?"

"That's the one. There's more than one way—"

"… to skin a cat?"

"Right. FAL charges PatProp a reasonable, if expensive rent. Millie gets a nice place to live, away from Houston where I can visit from time to time. I'll fill this place up with oil business contractors that owe me a favor so FAL will make a successful business out of your failure. All legal and proper."

❰❰❰❰❰

Don was in Houston on Jamail Jobey's discrimination claim against GFC when he got word that Papa and Minerva had returned to Austin. He was in the Bost & Bost conference room with Jamail, waiting for Gerhard Sturgeon, GFC's chairman, to appear for his deposition. He glanced over the list of questions that Wiley and Faye had supplied. He was looking forward to the morning, that is, if Sturgeon showed up.

Max Kilgore came into the room with smiles and handshakes for Don and Jobie. "Don, can we talk?"

Don followed Kilgore into an empty office. Two Bost lawyers were waiting, along with a man in a black suit and black tie who looked up at him dourly. "Don, this is Herman Goerbane."

The man nodded.

"Hi." Don looked at Kilgore and raised his eyebrows.

"The president of GFC America."

"I wax expecting Mr. Sturgeon."

"Don, is there a number for which you would settle this matter?" Kilgore asked.

"There is always a number, Max," he said. "What's the offer?" *Sturgeon really doesn't want to go on record about GFC's race discrimination, does he?*

Don took the company's offer back to Jobey. Kilgore scurried back and forth between Don and Goerbane, and they finally agreed on two million dollars as the cost to GFC for terminating their only black executive in North America and Europe.

Don called Faye in Velda and asked her to find Wiley on his honeymoon and give him the good news. Then he and Kilgore began the tortuous process of hashing out the settlement agreement, line by line.

"Things are looking up," Faye said when he told her the settlement was signed. "The office building sale has closed. We'll have a good fee on the Jobey case. Congratulations, Mr. Cuinn. Take some time off. Relax."

"I wish I could. There's a problem or two in Austin that require my skills."

"I told you that Nordstrom woman was trouble, Mr. Cuinn."

Don took a commuter flight from Houston Hobby airport to Austin, arrived on time and strolled through the airy Austin airport in no hurry to face his relatives. He pulled his carry-on, with his old briefcase strapped on top, down the concourse, through the throngs of travelers trying to get to their gates. He needed to compose his thoughts for his first meeting with Papa. He would do that while he waited for Thelman and the bumblebee cab and during the long ride to town. He looked forward to seeing the old hippie. He considered a stop at the Salt Lick for a sliced beef sandwich, or a few minutes at Earl Campbell's place for a beer, but he did not want to keep Thelman waiting, so he decided against it.

A wiry guitarist and a skinny washed-out blond in scruffy jeans were performing at the little stage next to the escalator. *Not bad*, he thought, then went down the escalator, trying to recall where the taxi stand was located. To his surprise, a man in a black suit and a chauffeur's cap stood by the exit holding a sign with his name on it. Don approached him. "Are you waiting for me?" he asked. "I'm Don Cuinn."

"I am Thompson, sir. Your car is outside. Here, let me help you with that." He reached for Don's carry-on.

"It's okay, I have it. Did you say my car?"

"Yes, sir. The Wisconsin, uh, I mean the Rothschild car. It's just outside."

Minerva Wisconsin may not be as rich as Anne Morgan Patson, but she does have style. "Just show me the way, Thompson," Don said.

The black Mercedes S-600 was at the curb. The purple cab with the bumblebee on top was parked directly behind the Mercedes and Thelman was leaning against the old cab's front fender, violating both the no parking and no smoking ordinances. "Just a minute," Don said to Thompson. "I need to take care of something."

"Hello, Thelman," Don said. "Hey, listen, I'm sorry, but somebody sent that car for me. How much do I owe you?"

Thelman eyed him suspiciously. "You called me, you owe me the full fare."

"Come on, Thelman. There's probably another adventuresome soul who'll ride with you." He took out his wallet. "How about twenty dollars, for your trouble?"

"The first time you came down here, you got off a private plane. This time you're getting in a stretch Mercedes. You're a member of the one per cent. Give me my sixty bucks or I call the cops."

Don dropped a twenty-dollar bill on the purple cab's hood. "Call 'em, Thelman."

Thelman scooped up the twenty, thought a minute, then yelled at Don. "Remember the poor Tonkawas!"

Thompson sighed with relief when Don made it back to the Mercedes. "Shall I call the authorities, Mr. Cuinn? That man shouldn't be allowed to drive a taxi."

"No, no," Don said. "Thelman's okay. Actually he's right." He took a fifty out of his wallet "Here, give him this."

Thompson waved the bill at Thelman but the old hippie drove off. He shouted out the window, as he gave Don the finger, "Keep your fucking money!"

"Sorry, sir," Thompson said. He opened the door of the Mercedes.

In the roomy back cabin, shielding his eyes from the sun, sat Papa. He reached out to Don and they hugged. "Get in, please. Oh, Don, I am so glad to see you." He was dressed in a charcoal gray pinstripe suit with vest and silk tie, none of which Don had ever seen before. "Would you like something to drink? Thompson, we have drinks, do we not?"

"Anything you would like, Professor."

Papa raised his bushy eyebrows in amusement. Don noticed they were less bushy, in fact they were trimmed, and his hair had been cut by someone other than Dorrie Louise. "When in Rome," Papa said with a smile.

"Rome's pretty nice, Papa," he said. "Nothing for me, thanks." He took the old man's hand, "Married life agrees with you."

"Do you think so? I believe so. However, it does not agree with your mother."

"I guess not." He buckled his seat belt as Thompson accelerated smoothly through the airport traffic. Cool air flooded the cabin and the darkly tinted windows gave the outside world a different dimension. "She insisted I come down here and make you divorce your new wife."

"Oh, dear," Papa said. He smiled at Don. "Your mother is very protective of me. It seems that Lena left me in her care."

I wonder what Lena would have said about Papa's new station in life. I suspect she'd light a Camel and say, "I'm not surprised. Nothing is too good for Papa, and that includes a new, rich wife."

"How in the world did all this happen, Papa?"

The old man shot his cuffs and examined his monogramed cuff links. "I never felt the need for clothes, you know, Don? My tweed jacket and a dark suit for weddings and funerals were quite enough. And yet," he held his hand up so that Don could see the cufflink, "things like this do have a certain beauty."

"A gift from Minerva?"

"Yes, of course. Seville Row. Being her consort requires standards of attire…. apparently."

Thompson pulled the Mercedes smartly onto the highway and accelerated. The silent engine moved them with the comfort of speed under grace.

"You didn't marry her for money, or for clothes."

Papa smiled. He took off his stylish new glasses and cleaned them with the striped silk tie. "Didn't I?" He put the glasses back on his Roman nose. "There are other perquisites, of course."

Thompson had navigated the interchange at I-35 and was heading south, toward San Antonio, not north, to downtown Austin. *Maybe I'm disoriented*, Don thought.

"What perquisites, Papa?" he asked.

"Well, Minerva has friends in the publishing world, and a volume of my verse is going to be released next year."

"That's good."

"Perhaps. I've gone so long without critical eyes on my work." He sighed. "She says there will be a review in the *Times Book Review* and a journal or two."

"She gets around."

"She does. This evening, for example, I'm giving a reading before a gathering of Austin's intellectual elite at the Hilby House. You are invited, of course. There will be drinks. The audience will need them."

"I'd love to hear you read, Papa, but this sounds like Minerva's deal." The car slowed and exited the interstate. "Where are we going?"

"There's something I want you to see." They exited the Interstate, crossed over it and in a few minutes, stopped. "Put down your window."

Don pushed the window control and the bright sun filled the back seat of the car. In front of them was a giant billboard advertising *Austin Next*. Plastered across the billboard were the words: "A Minerva Properties Development." Beyond the sign, the road had been paved, the bridge was open, and construction crews were at work. "Minerva Properties?"

"Minerva is also well acquainted in the world of finance and banking."

"How did she manage it?"

"Her company is an active developer. You know the properties of her first husband, north of the city? She became aware of this property's problems and decided she could profit by buying the banks' positions."

"Where does that leave the investors?"

Papa smiled. "That is the best part, Don. Minerva has agreed to keep the investors whole. They have the option of continuing their investment or, if they so choose, Minerva will refund their money."

"Jesus, Papa, she must have really wanted to marry you."

"Who wouldn't, Don?"

Don laughed.

"It did not hurt, of course, that she expects to make a substantial return on her investment."

"I think I'll have that drink after all."

Thompson drove them slowly into the rejuvenated development. "Stop here, please, Thompson," Papa said. He opened the door and climbed out, declining Thompson's offer of help. Don joined him. "Let's walk down here."

Papa led the way onto the famous Bridge To Nowhere. He pointed to a fenced area beneath them. "That is the Tonkawa Burial Ground."

Don climbed onto the guardrail and looked down at the archeological site. Stonemasons were busily laying rock walls around the excavation. New oaks and shrubs had been planted nearby and a small bubbling creek ran down an incline by the site. A small wooden gazebo overlooking the site was under construction. "It's beautiful, Papa."

"Yes, I think so." He wiped a tear from his eye. "Minerva has also arranged for a memorial near the Jewish area of the Montingac cemetery. In France."

"Where you lived before your father sent you and your mother to Cuba?"

"Yes. There is a connection, the Tonkawas and the French Jews. Both persecuted, both forced to leave their homeland. I am writing a poem."

"You should." He took Papa's hand. "I'm glad you are writing."

"It's a great comfort to feel that urge to create again. It's the first time I have since Lena's death." He turned back to the car. "Your mother has a large investment in *Austin Next*. I hope she will leave it with Minerva, but I will not be surprised if she decides not to. I will leave my own money, of course, but Dorrie Louise's dislike of Minerva may be clouding her judgment. What do you think?"

"It's entirely up to her, Papa." He leaned over and whispered to Papa. "What Minerva is doing is wonderful, but that's why you married her, isn't it? You married her to get your friends' their money back."

Papa smiled. "Oh, it's not too great a sacrifice. I have the company of a beautiful, if opinionated, woman."

"You seem to attract that kind. First Lena, then Mama, now Minerva."

Papa smiled. "I suppose that is true. In any case, I can write, and I can devote myself to saving the Hieronymus Parcel."

"Minerva won't buy it?"

"Sadly, no. Apparently there's a limit to my charms." They walked slowly back to the car. Papa was breathing heavier from the exertion. "How is your reporter friend progressing with his investigation?"

Don opened the door and helped Papa into the cool car and the smell of expensive leather. "Actually, if you can drop me off at the magazine office, I'll find out.

Thompson nodded when Don gave him the address.

Papa settled back into the seat. "Will you be staying with Miss Nordstrom?"

"I'm not sure, Papa. I'll call her," Don said.

"I like her. I think she is good for you."

Don buckled his seat belt and smiled at the old man. "I like her too, Papa. But Mama likes her about as much as she likes Minerva."

"How symmetrical."

CHAPTER EIGHTEEN

E ven Don, who usually took no notice of such things, could tell that from the time of his last visit, the closefisted new owners of This Texas had succeeded in eradicating every last trace of the esthetics and personal taste of the magazine's founder, Drayton Philby.". The desk and chairs in the reception room could have been rescued from a condemned Motel 6. No more Oriental rugs or black slate tables.

Don announced himself to the receptionist, who greeted him with a suspicious eye. "I'll see if Mr. Denning is in," she said.

Don sat on an uncomfortable chair and thumbed through a copy of last month's issue of *This Texas*. In a *pox on both your houses* editorial, the magazine announced its departure from the liberal-leaning politics of the prior publisher. "Our only creed is the truth and our only bias will be against hypocrisy, greed, and pretension." *So far so good,* Don thought. *Now do that and sell ads.*

"Not a bad start, do you think, Donnie?"

He looked up from the magazine at the sound of the familiar voice. It was Anna Kaye. He stood and they hugged. She was dressed in a conservative dark suit and tailored blouse. Seeing her fully clothed only reminded him how beautiful she was naked.

"Surprised to see me, sweetie? I got your message. I meant to call you back, but, I've been so busy, you know."

"Me too, Anna Kaye."

She handed him a newspaper. The first page of the Metro section had an item that Wesley Bird had been charged by the federal government with securities fraud.

"I almost feel for him," Don said. "Not even first page news. What next?"

"June Fennel, late of the DA's office, thinks they're trying to get Wesley to roll and implicate Braeswood."

"June resigned?"

"Yes, she did.

"Will Wesley turn on Braeswood?"

"Who knows? I haven't talked to him since the sentencing. I've given up my consulting business."

"What the hell?" he managed.

"I work here now. That's a surprise, I'll bet."

"Work here? Doing what?"

"I'm the Director of Public Affairs."

"What's that mean?"

The receptionist interrupted them. "Mr. Denning is out all afternoon."

"I'll have Charlton call you, Donnie," Anna Kaye said. "I heard him say that he and his partner had to go shopping for new curtains."

"Ask him to call right away. Papa is ready to rally his troops."

"I heard about the Professor and Minerva Wisconsin," Anna Kaye said. "That was a surprise, I'll bet. Their marriage is big news. At least in Austin."

"And as we know, that's the world."

She smiled. "Well, it isn't Velda, I admit." She looked at her watch. "Do you want to get a bite? I need to talk to you."

"Sure. As long as it's barbecue."

"Curtis' or Pruitt's?" she asked.

"You need to ask? Curtis'. Always."

"You're old Austin all the way, aren't you? I'll leave word for Charlton to join us if he gets back in time."

On their way to Curtis', Don told her about Papa and Minerva. He exaggerated the stories a little bit, just to hear her throaty laugh. He leaned against the door of the yellow Fiat and admired her as she maneuvered down Lake Austin Boulevard through the Lamar intersection traffic, happily cutting off delivery trucks and gunning to beat the lumbering Capitol Metro bus to the next intersection. The power plant and its new condo tower rose in the east. "Want to go see the power plant?" he asked.

"No, thank you," she said. "I don't work for them anymore."

"We could still visit."

She glanced at him. "We had fun, didn't we?"

Had?

Anna Kaye pulled sharply into the gravel parking lot in front of the Faithful Matl BBQ, also known as Curtis'. She found half a parking spot between a 1995 Chevy pickup with a dented tailgate and a shiny new Caddy Escalade. Don squirmed out, brushing against the old truck, careful with the door. Anna Kaye on the other hand, threw her door wide open. Don heard it hit the Cadillac's door and saw a smear of yellow paint on it. Anna Kaye led the way past the ten foot stack of post oak and into, by its own account, the only authentic keeper of the flame of the original Matl BBQ. The coals from the piles of post oak that were burned, every day, day in and day out at Matl's had never gone cold, in the hundred years the place had been open. Willie Matl, the founder, had two sons, Curtis and Pruitt, who hated each other, and after their father's death, went their separate ways and opened their own restaurants a few blocks apart, each claiming to be Willie's rightful successor.

The traditionalists preferred Curtis', certain that the brisket at Pruitt's could never measure up to Curtis'. Newcomers, especially Californians, preferred Pruitt's. They said that even if the brisket was a tiny bit less flavorful, he made much better sausage. They also liked the upscale surroundings and the waitresses in jeans and polo shirts. It was good to get a knife and fork, and a real napkin. Those things, plus the weekend buffet with cheese grits and made-to-order omelets, made Pruitt's the more fashionable place to go. Also, it didn't flood.

There was a rickety deck in back of Curtis' overlooking the creek, which usually had water in it, along with brush and trash. On rare, but distressingly regular occasions, the creek flooded, sending water through the back door, out the front door through the parking lot, and into the street.

By the time Don and Anna Kaye got to the head of the line, they had their orders carefully in mind. They knew not to converse with Curtis. He had refused to serve customers for far less. "Go on up the street," he told one loquacious tourist. Curtis weighed three hundred pounds, much of it in his beefy forearms, muscled and bronzed from years of tending the smoky grill. He waited silently for them to recite their order.

"Chicken. One quarter," Anna Kaye said.

"Half pound of brisket, three links," Don said.

Curtis nodded, sliced the brisket, cut the sausage links, quartered a chicken with a single stroke of his long knife, wrapped the food in butcher paper and marked the amounts. By the time they reached the cash register, grease had soaked through the butcher paper. Curtis' wife, a two hundred pound version of her husband, tended the cash register. She regarded them balefully, as if doubting they could afford the twenty-dollar tab. She examined Don's fifty-dollar bill under an infrared light, marked it with a pen, and gave him his change. *That was Thelman's fifty,* he thought with a pang of conscience that he suppressed when he smelled the brisket. They took pickles and onions from the sparse condiment tray and sat at one of the communal tables. They had the table to themselves.

"Do you think Curtis will ever start serving sides?" Don asked. He wrapped a piece of white bread around a thick piece of brisket. "Some slaw would be good with this."

"If you want slaw or knives, go to Pruitt's."

Don glanced at Curtis' wife, who was listening to them.

"Hush, now," he said. "Big pitchers have little ears."

Anna Kaye laughed. "I'm not afraid of her."

"You should be."

They ate quietly. Don did not understand why Panhandle barbecue joints couldn't match Austin brisket, but it was no contest. He finished the brisket and speared a sausage link. "Do you like working for *This Texas?*"

She wiped a bit of sauce from her chin. "I do. Dave is going to make a go of it."

Don folded up the butcher paper and wondered if a few pounds of brisket would survive the trip back to Velda. *Probably not. Pity.* "Are you two still running together?"

"The first thing every morning, before it gets too hot."

"Every morning? Right." He carried their trash to the metal trash can and deposited it carefully. He refilled their ice tea, squeezed a lemon slice over his hands and dried them on a paper napkin. "Where's his wife?"

"She's gone back to Akron. Their marriage is on the rocks."

They sat silently for a minute, finishing their tea. Finally, he looked at her and said, "You're fucking him, aren't you?"

She colored and stared at him. After a long pause, she said, "Why is it any concern of yours who I'm *fucking*, as you so elegantly put it?"

He picked up the empty tea glasses and put them with the other dirty dishes on the metal tray by the bar. He sat back down. She stared defiantly at him. "So tell me," he asked, "did he give you the job after you started screwing, or is that just your way of showing your appreciation?"

"What is this, Donnie? Are you jealous?"

"As I recall, the last time we talked, you said I was the love of your life."

"It's too bad you couldn't reciprocate." She stared at him with pursed lips. "What would you have done if I had agreed to move to Velda?"

"You never would have."

"You counted on that, didn't you?" When he didn't answer, she went on. "Donnie, you have a shrine to Cecilia in your bedroom. I saw it."

"I have a picture of my dead wife."

"No. It's a shrine. I could never compete with her."

"You said you loved me."

"I did. I do. What difference does that make? You left me once for Cecilia, when she was alive. Now, a second time? Who could accept that? Are you going to worship that dead woman the rest of your life?"

The image of Cecilia dead on the side of the road outside Acapulco, her father and brothers and the driver, all gunned down by shooters from a drug cartel, flooded his mind. What was missing was his body. He should have been there with her. "Yes," he answered. "I guess I am."

"Then go live in your crappy little store in your crappy little town and leave me the hell alone." She was crying. He offered her his handkerchief but she shook her head.

"Please stop crying, Anna Kaye," he said. "I don't know why I said that. Maybe I'm afraid of falling in love with you. I have this dream, where I see Cecelia dead, gunned down, on the side of the road, in Mexico. Some nights when I'm with you, I don't have the dream. God, is that it? Am I afraid that if the nightmares stop, I'll lose my last connection to Cecilia?"

He reached for her and she nestled her head into his shoulder, still crying. "You can sleep with whoever you want. I should be happy you've found someone." He muttered half to himself, "I am happy. No, I'm not happy. I'm jealous. Why do you have to go jogging with that rich war hero with two missing legs?"

She raised her head and her sobs turned to laughs. "Donnie Ray Cuinn, do you know how ridiculous that sounds?"

He laughed too. "Jesus. I'm really screwed up."

"We're both screwed up," she said. She took the handkerchief and blew her nose in it, then handed it back to him.

He took it carefully and grinned. "Friends?"

"Always," she said. She wiped her eyes and looked up just as Charlton appeared at the table. "I need to go," she said. "Good luck with the Hieronymus Parcel story," and rushed out the front door.

"What's wrong with Anna Kaye?" Charlton asked.

"A slight misunderstanding. As usual, I was a horse's ass, but I think we got it sorted out. Sit down. Do you want some brisket? It's the best in town."

"I'd like some, but that man over there, the big guy? He told me to get out."

"You tried to talk to him, didn't you?"

He left a confused looking Charlton at the table and returned to the grill. "A pound of brisket, please."

Willie stared at Charlton and then back at Don.

"Cut him some slack, Willie. He's from West Texas. He doesn't know any better."

Willie nodded and knifed one of the briskets on the back of the grill. Don watched him slice the tender beef. He paid and waited with amusement while Charlton attacked the brisket like the survivor of a death camp.

"Please tell me I can come back here," he said between bites.

"You'll be fine as long as you don't try and engage Willie or any of his kin in conversation."

"That'll be hard," Charlton said, "but I'll certainly try."

When the pudgy reporter had savored the last bit of meat, cleaned his hands, folded the trash neatly and deposited it in the trash can, he sat back and smiled. "Would you like to hear about our trip to Bermuda?"

"That's what I've been waiting for. Let's go out back."

The back porch was empty. They sat at a table overlooking the innocent looking little stream that ran below the wood porch. Old deformed oak trees, roots exposed, shaded the porch. "Did you both go to Bermuda?"

"Yes, of course. Dave insisted I take Graff. I never realized what a wonderful man Dave is—so understanding—so generous. And, of course, so good looking."

Oh, for Christ's sake. Don't tell me you're in love with him too.

"Anyhow, we had a marvelous time, and I found out a lot. You remember that we suspected that Dockery Ashley owned the company that got the leases from Anne Morgan Patson?"

"Barbary Coast, Inc. Of course I remember. I told you."

"Don't get uppity. We had a good week in Bermuda, my contact and I down there. We got access to confidential records, and found some very interesting stuff. It's clear that your information is correct."

"How'd you do it?"

"My contact has his ways. For a fee."

"Ah."

"However we don't have proof that Judge agreed to sell the Hieronymus Parcel to Anne Morgan Patson."

"Why else would she give him the leases?"

"Who knows? But without that link, we would have nothing we can print."

"Just suspicion. I get it." Don sighed. "So that's it?"

Charlton chuckled. "No. I saved the best part for last. We kept digging, and we found where Judge transferred half of his stock in Barbary Coast to a second Bermuda company. You will never guess who owns that company."

"Not the other H.H. Company directors?"

"They own half of what Anne Morgan transferred to judge."

"Can we prove that?"

"I think so. Dave thinks so. Of course, the magazine's lawyers are worried whether it will stand up in court. And I haven't told you the clincher." He reached into his shoulder bag and removed a folder. He handed it to Don. "Read this."

Don opened the folder. In it was a memo. It read:

To: Dave Lewis
From: Charlton Denning
Subject: Interview with Dockery Ashley re: Hieronymus Parcel

I called Dockery (Judge) Ashley's office for an interview to discuss "local business issues." He agreed to see me. His office is a large office suite on the top floor of the Crystal Tower office building. It overlooks the state capitol. FYI- Dockery at one time was one of the most powerful unelected persons in the city, if not in the state. His kingmaker days in Texas politics are finished, but he clings to his position as president and director of the H.H. Company, the non-profit company that owns the Hieronymus Parcel and is a large distributor of grants to many local charities. He and his two fellow directors pay themselves handsomely. Administrative expenses take a large part of H.H. Company's revenues each year.

He came around his large desk and shook my hand. Ashley is a large man, with florid complexion and a jowly face. He wears horn-rimmed glasses and shaves his head. He examined me closely, ushered me to a seat on the overstuffed sofa, and settled into a large chair across from the sofa. I took out my recorder and placed it on the coffee table. He looked at the recorder and nodded his agreement.

The following is the transcript of that recording.

"*So, Mr. Denning, you work for the new owners of This Texas?*"

"*Yes, sir. I've worked for the Lehrer publications for many years, in San Diego and in Velda, before coming here.*"

It'll be interesting to see if Kingston Lehrer's, uh, eccentric views find a readership in this part of the state. Is he still campaigning against the post office and the fire department?"

"*At This Texas, our only creed is the truth.*"

"*Like beauty, hmm? In the eye of the beholder. All the same, quite a change for you from the Panhandle. Did you cover the thriving business scene in Velda?*"

"*Mainly the oil and gas industry. For example, the Patson company is very active in Velda County. I'm sure you know the family.*"

"*Everyone knows the Patsons.*"

"*Is it true that the H.H. Company is going to sell the Hieronymus Parcel?*"

"*Where did you hear that?*"

"*Oh, on the street. Rumors, you know.*"

"*I never comment on rumors.*"

"*It is for sale, isn't it?*"

"*I'm not free to say.*"

"*You're the chairman of the H.H. Company. Surely you can tell me if you are planning on selling the company's most significant asset.*"

Note: He sat up in the chair and stared malevolently at me. For the first time, I saw the real Ashley.

"*Where is all this coming from?*"

Note: He seemed to be considering whether to end the interview. Apparently he decided not to.

"*Whether the parcel is ever sold is up to the directors. I only have one vote.*"

"*Let me ask you about a different matter.*"

"*I'd prefer that,*" (note: he said this with a small smile.)

"*Austin is in a boom. Land values are skyrocketing. People are moving in by the thousands."*

"Like you."

"Yes, sir, like me. When the economy is doing so well, and times are so good, why is it that you, personally, are having such a hard time financially?"

"I don't have any idea what you're talking about."

Note: I handed him a sheaf of papers. They included a million dollar home equity loan on the famous mansion in old Austin, recently filed in Travis County; a notice of foreclosure on certain real estate in Brown County, Texas; a credit report showing large overdue balances on four credit cards; and finally, a divorce petition filed by his wife Wilda, alleging that Dockery had mismanaged her inheritance. He examined the papers, sighed, and handed them back to me.

"Many people have temporary financial reverses. A few bad investments. Unfortunate market timing. That sort of thing. Do you think there is some kind of magazine article in all that trash?"

"Returning to the matter of the Hieronymus Parcel. "Why would you ever sell it? So much beautiful land, right in the center of the city. Why not leave it as green space?"

Note: Ashley shook his head. He seemed back on more familiar ground. *"Hiram Heironymus left that property to benefit the poor children of the city. Having a green space on the prosperous side of town isn't of much benefit to them, is it? As directors of the company in charge of those assets, we have to decide whether to monetize the assets, and use that money for good purposes."*

"Many people in the neighborhood would like to see it kept as it is."

"I know, I know. But should we let the wishes of the privileged few override the needs of poor children? It's the same group of leftists who wanted the primate preserve closed and the research stopped."

"Why did the company allow that in the first place?"

"Times were different. The scientists convinced us that lives were in the balance, that they would find vaccines and important information so diseases of all sorts could be cured."

"And did they?"

"In fact, they did. But society concluded that those good things did not justify experimenting on animals. It didn't help when those activists opened the gate and some chimpanzees escaped. The same activists, by the way, who are so opposed to the sale of the Hieronymus Parcel."

"That must have been something, those chimps running loose all over Tarrytown. How many were there?"

"Oh, I don't know. I'm sure it's in your notes there. Two dozen?"

"Quite a job getting them all back. How long did it take?"

"A couple of days. The damn chimps were scared out of their wits, thrown into the company of all those liberals. But we got them back. At the same time, the new NIH report came out, banning grants for most animal research, so we shut the laboratory down. Now, the buildings sit there, of no use to anyone. The parcel is a perfect site for office buildings, condominium towers, retail shops, a new city center, vibrant and prosperous!"

"Some people want the Monkey House turned into an animal shelter and the rest of the land kept as a park, with ball fields and jogging trails."

"How many meals would that buy for the hungry?"

"Let me understand. The only reason to sell this land is to help needy children?"

"Of course. That is, if the directors decide to sell it. Why else?"

"It has nothing to do with the large salaries the directors draw and that the H.H. Company is running low on cash?"

"That's an insulting insinuation."

Note: He waited impatiently while I made some notes. I looked up at him and returned to recording.

"Have you ever heard of a company called Barbary Coast, Inc.?"

"Why do you ask that?"

"Because the Patsons have deeded some valuable oil propertiees to it."

"Why would that possibly interest me?"

Note: I took out a copy of the documents from Bermuda.

"It would interest you, I suppose, because, according to the Barbary Coast company records, you are its sole shareholder. Those leases must come in very handy, considering your financial losses, is that right?"

"This interview is over. Good day!"

"I have one more question. I have a document in which you assign half of your interest in the Patson leases to your two fellow directors. Do they know you're getting paid twice as much as they are to sell the Hieronymus Parcel to Anne Morgan Patson?"

"Leave or I'll have you thrown out on your ass, you fat fag. Git."

"I'll ask the other directors that question, sir."

END OF INTERVIEW

Don hugged the grinning reporter. "Charlton, you're a wonder. He never denied it, did he?"

"No. He fumed and threw me out, but he didn't deny it. Dave believes we have enough to make a hell of a story. A cover story."

"Wonderful. When is the article coming out?"

"It's being set now. Ashley's lawyers have threatened to sue. They say we stole the documents."

"Did you?"

"I certainly didn't."

They got up to leave, making their way through the empty cafe. After they left, Curtis' wife slammed the door behind them and they could hear Curtis shouting at her. She yelled something back, and the daughter chimed in, the roar of their voices, repressed until the last customer left, filled the air. Don turned to Charlton. "You never know. Maybe there's a human interest story there for you."

"Do you think?" Charlton said. "I'd rather have Judge Ashley mad at me than Curtis Matl."

CHAPTER NINETEEN

By the time he returned to Austin to attend Minerva and Papa's party celebrating their marriage and the unexpected solvency of *Austin Next,* Don had promoted Wiley to partner in Rosen & Cuinn, now Cuinn & Franklin, moved Wiley into his old office and himself into Jake's, moved his belongings back to the old Thorpe store in Antelope City, completed the sale of the Hansro Building to Phil Patson, watched Millie Stein set up housekeeping in the penthouse, received and disbursed the Jamail Jobey settlement check and looked over Wiley's handiwork in three probates and four divorces. Everyone in Velda was either dying or divorcing, it seemed. He missed Anna Kaye, but he was solvent, and Faye had taken a recess from criticizing his financial management of the law firm.

Papa and Charlton had each sent him copies of the new issue of *This Texas.* "*Monkey Business at the Monkey House,*" the cover blared. Superimposed over a photograph of the Monkey House was a picture of Judge Ashley and another of Anne Morgan, an oil well linking them.

Charlton had texted him daily with the threatened lawsuits, community reaction, and general uproar caused by his article. No one knew what Judge Ashley might do next. He had been to Akron to complain in person to Kingston Lehrer, but Lehrer laughed in his face. "K.L. hates government in all forms," Charlton told him on the phone. "The only thing he likes better than exposing a politician is making money. Ad sales are through the roof, so here he gets to do both things."

"Ashley's not an elected official," Don reminded him.

"He is as far as the chief is concerned. Needless to say, Dave Lewis is a hero."

Needless to say.

The large crowd gathered slowly at Hiram Hieronymus Hall. The ballroom of Cartwright House was named in honor of the philanthropist, who had donated the land and money for the first buildings at Cartwright House. The main elevator was still under repair, a warning tape over the door, and that delayed things. People in various stages of elderliness, some walking slowly, some behind walkers, some in motorized wheelchairs, and a few upright and looking fit, made their way into the hall. Don had brought a coat, but of course had forgot to bring a tie, and was seriously under-dressed. *You need a keeper*, he thought. He hugged Papa, and Minerva gave him a continental two-cheek kiss. "Don, dear, so good of you to come."

"My pleasure, Minerva," he said. He looked around. "Quite a crowd."

"All our friends," she said. She smiled at him and turned away to greet some latecomers.

"No Mama?" he said to Papa.

"Alas, no. She still has not forgiven me. Even an autographed copy of my new book couldn't entice her." He motioned to the table near the entrance, draped with a gold linen cloth and stacked with copies of *Rothschild's Poetry* for the guests. "Did you get yours?"

"I did, Papa, and I enjoyed it very much." He hugged the old man again and said, "She'll come around, I'm sure."

In fact, he was not sure at all. His mother was a stubborn woman. She had decamped to Brenham, the home of Don's oldest half-sister. She wrote Don that she was "finished with that craziness up there."

The crowd parted to make way for Anna Kaye, sashaying in on the arm of Dave Lewis. She was striking in a low-cut dress slit up the side almost to her hip. Charlton and Graff followed them in matching electric blue tuxedos. Charlton had a newspaper in his hand, which he was waving. "Professor," he called, "this is for you."

Anna Kaye leaned forward for Don to kiss her cheek. She whispered, "Are you angry with me?"

"Are you angry with me?" he answered.

They laughed.

Don looked over Papa's shoulder at the early edition of the next day's paper. The headline read, "H.H. COMPANY DIRECTORS RESIGN: HIERONYMUS PARCEL FUTURE UNKNOWN."

"You won, Papa," Don said.

"I must tell everyone," he said.

Don helped him to the podium and turned on the microphone. Papa cleared his throat. "Thank you all for coming. This is a special celebration, made more special because of this news story, which will appear in tomorrow's newspaper. He read in his melodious baritone voice:

"The H.H. Company announced yesterday that its officers, including the influential advisor to governors, senators and presidents Dockery Ashley, have submitted their resignations and will no longer be involved in the affairs of the company. The non-profit company owns the Hieronymus Parcel. It was once the site of the controversial Primate Preserve.

Local citizens, led by a group of retired educators, professionals and state employees living near the property objected to the use of chimpanzees for research being conducted by the Primate Preserve, which ceased operations on the property after the escape of a large number of chimpanzees into the neighborhood. The chimps were captured, but the Primate Preserve gave up the fight shortly thereafter and moved its research to a location outside the United States.

The conflict with the community then shifted to the future use of the Hieronymus Parcel, with neighborhood groups calling for the property to be devoted to recreation and affordable housing and the company officers insisting they had a duty to sell it to the highest bidder, whether or not commercial developers use the proceeds for charitable purposes.

The latest event, which led the attorney general to call for the officers' resignations, was an article in *This Texas*, alleging that

Ashley and the two other directors had received valuable oil properties from wealthy heiress Anne Morgan Patson's oil company in exchange for their agreement to sell the property to Patson. The attorney general, who has oversight of charitable corporations in Texas, will ask a Travis County court to appoint new directors of the company, who will then decide whether or not to sell the property.

Papa's eyes welled with tears as the crowd broke into cheers and applause. "You did it, my friends!" Papa shouted. "STC did it."

Minerva led Papa through the room. Everyone was laughing and crying and getting tipsy on the champagne that waiters poured with abandon.

Out of the crowd, June Fennel appeared at Don's side. "Great night," she said. They touched their glasses in salute. "To STC, whatever that is." She took a long sip of the champagne. "This is good bubbly.

"1990 Cristal Brut."

"Is that expensive?"

"I would imagine. Nothing's too good for Minerva. What brings you here?"

She motioned to one of the waiters for another glass of champagne. "I've been offered a job, working for your stepmother."

"Minerva? She's not my stepmother. At best, she's my surrogate father's second wife. What do you mean, working for her? Doing what?"

"She's a big real estate developer, Donnie Ray." She reached up and brushed his hair back. "You don't mind if I call you Donnie Ray, do you?"

Her hand was cool on his forehead, which seemed warm all of a sudden. "I prefer Don."

"I prefer Donnie Ray." She looked out at the room. Minerva and Papa were making a grand procession. Laughter and hurrahs followed them. "Minerva Enterprises is a large land developer, and large developers need lawyers."

"You're a prosecutor. What do you know about land development?"

"I know about thieves and crooks and scoundrels."

"Oh. Then I guess you're qualified." He looked at her for the first time. She was good looking in a frank, business-like way. The opposite of Anna Kaye's glamour girl look. *The last thing I need is another Austin girl-friend.* "Speaking of scoundrels, what do you hear about my old buddy?"

"Wesley Bird? I believe he is now in federal custody. They have him locked up, pending another bail hearing."

"They want him to testify against our former governor?"

"Honestly, I don't know," she said. "I do know they use little fish to catch big fish, and Wesley is definitely not a big fish."

"Braeswood better watch out."

"Exactly."

There was a commotion at the other end of the room, by the entrance. People were talking loudly, and he heard a woman shriek.

"What is happening?" a woman asked.

At first, Don thought someone had fallen, or maybe two wheelchairs were involved in a head-on collision, but then he saw the men.

Five men, dressed in camouflage with bandanas covering their faces, were waving handguns. They were trying to herd the room full of residents away from the entrance and back to the other end of the room.

"Minerva," a man shouted. "Is this some kind of joke? If it is, it isn't funny."

Don started toward the disturbance but felt the restraining hand of Dave Lewis on his arm. "Wait, Don. They have guns."

Don stopped. Someone dropped a glass of champagne on the floor. It shattered and the crowd went silent, watching the men. "Everybody line up along the wall, where we can see you!" the man in the center ordered. He was taller than the other four men, and wore a billed cap pulled low over his face. Gently at first, then more roughly as they grew impatient with the elderly people's slowness, they shoved the guests against the wall.

"What did he say?" a woman asked in a frightened voice.

"You, there," the leader said, pointing his gun at Don and Lewis, "sit down on the floor where we can keep an eye on you." They pushed the waiters into the same area, where the younger people all sat in a circle with their hands over their heads. "Don't move, or people will get popped."

"What do you want?" Lewis asked. "Can't you see it's a bunch of old people? Leave them alone?"

"Shut up," the intruder nearest to him said. When Lewis started to say something else, he hit him across the side of his head with the barrel of his gun. There was a nervous buzz. One of the male waiters tossed Lewis a napkin and he held it to the bloody wound. "Shut up, I said!" the leader yelled at the crowd, who backed nervously against the wall. "Behave yourself, and nobody'll get hurt."

"I want to go home," a woman cried in a small voice.

"Shut her up!" the leader said to the man standing next to his sobbing wife, who had shrunk into her wheel chair. The husband leaned down and stroked her head. "Quiet, Millie. It'll be all right," he said softly.

Papa spoke up. "The guard will have called the police by now. You should up and leave, before they get here."

The leader laughed. "What guard?" He motioned to the intruder standing nearest the entrance, and he shoved Montibello into the room. The man pushed him into the circle beside Don. "God, I am so sorry," Montibello said. "I looked up and saw this man at the door. I went to see what he wanted, and they jumped me."

"All right, folks," the leader said. "You're going to give us your cell phones and your jewelry and your billfolds, and then we'll be out of here and you can go on with your party. Cooperate and nobody gets hurt." Two of the men started around the room, holding pillowcases, in which they ordered the residents to put their valuables. Minerva went first. Standing regally, she unclasped her diamond necklace and put it and her ruby ring and diamond wedding ring and diamond tiara in the bag without a sound. Papa Rothschild followed suit with his gold ring and new gold cuff links. Some of the other women obeyed the men's orders but some did not. "Not my wedding ring, please not that. My late husband…"

"Shut up, bitch, or you'll be late too. Give it here!"

The men made their way around the room, collecting rings and necklaces and even earrings from the guests. "Money, old man," one said to the former dean of the education college.

"I don't have any money. We never carry money here. We don't have any need for it."

"Don't lie to me! Give me your money."

One of the men yelled to the leader, "None of the guys have a billfold, Pete. They leave their money in their apartments, they say."

"Well then, everybody will just have to wait here while we take them one at a time to pick up their money."

A moan of despair filled the room.

"That'll take a long time, Pete."

"I told you not to use my name, fool. Finish up with the jewelry and then we'll clean out their apartments. We have all night." He stopped in front of Anna Kaye and took her in. "Hey, Baby. Aren't you something?"

Anna Kaye stared defiantly at him.

Careful, Anna Kaye, Don thought. Lewis swore under his breath.

The man stood very close to the tall blonde woman. "Nice earrings. Want me to take them off for you?"

When she didn't answer, he whispered something to her.

She backed away from him as best she could and said, "In your dreams, you motherfucker." She tore the earrings off and tossed then into the bag.

"I like a woman with fight." He turned to the others. "Hurry up. We need to get done here before the shift change."

The collection was interrupted by a wail, this time from Papa. «*Mon fils, vous m'entendez?*» (My son, do you hear me?)

"*Oui père. Je vous entends.*" (Yes, father. I hear you.) All those afternoons when Papa insisted on teaching Don conversational French, telling him that every educated man should know French.

Don looked at Dave Lewis, who nodded that he understood.

"*Vous tous qui comprend, écoutez-moi.* "(All of you who understand, listen to me.)

"Hey, who's talking?" Pete shouted from the other side of the room. Shut that up, or you'll be sorry."

But Papa went on, "*Je suis debout par le contacteur d'éclairage.*" (I am standing by the light switch.)"*Quand j'éteints les lumières, attaque et forcez-les par la porte.* (When I turn off the lights, attack them and force them out the door.) *Allez ouvrir l'ascenseur et nous allons les jeter en bas."* (I will open the elevator and we will throw them down the shaft.)

D'accord? (Do you understand?)

"Oui, professeur." The answer came from all around the room. Don looked at Lewis, who mouthed silently, *Let's get 'em.*

"I said, no talking! Shut up!" Pete ordered. He found Papa. "What did you tell them, old man?"

Papa raised his hands toward the sky. "I was praying." Around the room, men raised their hands as if praying and repeated after Papa, «*Oh mon Dieu, frapper ces criminels! Frapper ces criminels! Frapper ces criminels"* (Oh God, strike down these criminals! Strike down these criminals! Strike down these criminals!)

"Stop talking. Shut up, you hear me? What'd you say? What language were you talking?"

"The language of every educated man in this room," Papa said. He lowered his arms and turned off the lights.

The room plunged into darkness. A roomful of old men, quickly followed by Don and Lewis and Montibello and the waiters rushed the startled intruders. Shouts of panic and women's screams shook the ballroom. Don reached for the intruder nearest him and grabbed one leg. He felt Lewis take hold of the other leg. They brought him down to the floor, banging his head on the wood surface. Don heard the man's gun scoot out of reach. They pulled him to his feet and forced him ahead of them, through the melee toward the entrance, behind which an emergency light was flickering dimly.

All around them, people were panting with exertion. One gunman screamed in panic when a group descended on him and began beating him on the head and shoulders with their canes and walkers. A gunshot lit the room for a second, but Don couldn't tell if it hit anyone. Women screamed, men fought, people were scuffling.

When the action subsided, the intruders were huddled in front of the broken elevator, penned against the yellow warning tape, outlined in the glow of the emergency light. Papa had managed to open the elevator door and the residents were threatening to shove the robbers down the elevator shaft. The robbers stood in a semi-circle in front of the open elevator. The shaft loomed behind them.

One still had his gun and he pointed it at the crowd. "Gimme that," Pete said. The robber with the gun tossed it to Pete. Pete turned toward the open elevator shaft to catch it. When he did, the gun was grabbed in midair by the long arm of a six-foot chimpanzee, with glowing red eyes and a grinning mouth full of large white teeth, hanging on the elevator cable by one arm. The ape examined the gun, shrieked loudly, dropped the gun down the elevator shaft and scrambled up the cable, out of sight. The residents fell on the surprised robbers again, with their full force anger, cursing them in French and English and subdued them quickly. The residents trussed them with their belts and suspenders.

The crowd left the waiters and Montibello to guard the intruders and gathered around the serving tables, pouring champagne and talking happily. Papa hugged Don, then lifted his glass and said, "To Rufus. Thank you very much. And thank you all. What we accomplished here tonight is a testament to our autonomy and independence!"

He smiled at Don, who shouted, "Don't mess with seniors!"

The room erupted in applause.

𝕮𝕮𝕮𝕮𝕮

Most of the Austin police force, including the chief, arrived. Chief Orr praised the residents and accepted a glass of champagne himself. "These guys didn't know who they were taking on, did they? They were armed. How did you manage to do it?" He motioned at the robbers, who were being handcuffed by the officers. "And what's this about some giant ape stealing their gun?"

Papa laughed. "A giant monkey? I believe the man with the gun saw a shadow and panicked. My question is, why did these intruders come here tonight?"

"I think I have the answer to that. Their leader was carrying this." He showed them the previous week's society column from the *Old Austin* weekly newspaper. Highlighted in yellow in the Upcoming Events section was a description of Minerva and Ralph Rothschild's upcoming party at Cartwright House for the launch of Professor Rothschild's new book. "We've been looking for these guys. They specialize in burglarizing west Austin homes when they know the owners will be away. They must get their leads from the *Old Austin* weekly."

"I guess they'll be getting their copies delivered to the state pen after this," Don said.

"That'll be a first," Chief Orr replied. "But Professor," he said, "several people are certain they saw a big monkey in the elevator shaft. Are you sure there wasn't one?"

"I was standing by the elevator shaft the entire time. I can assure you there was no monkey, giant or otherwise."

"Well, in any case, we're going to have a look around. There were rumors that when those monkeys escaped from across the road a few years back, they might not have got them all back, that maybe they have missed one. Could that be your elevator shaft monkey?"

"Anything is possible, Chief, but I doubt you will find a missing *monkey* lived all that time at Cartwright House."

«««««

Minerva took on the task of returning their valuables to the partygoers. She placed the jewelry carefully on a serving table and called women's names. "Millie, here are your things," she said to the woman in a wheelchair. She seemed to know who went with every piece.

Don stood by Papa, watching the police taking statements from the excited residents.

Don leaned in close and whispered. "You're the last person I thought would lie to the police."

Papa shook his head. "I did not lie. There was no *monkey.*"

"Oh, I forgot. A chimpanzee is not a monkey. Is that it?"

"I saw no monkey. That is the truth."

"Well, whatever he was, monkey or chimp, we all saw him."

"Did we? Maybe it was the play of shadows in the elevator shaft. The mind can play tricks sometime."

"You know there was a chimp, don't you, Papa?"

Papa brushed back his hair and straightened his tie. "Rufus?"

"Where is he?"

"If there is a Rufus, he's probably gone back to his hiding place, wherever that is."

"How could a chimp live here for years?"

"I suppose it's possible. There was always some confusion about how many chimps escaped and whether they were all found. Are you aware there is a sacred Balinese Hindu site that is a sanctuary for monkeys?"

"No, I wasn't. Why?"

"It is called the Ubud Monkey Forest. There is a large Hindu populace in Bali. The Hindu religion holds many animals to be sacred, including monkeys. There are many such sites all over Asia."

Don thought a minute. "So you're saying there's also one in Austin?"

Papa smiled, but did not reply.

"And," Don went on, "the staff at Cartwright House comes from all over the world. There are probably some Hindus, right? Who might not know the difference between a monkey and a chimpanzee?"

Papa smiled but didn't answer.

Don went on. "If you believe monkeys are sacred and a giant one appears, you might be very impressed, don't you think, Papa?"

Papa cleared his throat. "I see Dean Livermore wants to speak to me," he said. "I will say, Don, that we have an extraordinarily large budget at Cartwright House for bananas and other fresh fruit. Larger than for any comparable facility."

"That's probably why you are all so healthy."

"Or perhaps we live in a holy place, favored by the gods."

"That would make a good poem."

Minerva patted Papa on the shoulder as they passed. She smiled up at Don. "Aren't you glad you came?"

Don kissed her on the cheek. "Thank you for everything you've done for Papa."

"Ralph is a talented poet whose work is finally being recognized. He is also very brave, isn't he?" She handed Don a notebook. "This was at the bottom of the pillow case those men were putting our jewelry in. What do you think it is?"

Don opened the notebook. He recognized immediately the backward scrawl. It was Wesley Bird's handwriting. He had known that handwriting ever since their first class together at the University. He remembered the funny notes they had passed back and forth, planning the rest of the day when they finally got out of class. Those notes were funny. This notebook was not.

There was a name at the top of each page. The name on the first page was Papa's. It read:

Ralph Rothschild

Retired English professor

Cartwright House

Relatives: Dorrie Louise Smith (friend, roommate, keeper?)

 Stepson? Donnie Ray Cuinn, Velda, TX.

 Dorrie Louise's three daughters (Names?)

Don turned the pages. He felt the familiar anger at Wesley's betrayals. Each page had the name of a Cartwright investor in his scheme, with their children and grandchildren's names and addresses. "I'm sorry, Minerva, but I think this explains why these guys raided your party."

Furious, he confronted Pete, the intruders' leader, who sat hand-cuffed, waiting for the police to take him away. "

"Did Wesley Bird send you here?"

The man shrugged. "Nah, man, the All-American didn't send us. But when we saw how much money these old folks had, we decided to rob them. Huge mistake, man."

Don held up the notebook. "Where did you get this?"

"From the All-American."

"You said he didn't send you."

"Like I said, he didn't send us. I was in jail with him. He gave me the book. Said he'd pay me twenty grand if I'd pay a call on those dudes, 'press on them if they loved their kids or grandkids, they ought not testify against him in that fed case he has coming up."

Don squatted down in front of Pete and looked him in the eye. "Wesley Bird offered you twenty thousand dollars to frighten people who might testify against him?"

Pete smiled. "What he said. 'Course I don't know if he's got that much bread. Doesn't matter. I'd never do it. Too risky."

"Too risky to intimidate a witness, but not too risky to try to rob a roomful of old people?"

"He's mixed up in a federal case. I wasn't going to do it, just gonna wait and see. See if he beat the rap. He's got a rich wife. Did you know that? If he got off, I'd show up at his place for my money." He shrugged. "He'll get off, you'll see. "

Don stood up. "He might not this time, especially when you tell the U.S. attorney what you just told me."

⟨⟨⟨⟨⟨

The party began to break up. It was almost ten, past the normal bedtime of the Cartwright residents. Don said goodbye to Charlton and Graff. "You'd never have an evening like this in Velda, Graff."

The skinny man hugged Don. "Say hello to Velda for me. Tell them Austin is a very exciting place."

"I'll tell them." He hugged Anna Kaye and shook hands with Lewis. "Take good care of her. She's a load."

"I know. I will. Thanks for Charlton and the big story. It'll keep my father-in-law off my back for at least a month."

He watched the four of them make their way slowly to the entrance, laughing and hugging one resident after another.

June Fennel appeared at his side, and he handed her Wesley's notebook. "See this gets into the right hands, will you?" He explained what was in it, and what Pete had told him. "What'll happen to Wesley, do you think?"

"He'll turn state's witness against Braeswood now. He doesn't have any choice. He'll be lucky if he avoids serious prison time. Witness intimidation is frowned on." She looked around at the remains of the party. "Stay right there," she said.

He watched her walk across the room to an uncleared bar station. *It might be the champagne, but she's a good-looking woman.*

She returned in a moment, cradling an unopened bottle of the Cristal champagne. She brushed his hair back from his forehead. She had a habit of doing that, it seemed. It felt nice. He grinned, a little foolishly.

"So, Donnie Ray Cuinn," she asked, "would you like to go to my apartment?" She held up the bottle. "We could uncork this." She smiled mischievously. "And discuss the evening's events."

He surveyed the room, taking it all in one last time. He thought for a second, then said, "Sure, why not?"

What could possibly go wrong?

THE END

ABOUT THE AUTHOR

BOYD TAYLOR is a writer who lives in Austin, Texas. In his prior life, he was a lawyer and corporate manager.

This is his third book recounting the lives and times of Donnie Ray Cuinn, first as an erstwhile grad student, and then as a lawyer in a small Panhandle town. The earlier books were *The Hero of San Jacinto* and *The Antelope Play*.

Boyd welcomes question s and comments from his readers. He can be contacted at antelopecity@icloud.com and followed on Facebook at https://www.facebook.com/TheHeroofSanJacinto